NEW BEGINNINGS AT WILDFLOWER LOCK

HANNAH LYNN

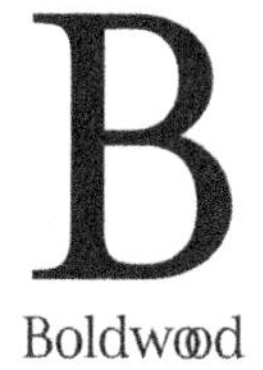

First published in Great Britain in 2023 by Boldwood Books Ltd.

Cover Design by Alexandra Allden

Cover photography: Shutterstock

A CIP catalogue record for this book is available from the British Library.

Paperback ISBN 978-1-80549-641-0

Large Print ISBN 978-1-80549-643-4

Hardback ISBN 978-1-80549-640-3

Ebook ISBN 978-1-80549-642-7

Kindle ISBN 978-1-80549-644-1

Audio CD ISBN 978-1-80549-635-9

MP3 CD ISBN 978-1-80549-636-6

Digital audio download ISBN 978-1-80549-639-7

Boldwood Books Ltd
23 Bowerdean Street
London SW6 3TN
www.boldwoodbooks.com

To Kath, thank you for everything.

1

Daisy May pressed her phone to her ear as she fought her way through the horde of bustling London commuters.

'I can't talk right now, Mum,' she said, narrowly avoiding a briefcase as it swung through the air and towards her knees. 'I'm just getting on the Tube. Yes, the job is fine. I promise I will call you when I get home.'

Her mum's voice crackled down the line.

'You're breaking up, Mum. I'll ring you when I get home. I can't hear you.' She glanced at her screen before pressing the end call button, then picked up her pace as she headed towards the trains.

At some point, Daisy hoped her mother, Pippa, would learn that five-thirty was not the ideal time to ring. Especially given the hours of her current job. Then again, the job was probably why Pippa was ringing. Four months was the longest Daisy had worked anywhere in the last three years, which at twenty-four was hardly something to be proud of. No doubt her mother was starting to worry that Daisy was getting itchy feet, the way she'd done with all her other jobs. But so far, that hadn't happened.

Daisy's twenties had felt as if they'd sprung out of nowhere.

And with them, a whole heap of adulting she hoped to avoid. It wasn't just the normal life maintenance like bills and jobs that kept her down. Every week it felt like another friend was getting engaged or moving in with the love of their life. And she was still here, trying to find a job she didn't despise so much, she wanted to quit after the first week.

'Can you move?' A jolt from the side jerked Daisy back into the moment and she realised her train was at the platform. As the doors hissed open, dozens of commuters pushed past one another. Those who were trying to get on had zero regard for those that were trying to get off. Had it been any other situation, the sheer lack of manners would have warranted a few curt words from Daisy, but this was London on a Friday evening, people desperate to get home after a week spent working a job they probably didn't like all that much either. Some days, people deserved a break.

The doors beeped, announcing their imminent closure, spurring Daisy into action. With an uncharacteristically energetic hop, she jumped onto the train and squeezed in right at the end of the carriage.

It was a fairly straightforward journey from the office to her flat, with one change followed by another seventeen minutes on the overground. After that, it was a ten-minute walk home.

Despite the erraticism in Daisy's career, her flat had been a constant since she'd moved to London. It had been the first place she viewed when she'd packed up her life and moved here three years ago. It was pure luck – or perhaps fate – that she found somewhere in her price range in the location she was after, but it hadn't been without its flaws. The landlord had been desperate to get the place rented after his last tenants had walked out without warning and left him high and dry, apparently not having emptied the bins or hoovered for the best part of a year. So Daisy agreed she would clean up the place and in exchange, the rent would be more than fair. Thankfully, the landlord hadn't put the rent up once in the three years she'd been there and all it had taken was a good steam clean, a bit of elbow grease, and some heavy-duty air fresheners to make the flat liveable.

And cheap rent wasn't the only bonus.

As she approached her front door, she spied a small plastic bag hung on the handle. The shop below, which had been everything from a hairdresser to a jeweller, was now stable as a funky, high-end bakery. Not only did that mean that she was woken each morning by the smell of fresh bread, but a couple of times a week, she would come home to find a bag like this hanging on her door.

She picked it up and took a quick peek inside. Since its opening, the bakery had formed an impeccable reputation, but anything that hadn't been sold that day, or wasn't up to their exacting standard, could end up in her bag. A quick rifle around gave her an overview of what treats she had in store. There were definitely croissants. And by the looks of it, some quiches too, which meant both dinner and lunch tomorrow were sorted. One time, they left her an entire red-velvet cake, which she had taken into the office the next day. That was her previous job, and she'd left the week after. In part because no one thought to thank her for the cake.

Feeling grateful that she didn't have to worry about doing any food shopping, Daisy turned the key and let herself in. She picked up a bundle of envelopes from the floor and dragged herself upstairs, where, as always, the smell of fresh pastries had permeated through.

The modest-sized flat consisted of an open-plan living area, with a small, round dining table and a pull-out sofa bed that had probably been the best investment of her life, given how often Bex slept on it after a night out.

Remembering her promise to call her mum back, Daisy kicked

off her shoes, dumped the post on the dining table, and headed to the kitchen where she flicked on the kettle. Evening phone calls with her mum always required a cup of tea. No doubt there would be lots Pippa needed to tell her, like how her neighbour's hip replacement had been delayed again, and whether the couple from four doors down had got back together after they broke off their engagement. Yes, a cup of tea was definitely needed for that, if not something slightly stronger.

She left the kettle to boil and moved back to the pile of post. With a tired groan, she scanned through the contents. There was the usual mix of circulars and takeaway menus, along with a letter from her bank about their latest deals, and a large piece of paper inviting her to a group chat to talk about UFO sightings. As she expected, there was nothing worth opening, let alone keeping, and she was about to drop it all in the bin when she spotted something unexpected. An A4, brown envelope that had become folded up in the mix.

Flattening it out, she saw her name and address typed neatly on the front. On the reverse side were the sender details: FCS Solicitors and Co.

She had never received a letter from a solicitor before, but had seen enough from television shows to know that it was unlikely to be good news. Staring blankly at the nondescript envelope, Daisy racked her brain, trying to figure out what a solicitor could want with her. Whatever was in the envelope felt a lot thicker than just a single letter.

'Oh,' she said as a sinking feeling settled in her gut. Maybe this was to do with how she'd walked out on her last job without giving the full two weeks' notice. Of course, it wasn't her fault. They had withdrawn her application for vacation only three days before she was due to go and either she quit there and then, or she lost all the money she'd paid for the holiday. It wasn't as if she felt any loyalty to that place though, not after they docked her pay twice for being four minutes late back from her lunch break. She looked at the envelope. Surely they couldn't be so petty they were going to sue her? And if they did, how the hell was she going to afford that with the rent and the cost of living constantly rising?

Unprepared to open it just yet, she went back to the kettle to fix her cup of tea, yet as she poured the water, the large, brown envelope continued to stare at her. What would happen if she just ignored it? Could she do that? They didn't send bailiffs around for things like that, did they? And even if they did, it wasn't like she had anything they could take.

'Crap!' Water from the kettle ran over the edge of the mug and onto the worktop, only narrowly avoiding her hand. Daisy grabbed a tea towel and mopped the mess up, although even when the spillage was rectified, she didn't pick up her drink. Whatever was in that letter wouldn't go away just because she ignored it. So, with a steeling breath, she marched over to the table, picked it up and slid her finger beneath the seal.

Her eyes scanned down the front sheet of paper, once, then twice, then a third time, a deeper and deeper crease forming between her eyebrows with every read. When she was certain that there was no mistake, and she was in fact able to read correctly, she dropped into a dining chair and picked up her phone.

'I need you,' she said. 'I need you now.'

2

The minute the doorbell went, Daisy raced downstairs, only narrowly avoiding the coats and shoes she'd dumped on the way in.

'Tell me you brought beer?' she said as she swung open the front door. 'You're going to need beer to hear this.'

'I brought wine. You know I always bring wine. Now what is going on? Why the hell were you so cryptic?'

When Daisy had rung her best friend, Bex, less than half an hour before, all she had said was that she needed her. Now. Those few words, with no further explanation, had been enough for Bex to grab one of her garishly coloured coats and head straight out of the house. That was how their friendship worked. And it was a friendship that had stood the test of time. Bex had joined Daisy's primary school when they were in Year 3, and while they hadn't been great friends there, they grew closer at secondary school, and closer still when Daisy moved to London. Bex had been there to help her pick up the pieces when her life came tumbling down, and Daisy had helped Bex through her endless string of dates and short-term relationships, all of which continued to convince Daisy that she was better off being single. Possibly forever.

'Where's Claire?' Bex asked, as she trudged up the stairs behind Daisy. 'I thought you were going to ring her. Is she not here already?'

'Claire and Ian are having a date night,' Daisy said, pacing from one side of the open-plan flat to the other, before pausing in the kitchen to grab a pair of wineglasses. A nice craft ale was definitely Daisy's choice of drink, but at that moment, she wasn't going to turn down anything.

'I'll pour. You talk,' Bex said as she pulled a bottle of rosé out of her bag. Daisy nodded, only half hearing what she was saying. She was having difficulty concentrating on anything other than the contents of that brown envelope.

Given how often she had stayed over, Bex didn't need to ask where the corkscrew was. When she'd finished pouring, she handed a glass to Daisy, who took a long sip, before placing it back down on the countertop.

'We need to move to the sofa,' she said. 'You're gonna need to sit down to hear this.'

Bex moved across to the living area and took a seat on the sofa bed, although Daisy herself was in no mood to sit.

'My grandad's died, and he's left me something. A boat.' The words sounded even more ridiculous aloud than when she'd read them on the page, so she repeated them. 'I've been left a boat.'

From the way Bex tilted her head, she obviously found the statement as confusing as Daisy had.

'What do you mean? What kind of boat? And your grandad? You mean your dad's dad, or your mum's? I didn't think you had anything to do with either of them. Are you sure it's not some kind of prank? You know, like when people claim they will send you a hundred thousand pounds if you give them your bank details?'

It certainly would be easier if it was a prank, but Daisy knew it wasn't. And Bex was right about her having nothing to do with either of her grandfathers. Just like she was, her mum had been raised alone by her mother, almost as if it were a family tradition.

'My paternal grandfather,' Daisy said, her voice cracking.

At this, Bex's eyes widened and a hundred unspoken words passed between them. Bex knew better than anyone what that meant. After all, she had been there.

'You mean the one you spoke to.' She voiced the words that both of them were thinking. 'The one we met at your dad's funeral?'

'That's the one.'

Her stomach corkscrewed as she thought back to that day. It wasn't a day she thought about very often any more. In fact, she had tried her hardest to push it to the back of her mind. That feeling of complete and utter loneliness. Feeling like an imposter standing there, surrounded by complete strangers, feeling as if she was the one out of place at her own father's funeral. There were people crying. Not just old people: young people, too. Dozens of people there, for her father. Her father, Fred, who she'd never even known. Who had walked out of her life before she had even formed her first solid memory of him. That funeral was the only real memory.

Bex let out a low whistle, which she followed with a long draw on her wine. 'Okay, so this was definitely unexpected. What has your mum said? Have you told her already?'

It was Daisy's turn to take another sip of her drink. A big one, which resulted in her reaching for the bottle again, despite the fact her glass was still a third full.

Her mother.

To say her parents had a strained relationship would be putting it mildly. In fact, any mention of her father would see Pippa seizing up. It wasn't anger, no; it was worse than that. It was coldness. A stoniness that didn't exist anywhere else in her mother's persona.

'He isn't worth our energy.' That was a line she would respond with almost every time Daisy tried to bring him up. 'He's not worth your energy or mine.' Or, 'It's easier for everyone that he's out of our lives.' That was a line she used to use a lot, along with, 'Forgiveness works both ways.' Daisy never really understood what she meant by that, but she'd never been brave enough to ask. Whatever her father had done, she knew it wasn't good.

After a while, she stopped asking about him. After all, Pippa was right. He had left them when she was less than two years old and cut himself out of her life entirely. No Christmas cards, no birthday cards. No Saturday visits to the zoo together. Nothing. During the parents' races on school sports day, Pippa would run in both the fathers' and the mothers' race, insisting that a child did not need both to be happy. When it was Father's Day, she would go all out, cooking fancy meals and taking them on day trips to ensure Daisy never felt she was missing out.

And so when Daisy's grandfather had knocked on her door when she was seventeen, and informed them that her father had died unexpectedly of a heart attack, Daisy hadn't known how to respond.

'Of course I haven't told her,' she said, replying to Bex's question. 'How can I? You know what she gets like if anyone mentions my dad. She won't even let us say his name. I can't imagine how she'd react to this, but I'm willing to bet it wouldn't be positive.'

The pair fell into a heavy silence, which said something. Bex always knew exactly the right thing to say. The brightly coloured clothes she wore were a reflection of the optimism and energy that she approached life with. If she was staying quiet, that was a bad sign. Daisy had always thought it a shame that Bex went into accountancy when she was so very good at talking to people. She had a natural ability to put people at ease, regardless of the situation.

That was why Daisy had asked Bex to come with her to her father's funeral all those years ago. Daisy had known straight away that no amount of begging would persuade Pippa to go to the funeral of a man she couldn't even speak the name of, and Daisy didn't feel brave enough to go on her own. Bex hadn't hesitated and had supported her every step of the way. Eight years later, and her mother still didn't know Daisy had gone that day. It was the one big secret she kept from her. Although, now it looked like she was going to have two secrets.

'Do you think you should tell her?' Bex said, finally breaking the silence. 'Do you think she'd want to know?'

It was the question that had been rolling round Daisy's head since she saw the letter. Would her mother want to know? Or rather, did Daisy want to tell her?

She could recall the day her grandfather had come round as if it were yesterday. Sitting at the top of the stairs in the two-bedroom terrace she had grown up in, listening to this man she didn't know calling her mother by her first name, as if they were old friends. She had heard the grief in his voice. Grief Daisy had wanted to feel too. But how could she grieve for a man who made no attempt to have a relationship with her? How could she grieve for someone who had abandoned her? He was a stranger. Still, she remained where she was, leaning over the banister, trying to catch the quiet words.

'He never got over it,' he had said. 'You know that, Pippa. You know he never got over it. None of us did.'

'Well, we all had things to get over,' Pippa had replied with a bitterness Daisy didn't know her mother possessed. For a moment, there was a silence that echoed through the house, making the walls feel emptier than they had ever done in her life. In the end, it was Fred clearing his throat that broke it.

'I've written down the details of the funeral. You know I'd like it if you attended. You and Daisy both. We all would.' Another pause followed, after which her grandfather spoke again. 'Well, I'll see myself out.'

Daisy had scurried back up the stairs as her grandfather headed down the hallway. For a second, he stopped and turned his head, looking up at the exact spot where she had been sitting only a moment before. Then, without a word, he opened the door and walked out. A couple of minutes later, Daisy had come down the stairs with a false spring in her step.

'Who was that at the door?' she had asked, opening the fridge so that Pippa couldn't see her expression.

'Oh, just some salesman trying to get me to buy double glazing,' Pippa had replied, before screwing up the piece of paper in her hand and tossing it into the bin.

Later that night, when her mother was asleep in her bed, Daisy had crept downstairs and retrieved that crumpled up piece of paper. As the watery moonlight shone through the windows, she cast her eyes over the writing. It was the details of her father's funeral. And she was going to go.

3

Half the wine had gone, but Daisy was no closer to making sense of the situation. Her grandfather had left her a boat. She owned a boat.

'It's called the *September Rose*,' Bex said. 'I like it. It's better than some names people give these things. I saw one called *Fin and Tonic*. I mean, I guess it's kind of clever, but it does make you sound like a bit of a douche at the same time.'

Daisy was only half listening as Bex flicked through the paperwork the solicitor had sent. In fairness, she should have read through it all herself, but she had become transfixed by the very first page. And anyway, Bex was better at these things. Already she was three-quarters of the way through.

'So, from what it says here, you've got a residential mooring with this boat – I don't know if that's a good thing or not – and it's a wide beam. Again, no idea what that means, either. But the internet will.'

Passing the stack of papers to Daisy, Bex took out her phone and opened a search page.

'Wow,' she said, her eyebrows rising. 'I think you should look at this.'

Still feeling overwhelmed by the entire situation, Daisy looked up as Bex handed her the phone. The screen was opened up onto a page of different canal boats. They were only thumbnails, most of them of boats in the water, with various details typed beneath – mainly the length and year they were built. More than once, she read the words 'wide beam', and several other terms were repeated, like 'traditional' or 'cruiser'. But Daisy's eyes weren't lingering on the descriptions of the boats. She wasn't even really looking at the photographs. Her attention had been attracted to something else entirely. The prices.

'Do you see what I'm seeing?' she said to Bex, all while scrolling down to see more and more of what was on offer.

'If you're talking about how much these things cost, then yes, I saw.'

Daisy continued to scroll.

'There's one here worth a hundred and fifty grand.' Her jaw dropped open. 'Jesus. I've never been left anything before.'

'Your dad didn't leave you anything, did he?' Bex asked, although she quickly flushed at the question.

Daisy shook her head. 'Not anything that I know about at least.'

'I know she didn't like him, but Pippa would hardly keep something like that hidden from you. Would she?'

Daisy shrugged before quashing the thought.

'I don't think so. Most of the time, I don't think there's anything she keeps from me. Sometimes I wish she would. Particularly with all the losers she's dated. But she's different with my dad.'

During her youth, there had definitely been times Daisy had felt anger towards her mother for her reluctance to talk about her father. Pippa could barely choke out his name – Johnny – without coming out in hives and, more than once, they had got into a fight about it. But Daisy's opinion about her mother's reluctance to talk about things changed after she learnt what it was like to be truly heartbroken. After everything that happened between her and Paul, Daisy understood what it meant to have seen your life going in one completely straightforward path, only to have the road severed, twisted and forced into a direction you didn't even know existed. In the three years that had passed since then, Daisy had felt like she'd understood Pippa's reluctance to talk about her father far more. After all, Pippa had had to manage her heartbreak with a child in tow. And it wasn't as if she'd done a bad job raising her.

Growing up just the pair of them, Daisy had been proud of the fact that their relationship had been as tight as any mother–daughter relationship she had known. And as much as her mother worried about her, and her ability to hold down a job, Daisy also worried about her mother, and her ability – or rather lack thereof – to form a meaningful relationship. She had a habit of going for the wrong type of man, which was why it shouldn't have been a surprise that her father hadn't played any part in her life. Thankfully, over the last couple of years, Pippa seemed to have resigned herself to being single. And as much as Daisy didn't want to see her mother lonely, it was far better than seeing her being strung along by some no-good loser who was just out for a bit of fun.

'So, what are you going to do?' Bex said, bringing Daisy back to the moment. 'If it looks like this, we could go on some amazing holidays. You know, you can take these boats anywhere. We could sail to Europe.'

'Can you sail on a canal boat?' Daisy replied. 'Surely you need a sail to sail a boat?'

'Good point.'

Forgetting semantics, she was back staring at the numbers in front of her. One hundred and fifty grand. Her entire adult life, she had needed to be careful with money. She'd had enough to save for a package holiday with the girls every year or so and had been known to splurge now and then on a nice pair of shoes, but it was a long way from an extravagant lifestyle. And there was zero possibility of her getting on the property ladder. A hundred and fifty grand would change all that. She could put down a deposit on a flat. Maybe even with two bedrooms if she went far enough out of the city. And with a bit of luck, there would still be some money left over for a fortnight in the sun. Yes, this was amazing. This boat was going to change her life.

With Daisy occupying Bex's phone, Bex was back to scanning through the documents, and it didn't take her long to find something else.

'It says here it's moored at Wildflower Lock. Do you know where that is?'

'Wildflower Lock? No, I haven't heard of it.' Her eyes were still scanning down the list of boats. Some of them cost less. There were a few for around the seventy grand mark and one or two that came under fifty. But even that would be life changing. Fifty thousand pounds was still a deposit.

'I'm going to sell it,' she said, finally voicing the thought that have been rolling round her head. 'I'm going to sell it and finally stop renting and we'll celebrate by going on an amazing holiday. This is going to change everything. I can feel it. I can feel it in my bones.'

She could. It was as if energy was pouring into her cells. A sense of hope and optimism that she hadn't felt for years was flooding through her. This was more than luck. This was fate. And she was going to make the most of it.

'Great,' Bex said, picking up the wine bottle and filling up both their glasses. 'Although we should probably go and see it first.'

4

Daisy May was bouncing on her feet, shifting them from side to side as excitement bubbled through her. It wasn't particularly safe behaviour, given that she was driving a car. But she couldn't stop. She felt like a kid at Christmas, desperate to see what presents had been left beneath the tree, certain that Santa had fulfilled her wishes and brought every item on her list and more.

'How much longer until we get there?' Bex asked.

'Four minutes,' Daisy replied, glancing at the sat nav, her stomach twisting with excitement. 'Although that's just to the car park. We're going to have to walk to Wildflower Lock from there. I'm not sure how much further that's going to be.'

'At least we've got a nice day for it. Thanks for bringing me along with you.'

'Are you kidding? There's no way I would have been able to come here on my own.'

It was Sunday morning, nine days since Daisy had received the letter informing her about her inheritance. Although she had already signed the official paperwork and received the keys for the

September Rose, this was the first time she was actually going to see it. In truth, she could have gone the day before – and had desperately wanted to – but Bex had been busy with a lunch date with a guy she was certain could be the one. Daisy needed her friend by her side to do this. Besides, it was Bex who had organised the broker to come and look at the boat, so it only felt right she was there too.

Wildflower Lock was a convenient hour's drive away from Daisy's home in North London and the longer she had driven, the brighter the sky had become. As they weaved their way closer, a brilliant wash of blue shone above them and a gentle breeze swayed the trees, casting a constantly changing dapple of shadows on the road.

'I forget how green it is when you get out of the city,' Bex said, voicing Daisy's thoughts.

'Spring's always green. I'm not sure I'd be so keen to drive down these country lanes in the winter.' Not that she planned on having the boat for that long. The sooner she could sell it, the better. 'What time did you say the broker was going to meet us again?'

'Twelve thirty,' Bex replied with a glance at her watch. 'Which means we're going to be there early. It'll give us a chance to have a look around. Find the *September Rose*. Maybe your grandad left other things in there that are worth selling.'

Daisy hadn't even thought of that possibility. The boat could be full of treasures. She might not even need a mortgage after all. If the boat was worth as much as she hoped, and there were a few saleable items inside, then who knew what kind of future awaited her? Her mind ran away with all the possibilities. So much so that she nearly missed the turning.

'Turn!' Bex yelled.

Daisy slammed on the brakes and twisted the steering wheel,

taking the junction much faster than she should have. The road became a rumbling track, quickly opening up into a large car park which was substantially busier than she would have expected. *Wildflower Lock Car Park*, the wooden sign read.

'I guess the sunny weather has brought out the crowds,' she said, as she scanned the area, looking for a place to park. Getting out of the cars were families, dog walkers, and men and women with giant surfboards tucked under their arms.

'Do you think we can park up anywhere?' she asked. 'Maybe there's a special place for people who own a boat?'

'As you don't plan on owning yours very much longer, I suggest you just park anywhere you find a space.'

Conceding that Bex was probably right, Daisy parked next to a Range Rover, where a middle-aged man was trying to coax a greying Labrador out of the back, completely ignoring his wife's pleas to simply lift the dog down.

Daisy stepped out of the car, slammed the door shut and took a moment just to breathe it all in. The air had a definite tang here. A fresh crispness that was near impossible to find in London with all the smoke and car fumes. It smelt of the countryside. Of dew-covered grass and flowers in bloom. It was rejuvenating. It reminded her of the camping holidays she used to take with her mother to France. They would load up their little car, drive onto the ferry in dull England, and then drive off again in a whole new world. There was something so relaxing about that aroma. As if she could just close her eyes and fall asleep to it.

'I guess this is why they call it Wildflower Lock,' Bex said.

Following Bex's line of sight, Daisy's gaze fell upon the rows and rows of bushy purple flowers. Given that it was early spring, they were starting to bloom, and even from a distance, she could see the dozens of bees and butterflies flitting from one stalk to another. That, Daisy realised, was where the smell was coming from. Lavender. She walked over and brushed her hand against the delicate, violet stalks, releasing the aroma in eddies around her. There was something so familiar about that action. Probably just a touch of déjà vu. Not that she could ever recall being surrounded by this much lavender and certainly never stroking it. With a blink, she shrugged off the feeling and turned to Bex.

'I guess it's time we go find this boat.'

A winding path led up from the car park towards the canal and the lock itself. Unfortunately, the number of people increased as they bottlenecked through a narrow gateway. Daisy waited as patiently as she could, her feet tapping on the ground as the adrenaline flooded through her. Yet the moment they stepped through the gate, she stopped abruptly.

'Wow, this is incredible,' Bex said, although 'incredible' didn't seem to justify the sight in front of them.

Of course, she had seen plenty of canal boats before. It was hard to live in London and not. Camden, Islington and even Canary Wharf had their fair share of people who chose that way of life. She had only ever noticed the boats in passing, usually casting a lazy gaze across at them while she was hurrying to work or to meet a friend, or just walking home from a shopping trip. She had never really looked at them before. Not like this.

'They are beautiful,' she finally choked out.

'Which one do you think is yours?'

'I don't know. I guess we should find out,' she said, although she wasn't in any immediate rush to move. She was content to stand there and let the quiet sweep around her.

It was easy to see why these boats would sell for so much. Her eyes were drawn to one where the roof was covered in large, wooden planters, from which green shoots had started to spring. There were even bean poles set up, though nothing was currently growing on them. It was ingenious, the way the owners had turned the entire roof of the boat into a miniature allotment. Another boat was moving slowly up the canal and had been painted entirely in stars: not the childish type, with pointy corners, but actual patterns of constellations which had been labelled so people knew what they were looking at. Daisy found herself wondering if the inhabitant possessed a telescope. After all, you would be hard pushed to find anywhere better to sit and observe the stars. Every boat shone with its own personality. Not to mention their names. That was the *LC Amelia*, the *Nauti-buoy*, and the *Dusty Springfield*, although with its rather bland, grey exterior, Daisy struggled to see what link that particular vessel could have to the singer.

A strange sense of pride swelled through her at the knowledge that she owned one of these beautiful boats. Though only for a short while at least, she had to remind herself. The thought prompted her to look at her watch. It wasn't long until they were due to meet the broker, and she really wanted to find her boat beforehand.

But there were a lot of boats to look through.

'How do you think we should do this?' she said to Bex, who was currently ambling aimlessly away from her. 'Should we go in different directions, then ring each other if we find it?'

'Or we could just ask someone,' Bex countered, a more sensible suggestion. 'Your grandad kept the boat here for a while, right? Maybe somebody knows him.' She stopped to correct herself. 'Knew him.'

As Daisy considered the question, she scanned down the canal. There were boats as far as the eye could see, and on both sides of the canal, too. They could easily be searching for the best part of an hour and not get any closer to discovering which of these vessels was hers.

'That's probably a better idea,' she said.

With a quick look, Daisy spotted a woman hanging her washing on a line.

Talking to strangers wasn't something that Daisy generally had a problem with –changing jobs so often probably helped. She approached the lady, who was of a similar age to her mother, and cleared her throat.

'Excuse me, I wonder if you could help me?'

The woman didn't raise her head as she continued to peg a large sheet to the line.

'If you need your paddleboard licence, love, you need to go back to Papermill Lock. Or you can do it online, I think, but don't ask me how.'

'No, it isn't about paddleboarding,' Daisy said, suddenly not quite so confident as she had been, although she now realised it must have been paddleboards, not surfboards which people were carrying beneath their arms. 'I'm looking for a particular boat. I think it's been here for a while.'

At this, the woman stopped her pegging and actually looked at her. 'Is that so? What's she called love?'

'It's the *September Rose*. It was owned by Fred Collins.'

The woman's jaw dropped open by a full two inches. 'Good God,' she said quietly, before muttering something under her breath.

'Is everything okay?' Daisy asked. 'Did you know Fred? Do you know the boat?'

The woman was blinking, her throat pulsing as she swallowed repeatedly.

'Aye, we all knew Fred. Well, if it's the *Rose* you're after, you just keep going on up here.' She nodded up the canal. 'She's moored up next to the black shed. You won't be able to miss her.'

'This way?' Daisy double checked, just to make sure she was right.

'By the black shed,' the woman repeated.

Confident she knew where she was going, Daisy smiled broadly at the woman. 'Thank you. I better get going. I've got a busy day ahead.'

The woman remained tight-lipped as she nodded her head.

'I bet you have,' she said.

5

'Did you not think about asking how far away the black shed was?' Bex said, as they continued to trek down the towpath alongside the canal. It was a sensible point. Daisy was sure they had walked at least half a mile, and so far there had been no sign of a black shed. They had seen plenty of brown sheds. One white, and several that were so crumbled down, it was difficult to tell what colour they had even been before. But not a single black shed.

'Maybe you should go back or ask somebody else,' Bex said.

'She definitely said it was this way,' Daisy insisted. 'Let's give it two more minutes, then we'll ask someone.'

No sooner had she spoken than a small building came into view. Its wooden slats were in desperate need of a re-stain and some of the roofing felt was hanging off. But it was, most certainly, a black shed. And there, moored up in front of it, was one of the most beautiful narrow boats she had ever seen.

A swell of disbelief rose through Daisy as she drew to a stop.

'I think this is what they call hitting the jackpot,' Bex said.

For once, Daisy couldn't reply. Jackpot was right. It wasn't the biggest boat they had seen all day, but it was stunning. The light, powder blue reflected the sunlight so that the top of the boat was almost an exact match for the colour of the sky, while the bottom was a glossy back. The wood around the windows and doors was stained a golden hue, and the metalwork was polished to perfection. As she stood there, staring, Daisy drifted into a daydream. Not one where she was handed a mammoth cheque – which was the daydream that had been occupying her thoughts for most of the week – but one where she was standing on this boat, breathing in that lavender air while birds flew above her. The thought didn't last too long, though. After all, she knew nothing about boats, and to even contemplate keeping it was bound to be a disaster.

'We should probably have a look around before the broker arrives,' Daisy said, refocusing on the main objective: the money.

'After you,' Bex said, sweeping out her arm towards the boat.

Butterflies swelled in Daisy's stomach. She was genuinely nervous. Nervous about so many things. This was a part of her history. Her grandfather's history. At that thought, a pang of sadness struck her right in the sternum. Perhaps, if she had made more of an effort at the funeral, rather than hiding away, she would have got to know him more, maybe even visited him here when he was alive. Then again, it was unlikely. He had known where she lived. He'd proved that when he showed up on their doorstep. And what effort had he made to get to know his granddaughter? None. That was the truth. No, this boat was just a last-ditch attempt to eradicate the guilt he felt at having nothing to do with his family. She would be happy to sell it.

And with that mindset, she took a wide step, across the gap from the towpath and onto the boat.

A small door was fitted with two long glass windows, which allowed Daisy plenty of space to peer inside. There was a thin sofa, and a wood-burning stove in one corner. The floor was laid with the same light-coloured wood that had been used outside, while the ceiling was painted in a far darker colour, closer to midnight blue. Her grandad had taste, the interior more the type she'd have expected to find in a swanky bachelor pad than an old man's home. But then maybe her grandad had been a bachelor in his later years. She knew so little about him; it could easily be true.

'Okay, let's see which of these keys opens this up,' she said, pulling out the bundle that the solicitors had sent her. It was certainly a mismatched bunch. There were some small, modern, Yale lock keys, along with a selection of far older, and in some cases rusted, specimens. Unfortunately, at first glance, none of them appeared to match the lock on the door.

'Just try one of them,' Bex said. 'One of the thin ones?'

Following her friend's advice, Daisy picked the key that looked the closest fit, although it took less than a second to realise it wouldn't work. It might have been thin enough, but it was a good millimetre too long. Frustrated, she pushed her hand down on the door handle, only for it to swing open.

Her eyes widened with surprise.

'It's unlocked?' she said.

Bex stiffened. 'I guess the solicitors never checked before they sent you the letter,' she said. 'You could probably have a case with them for that. It could have been broken into. Anything could have been stolen.'

'I guess there aren't those sorts of people around here,' Daisy said, pushing the door open a fraction more.

'Come on, what are you waiting for?' Bex said, as Daisy stood there, staring at the door. 'This is good. We can have a proper look around now.'

Without waiting for Daisy to reply, Bex bounded down the steps.

'This sofa is really comfy,' she said, although she was on her feet only moments later. 'Oh my God, there's even a swanky coffee machine.'

Daisy picked her way down the steps and paused in the kitchen area of the boat. A kitchen that, while small, contained more mod cons than Daisy's flat. Something she wanted to rectify more than ever looking around her. Then again, having a landlord was likely to soon be a thing of the past.

Gradually becoming comfortable around these new surroundings, Daisy carried on down the boat. She had thought she would feel unsteady walking on it. That it might sway from side to side, but instead, being in the boat felt natural. She lifted her hand up and brushed the ceiling, drawing in a long breath of air. She hadn't expected to feel so at ease here. Such a deep sense of belonging. Perhaps her father had liked to be on the water as well, she thought.

The thought caught her by surprise. This last week, she had avoided thinking about the man who had deserted her and her mother. She certainly hadn't hoped that her inheritance would involve finding any deep connection with him. After all, why would she want to be connected to a man who walked out on his family? She forced down any sense of sentimentality as she continued to look around the boat.

This was easily at the top end of the ones she'd seen for sale online. Yes, this was going to be a healthy deposit. There would definitely be enough money to have a holiday abroad, too. She might even take her mother, although she still had to work out how to tell her about this place.

'Come on, I want to look through the rest of it,' Bex said, showing no signs of her energy level dropping. 'There's got to be a bathroom in here, right? I wonder what it's like. Do you think there's an actual bath? If it's a roll top, I might actually have to move in here myself. Come. On!' She punctuated her words even more firmly this time. 'This is your boat. I can't see it all before you do.'

That was one thing Daisy agreed with. At this rate, Bex would go through the entire boat and find every nook and cranny.

'Okay, I'm coming,' she said, finally moving deeper into the boat and letting her excitement start to take hold.

The smell was divine. The smokiness of the wood burner sank deep into the grain of the woods of the boat, while the aroma of the freshly brewed coffee was so strong, it was difficult to believe the machine hadn't been used recently. She could only assume her grandfather was a man who loved his espressos.

'Open one of the doors! Open one of the doors!' Bex said, still bounding around. Unable to fight her friend's infectious energy any more, Daisy did as was asked of her and moved towards the back end of the boat. There were three doors, all finished in the same light stained oak. Her grandfather certainly had a consistent aesthetic. A small swarm of butterflies worked their way further up her chest as she took in a quivering breath. Only to pause. 'Can you hear water?' she said.

'We're on a boat. Of course there's water.'

'No, I don't mean like that, I mean—'

Daisy cut herself short. Bex was right. They were on a boat. But this sounded like running water. Like a shower or something. No doubt there was somebody filling a tank or using a hosepipe nearby, or a lock, emptying somewhere in the distance. Either way, it wasn't going to distract her now. She was exploring her very own narrowboat. And, as her ownership of the vessel was likely to be incredibly short, she wanted to make the most of it. With a giddy grin, she slid open the door to the right.

The steam hit her first. A face full of clouded steam so dense, it momentarily blinded her.

'What the—' She stumbled back, blinking against the rapid

heat as she tried to make sense of the situation. Slowly, the clouds began to lessen, and her eyes strained as she tried to take in the view. Little by little, shadows and shapes came into focus, although as the scene cleared, she realised exactly what she was staring at.

And it wasn't an empty bathroom. It was a definitely-not-empty bathroom.

'What the hell are you doing in here?'

6

Daisy stumbled backwards, only there was nowhere to stumble back to. She hit the wall, and attempted to turn around, only to lose all sense of direction and end up facing the same way as she had been.

It didn't help that she couldn't seem to draw her eyes away from the figure in front of her. The figure that was hastily grabbing a towel to preserve a little of his dignity. When Daisy finally re-directed her line of sight so that she was looking at his face, he was wearing an expression of thunder.

'I... I think I might have got the wrong boat,' she stuttered, as she finally found her voice.

'You think?' The man stepped forward, the towel now firmly attached around his waist, his long hair wavy with water. 'You're trespassing. Get out of here now before I call the police. Bloody hen dos thinking they can go where the hell they want, like they own the canal.'

'We're really sorry. We're going now.' Bex grabbed Daisy by the hand and tugged her away, although Daisy was slower to move than perhaps she should have been. She just didn't like this man thinking this was some deliberate prank, as opposed to a genuine mistake.

'I really am sorry. I was looking for the *September Rose*. Obviously, this is not her.'

For the first time since she had opened the bathroom door on him, the man's expression flickered. The anger replaced by a hint of confusion.

'You're looking for the *September Rose*? Why?'

Bex was still tugging her hand, obviously keen to get out of there before the man made good on his word to call the police, but Daisy felt like she needed to give this man an actual explanation, along with clearing her name.

'I'm interested in it, that's all.'

The towel-clad man's face narrowed.

'Why?'

While she was fully aware that she was the one in the wrong, with the trespassing and everything, Daisy was finding this man's tone increasingly irritating. And the fact he wanted to know her private business meant she was absolutely not going to tell him.

'I've heard it's for sale,' she said, with just a hint of sharpness to her tone. 'Now, if you could tell me where it is, I will get out of your hair.' She pushed back her shoulders as she waited for him to reply, the urgency she'd previously felt to dash out of there as quickly as possible having faded.

'You haven't seen her yet?' the man repeated.

'Obviously not. Like we said, we thought this boat was the one we were looking for. We were told it was moored next to the black shed.'

He remained silent for a moment longer, his lips squeezed tightly together as he appeared to chew through a thought. There was something about his look – and the way his lips tightened –

that made her feel uneasy. Like he was deliberately trying to keep his face expressionless.

'She's moored next door,' he said eventually, pointing towards his kitchen and the door. 'If you give me a minute, I can get dressed and come and help you.'

'I'm perfectly capable of climbing aboard a boat.' The words came out a little sharper than she expected, but there was something about his tone that irritated her. Like he saw her as a damsel in distress. Like she should be grateful that he had offered to help her, even though she hadn't asked him to. She despised it when good-looking men assumed it was their right to sweep in and act like a hero whenever the opportunity presented itself, regardless of the fact most women didn't need a hero. Or want one.

His eyes narrowed. That same annoyance that had been there earlier crept back into his face. 'I wasn't implying that you weren't capable. I was simply offering to help.'

'Thank you,' she replied with deliberately less curtness. 'But obviously, I've taken up enough of your time. I should leave you to get dressed.'

With a final tip of her chin, Daisy nodded to Bex, who hurried ahead of her, before she turned around herself, and walked the length of the boat, towards the steps.

For some reason, her heart had started drumming again, but she kept her pace decidedly stately, and made a concerted effort not to look back. Not to even glance over her shoulder. Even so, she could feel his eyes boring into her. Were they brown or blue? She wanted to check, but she quickly shook the thought away.

Why on earth did it matter what colour his eyes were? She had only spoken to the man for two minutes, but that was more than enough to clock what a self-righteous know-it-all he was.

She took the steps out onto the back of his boat when he called again.

'Good luck!' he yelled.

Daisy sucked in a lungful of air and refused to look back. With her fist clenched at her side, she ducked out through the door and onto the back of the boat, but it was only when her foot landed on the riverbank that she finally felt able to breathe. A rush of adrenaline caused her to drop her hands onto her knees, although she had barely gained her balance when Bex broke into laughter.

'Well, I wouldn't mind waking up next to that every morning,' she said, in true Bex style, not even caring about the fact that they were still within earshot.

'You are joking?' she replied, straightening herself upright. 'Ignoring his obvious hero complex, any man with a body like that spends way too long in the gym. And what on earth was that last comment? Good luck? What was that supposed to mean? That because we're women we're incapable of handling a boat?'

'I'm sure he was just being friendly,' Bex said, but Daisy wasn't convinced.

She was still pondering the question when she remembered that she was on a schedule and needed to get to her boat before the broker arrived. Thankfully, she didn't have far to go. Turning on the spot, she looked to the next mooring. There was indeed a boat there, right next to the black shed, as the woman earlier had said. A boat that Daisy could not take her eyes off. All of a sudden, she knew exactly what he had meant by good luck. If this really was her boat, she was going to need all the help she could get.

7

The two women stood in silence, staring at the boat in front of them. From somewhere in the distance came shouts and laughter and even screams. Noises which normally would have drawn Daisy's attention. But right now, she couldn't move. Her feet were frozen to the ground. Her entire body was rigid as she tried to digest the sight in front of her.

'So, it's not in quite as good a condition as the other boats,' Bex said, finally finding something to say. 'But I'm sure a lick of paint would make a world of difference.'

Generally, Daisy admired her friend's ability to look on the bright side. But there were times when the reality couldn't be ignored, and it was going to take a darn sight more than a lick of paint to sort out this boat.

Daisy took a tentative step closer. At one point in time, the boat appeared to have been painted red and cream, although the red had now faded to a dirty orange-brown, the paint chipped off in most places, and the cream had dirtied to an almost identical hue. Yet there, obscured by the dirt and grime, a name was just about visible: *September Rose*. This really was the boat she had inherited.

Unlike the sturdy and attractive double-glazed windows on the boat next door, these ones were framed with timber that was cracking in some places and warped in others. While most of the glass appeared to be in one piece, it was so thick with dirt, the windows were practically opaque.

'At least it's all in one piece,' Bex said, still searching for something good to say. 'It could be worse. It could be sinking. And it's a good size. It's definitely wider than the others. And longer too. I'm sure you could fit a king-size bed in it – if you wanted to, that is.'

Gritting her teeth, Daisy moved a little closer. It wasn't just a case of a bit of dirt. While the boat they had seen near the car park had turned their roof into an allotment, this one had been turned into a scrapheap full of algae-coated ropes, and rust-coloured chains. Any hope Daisy had had of finding a stash of saleable items on the inside was dwindling rapidly.

Using the sleeve of her top, she rubbed a small circle in the dirt on the window, creating a hole that was just about clear enough to peer through.

'It's full of boxes,' she said, wanting to peer closer but aware than there were likely a thousand forms of pathogens breeding on the glass. 'I can't even see if there's any furniture in there.'

She let out a despondent sigh, the thoughts of a holiday sliding out of reach, but before she could allow herself to sink into a proper wallow, Bex sidled up and slipped her hand into Daisy's.

'I know it's disappointing,' she said. 'Particularly considering what we thought you'd got.' She offered a slight nod to the boat to the right of them. 'But you still have your own boat. And you might not get as much as you thought for it, but it's better than nothing, right? I mean, worst-case scenario, you sell this and get the best holiday of your life. Think of it that way.'

Bex was right. Of course this was better than nothing. Even getting a hundred pounds for this rusting, cobweb-ridden vessel would be a bonus she hadn't expected. But something had happened to her when she stepped on the other boat. This feeling of belonging. She would just have to quash it. If anything, having the boat in this state was a good thing. There would certainly be no feelings of doubt when it came to selling it.

Daisy was pondering what positive spin she could find to abate this sinking feeling in her gut when Bex's phone rang.

'It's the broker. He's here.'

The broker. Daisy's stomach sank further, although for Bex's sake, she forced herself to smile.

'I guess we better go meet him,' she said. 'You never know, it might be good news.'

* * *

'God, things like this make me so sad,' the broker said, as he ran his hand over the top of the boat. 'She would've been a beauty once. Got good bones on her, that's for sure. Lots of potential. Someone just didn't have the time to give her the love she needed. Or rather, didn't want to put in the time. In my opinion, people like that shouldn't be allowed to have a boat. It's like a pet. If you're not prepared to put in the work, you shouldn't get one.'

He was a short, stout man, whose suit was too long in the arms. He had the air of an ultimate salesman, what with his thick-rimmed glasses and large briefcase.

'My grandfather was very old,' Daisy said, feeling defensive of the man she had only met once, very briefly. She didn't actually know how old he was. 'I'm sure he did everything he could.'

'Of course, of course.' The broker lifted his hands apologetically. 'Didn't mean to cause no offence. Just something in this condition, it's a much tougher sell. Much tougher sell indeed.

Shame, because it's a special boat you've got there. Very good size, and like I said, good bones.'

'So, does that mean it will be worth a decent amount?' she asked optimistically. She wasn't bothered about waiting a little longer for it to sell, if it still meant there might be money at the end of it. Yet her comment was not met with the response she would have hoped; the broker threw back his head and laughed.

'In this state? I think you should count yourself lucky with whatever you get. Whoever buys it's gotta empty all these boxes out, get it out the water to blacken the hull, and that's assuming the engine still runs. It's not the cost that knocks the price down on these things so much as the time. People just don't have the hours to put in to these things, even if they're pretty basic tasks.'

Daisy studied the boat. They still hadn't gone inside. The bunch of keys weighed heavily in her pocket. Bex had, in a similar manner to Daisy, created a peep hole in the dirt and she was now pressing her eyes against the window as she tried to gauge as much as she could about the inside. But Daisy's mind was too busy whirring away.

'So you're saying if I did these things – blacken the boat, was it?'

'The hull,' the broker corrected.

'The hull. If I blacken the hull, clear the boxes out and clean the windows. Maybe gave it a lick of paint, it would be worth more? A lot more?'

The broker pulled his glasses down to the end of his nose, observing Daisy from above the rim. 'I would say it would be a much quicker sell, and I'd definitely be able to put it up for more. The question you need to ask yourself is, do you really have the time to do that? A young lady like yourself, I'm sure you've got better things to do with your weekends than come down here, scrub the deck and get your nails all dirty. If I were you, I'd cut your losses. I'll sort you a deal now. I'm sure I can get someone who'll take it for scrap.'

There were so many things he was saying that caused a prickle to run the length of Daisy's spine. To start with, there was the comment about her nails. Yes, they were painted, but that was because Claire had bought her daughter Amelia a gel manicure kit for Christmas and she practiced on Daisy every time she saw her. That certainly didn't mean she wasn't the type of person who couldn't get their hands dirty.

Besides, why would he make all those comments about the boat's potential, then say it would be turned to scrap? Obviously, he wanted her to sell it now, then he would do all the work himself and pocket the profits. She gazed at the boat once more, before casting her eyes to its neighbour. Would it really take that much work to turn it into something that stylish? At one point in her life, she had considered becoming an artist, so she definitely had some skills in that area. Perhaps this would be just the thing to bring that artistic side of her back to life after all these years. She could do the *September Rose* up to a half-decent state, then she would sell it, and reap the profit.

With a newfound air of confidence, she turned back to the broker and fixed her face with a smile.

'Do you know what? I think there might have been a change of plan.'

8

Daisy watched as the broker headed back towards the car park, his phone pressed against his ear, his salesman-like appearance at odds with the tranquillity of the river. Even with all the paddle-boarders and dog walkers, it really was an incredibly tranquil place.

Before now, Daisy had always thought riverbanks were lined with green reeds and water rushes, with very little in the way of flowers and colours. But as she took the time to observe her surroundings, she became aware of just how wrong she was. Tall stalks of indigo blooms pierced out between the green foliage while clusters of mauve flowers were dotted between the long rushes. Butterflies flitted from one yellow flower to another and even more exciting were the dragonflies. Daisy couldn't remember the last time she had seen a dragonfly in London. Certainly not for several years. And yet there were two, dancing above the water right in front of her.

'So, are we going inside, or not?' Bex said. Daisy blinked and brought herself back to the present. There would be plenty of time to look at dragonflies later, she told herself. For now, they had work to do.

After a quick look through the bundle she had been given, Daisy had found the key to the rusted padlock on the door and let herself in, but that was as far as she got. It wasn't that the route into the boat was blocked, but that the air was thick with dust. She covered her mouth and nose, coughing and spluttering out the breath she had just taken in.

'Perhaps we should just open the windows?' Bex used her sleeve as a mask as she stepped inside. 'Or I could always ring the broker back? I'm sure it wouldn't be too late.'

With the coughing fit under control, Daisy shook her head and walked over to the windows, where she flicked up one of the latches and pulled. She pulled again a second time, this time a little harder, though the window still didn't budge.

The dust had clogged the gap around the window, thick and black, and the wood had swollen slightly too, but Daisy wasn't going to give up that easily. Using both hands, and secretly praying the glass didn't shatter beneath her grip, she gave it another almighty yank. This time, it was enough, and the window opened inwards by half an inch. Another yank and it was fully open, although she knew it was going to take a lot more than one open window to sort this place out.

'So, any idea how you're going to attack all this?' Bex said, never one to beat about the bush. 'I mean, it's a lot to sort out.'

Daisy inhaled. She never normally minded backing out of a decision she had made, as she had shown by her countless number of jobs. After all, she had very much said goodbye to her pride after everything with Paul, and then again with the art school thing, but this was different. There was no way she was going to give that broker the satisfaction of her calling him back.

'The floor looks in good condition,' she said, pushing some boxes to the side so she could rest her hand against it. It was dry, which had to be a good sign. No doubt a sand and varnish would be enough to bring it up nicely. Not that she had any idea how to do either of those things properly. It would also be good if they could see slightly better, not to mention breathe a little easier. The one open window and door were hardly enough to get a decent draught flowing. 'Let's start by opening these windows and giving it time to air. It's not like we can do much more until we have some cleaning things. I'm not sure we should be touching any of this without rubber gloves.'

It was a little dramatic, but the morning had been far more overwhelming than Daisy had expected, what with entering the wrong boat and then the shock of this place. She didn't think she could cope with finding any more surprises hidden away in the cardboard boxes. She would come back later in the week, or next weekend even, when she'd had time to get her head straight.

With the first window already open, she picked her way over to the kitchenette area and tried the same yanking motion on the window there.

'They'll be okay to leave open for a couple of days, won't they?' she said, suddenly realising there could be a flaw in her plan. 'The rain won't be able to get in at this angle, will it? And it's not like anyone's going to try to break in.'

Bex paused from where she was straddling an unusually long cardboard box as she attempted to get a decent grip on window number three. She let go of it, looking at Daisy, before she replied.

'You could always ask him next door to keep an eye on the place? Drop in the spare key? It might help to re-introduce yourself and, you know, actually tell him your name or the fact you own the boat now. You are going to be neighbours.'

Daisy didn't reply. After all, it didn't take a genius to know where Bex was going with this, and she wasn't going to play into her hands by giving her any form of response.

This didn't stop Bex from pushing the matter further though. 'Maybe this is fate,' she continued as she attempted to yank the window open. 'I didn't see a ring on his finger and that boat was a definite bachelor pad. There wasn't a throw cushion in sight. And he was wearing a grey towel.'

'I don't think grey towels are a universal signal that somebody's single,' Daisy replied, annoyed at herself for getting drawn into the conversation. 'And even if he is, I don't do relationships, remember?'

'How could I forget? But maybe this boat might be good for you. A chance for you to let go of the past. Not all relationships end the way yours and Paul's did.'

Daisy yanked the window with such force, she toppled backwards.

'You really want to bring up Paul in a confined space like this?' she said when she found her balance.

'You're right, I'm sorry.'

Abandoning the window she was on, Bex clambered over several boxes until she was standing beside Daisy, and promptly wrapped her arms around her.

'There's no need to get cross with me. I'm your best friend, remember? I love you. I will always love you. I just wish you'd let somebody else love you, too.'

'I don't need anybody else's love. I'm fine just as I am. And I'll be even better when I've sold this for a chunk of money.'

It took a fair bit of climbing and balancing to get all the windows in the living area open, at which point, Daisy had a decision to make. Like the neighbouring boat, there were closed doors sealing off the other parts of the vessel. No doubt they would need airing just as much as in here, but to get there was going to be a real squeeze. And she wasn't sure she could deal with that just yet.

'How about we leave it here?' she said as Bex tried to brush the cobwebs from her coat. 'I'm not sure I can cope with seeing what else there is to do yet.'

'Thank God. I really did not dress right for this. I would have worn my climbing shoes if I'd have known.'

Chuckling, Daisy picked up her bag and offered the space one last look before she headed back to the door.

As she clicked the padlock back into place, Daisy felt substantially heavier than she had done all day. She was desperate to get back home, where she could get a takeaway and watch a horror movie.

Horror movies were always her go to when life felt a little overwhelming. Most of her friends found that odd; even her mother would choose a romcom for a bit of an uplift. But what was uplifting about seeing other people succeed in areas of their life where you constantly failed? No, horror movies were more uplifting, because at least, however bad her life was going, she wasn't being attacked by a man with hooks for arms.

'Why don't we go grab a coffee before we go back?' she suggested, recalling the coffeemaker in the boat next door with more than a hint of envy. 'I feel like I need some caffeine after this.'

'Why not? It might be nice to finish with a slightly better view of the lock, too?'

There was no way Daisy could argue with that.

When they had first arrived at the canal, Daisy had been so focused on finding the *September Rose*, she hadn't taken the time to study the scenery as much as she would have liked, but now she tried to take it all in. Just as she had suspected, the dragonflies danced in droves, while butterflies and the lavender bushes teemed with bees. But what surprised her most was the air. They may have only been an hour from London, but she could have been in the middle of the mountains, it was so clean. The crisp freshness that filled her lungs was so at odds to the fumy smog she was used to; she could almost feel it healing her various aches and pains with every breath.

Unfortunately, while there was wildlife aplenty, the canal lacked any kind of coffee shop and after twenty minutes of hopelessly scouring the canal, Daisy was feeling grumpier than she had all day.

'I guess we should just get home,' she said, and changed direction to head back to the car. For a day that had involved very little, she was feeling pretty exhausted, not to mention a whole heap of other emotions. Of course, she was excited about what was to come, but it was also pretty damn terrifying. 'I suppose I should look up what kind of paint I need to buy for this type of job. And if I can hire an industrial sander.'

As they climbed into the car, Bex was the next to speak.

'I hate to be the bearer of logical thinking here,' she said, clipping in her belt. 'But have you actually thought about how you're going to pay to get these repairs done? I mean, you said yourself, an abundant cash flow has never really been something you've had and projects like this swallow up money.'

It was true, but the thought of money only added to the feeling of terror she had been trying her best to ignore.

'It's not gonna cost anything to clear the place out to start with,' she replied, impressed with her evasive answering. 'After that, we'll know exactly how much needs repairing, then I guess I'll just have to work out how to get everything done as cheaply as possible.'

'Sounds straightforward,' Bex grinned.

'Perfectly straightforward.'

9

'I'm sorry I've got to cancel, Mum. It's a really last-minute thing. But I'll come round this evening?'

Daisy hurried about the flat, her phone pressed to her head as she tried to get things together. She had arranged to meet Bex and their other friend Claire at Wildflower Lock, and she was already running late. She needed to get off the call as quickly as possible, but more importantly, she needed to do so without arousing her mother's suspicion.

A full working week had passed since she had first been to Wildflower Lock and seen the *September Rose*, the dilapidated boat of which she was now the owner. A boat that her mother knew absolutely nothing about.

Lying to Pippa wasn't something Daisy did. In fact, they were the closest mother and daughter she knew, apart from Pippa and her own mother, but Daisy just didn't know how to approach the subject. Several times during the previous week, she had considered telling her, particularly because she knew there would be a lot of lying to do otherwise so she could work on the boat.

But while it may have been far easier in one respect to tell the truth, she had no idea how her mother would react. No, that wasn't strictly true. She knew Pippa would be angry. Angry at Daisy having any connection to her father and a past that had hurt her mother so deeply. And there didn't seem any point in upsetting her, not when Daisy was going to sell the boat anyway. Of course, in order to sell it, she had to do it up. And in order to do it up, she had to empty it. That was where Claire and Bex were going to come in handy. Together, the three of them were going to empty all the boxes. And judging from what Daisy had seen, it was going to be no small task.

The moment she hung up the phone to her mother, It rang again.

'Hey, Bex, is everything okay? I'm leaving just now.'

'I'm so sorry to do this to you. I'm gonna have to bail. Work has just called. We're getting audited for an account on Monday. It's all hands on deck.'

'Oh.' The disappointment hit Daisy hard, although she couldn't blame Bex at all. This was another reason that having a career seemed overrated. Being beholden to large companies and domineering bosses just wasn't her style. Not that it seemed Bex's either. 'Don't worry about it. Honestly, it's not a problem.'

'I feel so bad. I promised I'd help.'

'It's fine, there's probably not enough room for the three of us in the boat, anyway. Claire and I will get this sorted. Besides, you already did the first stint with me. Don't sweat it.'

'I really am sorry,' Bex repeated for what felt like the hundredth time. 'And if it makes you feel any better, I'm gonna be spending all day in a stuffy room looking at numbers and listening to men make sexist jokes while they pass wind.'

'You really make your job sound appealing,' Daisy said. 'I hope the audit goes okay. Let me know when it's done. We can have a drink on the newly cleared boat to celebrate.'

'A drink sounds good,' Bex replied, before wishing her good luck again and hanging up the phone.

Armed with a large roll of black bin bags, Daisy had just sat down in her car when her phone rang again. Instinctively, she knew who it was and what they were going to say.

'I'm so sorry. Ian just called. He's not going to get back in time to look after Amelia.'

Claire had attended secondary school with Bex and Daisy but had left at sixteen to marry her high school sweetheart. After eight years together, they were still going strong. Unfortunately for Daisy, Ian worked shifts as a lorry driver. The sporadic hours meant trying to pin Claire down was as easy as herding cats into a bath.

'Don't worry. It's not a problem,' she said, a sinking feeling twisting inside her. 'The boat is probably too small for all of us anyway,' she added, parroting the same line she'd used less than half an hour beforehand.

'I'm sure you and Bex will get loads done anyway, without me,' Claire continued. 'And I can't wait to meet the boat. We should definitely take it out together before you sell it.'

'Definitely.' Daisy skipped the remark about Bex. The last thing she need was for Claire to feel any more guilty than she already did.

'At least you've got nice weather for it. Promise you'll send lots of pictures?'

'My phone battery is charged ready for it,' she said, unsure why she was forcing herself to smile when nobody could see. 'And give Amelia a kiss for me.'

'Will do.'

So that was it. She was on her own.

More than once, Daisy considered turning around. What she had envisioned as a fun day, unloading the boxes with her friends, having a peek inside one or two of them to find out a little more about her grandad, and giggling away with the girls, had turned into her spending her Saturday on her own in a derelict boat.

Surprisingly, though, when she parked outside Wildflower Lock and inhaled her first lungful of floral scented air, her mood shifted.

'Morning,' a woman with a paddleboard said, dipping her chin as she passed by.

Daisy opened her mouth to reply, only to close it again. The woman must have been speaking to someone else, surely? After all, Daisy had never seen her before, and you didn't just greet random people, did you? Apparently, Wildflower Lock people did. Because before she had left the car park, three other people, two dog walkers and a kayaker, had also wished her a pleasant morning. The next time, Daisy tried getting in there before they could.

'Lovely day for it, isn't it?' she said to the next paddleboarder that went by.

'Oh, it's always a lovely day for this,' they replied.

It was amazing the effect that strangers could have on her mood. Daisy walked with a near spring in her step and a positive attitude that lasted all the way until she reached the *September Rose*.

Somehow, seeing the moss-covered, derelict boat was even more heart-breaking than it had been the previous weekend. The sun seemed to fall at the exact angle to catch the cobwebs and rust, making them glitter in the light, while bits of litter had gathered in the water around the hull where the boat had been stagnant for so long. At the thought of the work ahead of her, a deep churning began in her gut, but she tamped it down as quickly as she could.

'Okay, let's get this started,' she said to herself.

Inside the boat, their decision to leave the windows open had helped shift the musty smell a fraction, while the movement of air had at least displaced some of the dust. But that was where the good news ended.

The first issue was knowing where to start. It didn't help that the boxes were stacked irregularly. In some places, larger ones were placed on top of smaller ones, most of them at odd angles, some of them having already collapsed, and in other places, small boxes had been shoved into the cracks between larger ones. Knowing that just getting started was a big part of the battle, Daisy prepared herself, before picking up the box closest to her, only to discover it was substantially lighter than she'd expected. Opening it up, she found there was nothing save a few paper receipts. A spark of hope flickered on within. If she could just sort out which of these boxes were empty and stack the full ones, that would likely go a long way to clearing her a bit of space. After all, she still hadn't seen the state of the bathroom and toilet yet. Or the bedrooms. If they were as full as the living area, then it was likely going to take her the entire weekend for her to sort, if not longer.

It probably wasn't the most efficient way to do things, and had Paul been there, he would have scoffed at the ineffective manner in which Daisy was doing things, but she quickly found a rhythm.

Her method was simple and involved taking everything out of the boat to start with. With all the boxes outside, she would then identify the ones she knew were rubbish, like the box full of receipts, and the rest she would bring back in to sort with Claire and Bex, assuming they would be free one night later in the week.

For the most part, Daisy enjoyed the physical act of moving all the boxes around. Bizarrely, it reminded her of those brief weeks she had spent at art college, when they had been given a giant canvas to adorn however they saw fit. Daisy had spent an entire day moving the canvas around, trying to get a feel for it, and find an angle which she felt she could paint at. She had dropped out before the piece was ever completed, but that was a part of the memory she didn't like to ponder on for too long.

To start with, she approached every box tentatively, half expecting a spider, or worse still, a mouse or rat, to jump out. But the spiders were amazingly lethargic and made no attempt to run at her as they crawled out from beneath the cobwebs. Slowly, two large piles formed outside by her boat. The first were things that were going to be binned. The second, things that would probably be binned too, but not immediately. These required a further inspection, so she was going to place them back on the boat when she was finished.

As she stood in the living area, holding the last large box, she gazed around the boat. It was ridiculous how much larger it felt now it was empty. And it was easier to see where it needed work, too. The floor was – as she had initially thought – in good condition, which was not something that could be said for the ceiling or the sides, which were covered in a mismatch of chipped, wooden panelling. After this box, she would have to stop living in denial and open up the rest of the doors to see what waited for her there. A task she was actually looking forward to. And so, moving at a decent pace, she climbed out of the boat and was preparing to add the box to its current pile when she found her route was blocked.

There, standing on her boat, was her neighbour.

'What the hell do you think you're doing?' he said.

Again.

10

He was substantially more dressed than the last time she had seen him and now that Daisy wasn't so put off by the lack of clothes, she could see that his eyes were in fact brown. Almost identical to his stubbly beard and his long hair, which was worn in a topknot. With his ripped jeans and T-shirt, his look was incredibly relaxed, which was more than could be said about his demeanour.

'What is all this? What are you doing?' he snapped, repeating his initial question, despite the fact that Daisy hadn't even had a chance to answer him.

'What do you mean, what am I doing? What does it look like I'm doing? I'm clearing out the boat.'

'You bought her?'

Something about this man irritated her. It wasn't an irrational irritation. Yes, she had accidentally trespassed on his home, but surely anyone with half a brain would make sure their front door was locked while they were in the shower. Particularly if that front door was on a boat next to a public footpath. And now he was speaking to her in a manner that made her hackles rise. After all, what business was it of his whether the boat was hers?

'I wouldn't be clearing it out if it wasn't mine,' she said, curtly. 'Beyond that, I don't think it's any of your business.' She watched as he gritted his teeth in a remarkably similar way to how she was doing.

'You can't leave it like this,' he said, indicating the pile of boxes. 'It's a public towpath. You're blocking the route.'

'I'm not leaving it like this, obviously. I'm sorting it. There's plenty of room for people to pass.' She pointed to the thin strip of land she had left on the pathway.

'This is a hazard. People come down here with their families, on bike or with buggies.'

'And there's plenty of room for them to pass. It won't be here for long.'

'You need to move it now.'

'I'll move it when I'm sorted.'

'You need to move it all back now. You're not leaving it here.'

'I am.'

'No, you're not.'

In a movement that Daisy had not expected, the man grabbed the box out of her hands. Assuming it was heavy, he used far more force to pull it out of her grip than it actually required. As such, he tumbled backwards before catching his heel on another box that Daisy had placed there earlier. By the time he was upright, his face was burning red.

'That's it,' he said. 'If you do not remove all this right now, I'm giving you an official warning.'

Daisy couldn't hold it in. Who the hell did he think he was? He looked like he should be at some hippie festival, singing with a guitar around a campfire, not pestering her for the innocent act of sorting out her own inherited property.

'An official warning for what?' she laughed.

Like that, his demeanour changed. There was a shift in the way he was standing. His posture didn't seem to have changed so much, yet at the same time, he looked to have grown by an inch. Or perhaps it was simply the way he peered down his nose at her.

Then without another word, he turned on his heel and stomped back onto his boat.

'Idiot,' she muttered as she picked up the box he had dropped and put it back on the 'to bin' pile. Really, how ridiculous could some people be?

Back in the boat, she took a moment to admire how much she had achieved. Removing all the boxes had revealed a large wood burner, not unlike the one in the boat next door. Of course, she would need to get someone to check that it worked before she actually used it. She took a moment to imagine having the girls over for dinner, maybe a board game night. Of course, she needed to know how many beds it could sleep before she got too far ahead of herself.

With that thought in mind, Daisy knew it was time to tackle the other end of the boat.

Since returning to the *September Rose*, Daisy had avoided opening the doors to the back part of the boat for fear of what she may find within. She knew she had to face it at some point, of course, but the thought of an overfilled toilet, or a rat-infested bedroom, was something she hadn't been able to face straight away. Bracing herself for whatever was to come, she placed her hand on the back door handle and slid it open.

She paused, then took a step forward.

'Okay,' she said hesitantly before taking another step inwards. A small smile gathered on her lips. A small smile, which only increased the more she saw.

The first surprise – apart from the lack of rats – came from the number of boxes. There were still plenty, and they were still covering the floor, but they seemed to be more organised here.

There were plastic trays, so not likely to succumb to the weather as easily as the cardboard boxes. Several of the boxes had labels on too, like *bills* or *boat manuals*. It was definitely a step up from the living room.

The second surprise came in the form of the bathroom. While it wasn't to her taste, it was still white. White shower, white toilet – which was ridiculously large – and even a small, white bath. That was something she hadn't expected. But the third and final surprise was the real cherry on top.

'No way,' she breathed at the sight.

Not only were there two, small, narrow rooms stacked with bunk beds, but there was a full double bedroom. And Bex was right about one thing; it really could fit a king-size in. This boat could sleep six people. Six! Something that size had to be worth money when it was done up, didn't it?

With her spirits lifted to the highest they had been all day, Daisy headed into the master bedroom. She was about to look inside one of the large plastic boxes when she was interrupted by a knock on the door.

Placing the plastic box back where it was, she turned around. Her face fell.

'What do you want?' She wasn't going to pretend with niceties. Not after the way he had spoken to her earlier.

'I just wanted to give you this, that's all,' he said. He took two steps into the boat but didn't come any further. Instead, he waited and made Daisy walk across to him.

'What's this?' She looked at the envelope he was holding out.

'I'm sure you'll be able to read it well enough.'

As she took it from, his gazed moved to the boat.

'Wow, she really is beautiful,' he said, before seeming to remember himself and returning to his previously stern demeanour. 'Anyway. I should get going. I'm sure everything in there makes sense.'

With that, he turned and walked away, leaving Daisy with the envelope. It read,

To the occupier of mooring 114.

Mooring 114, that was familiar, she thought, before realising that she had seen it somewhere in the solicitor's letter. As tempted as she was to get back to the clearing, she was equally intrigued to know what was inside the envelope and so slipped a finger under the seal and pulled the letter out. As her eyes scanned down the page, her jaw locked into place.

'You have to be kidding me.'

11

Daisy's knuckles shone white through the skin as she clenched her fists.

Every expletive known to man ran through her head as she marched out of the *September Rose*, not even bothering to lock the door as she went. He was not going to get away with this, she told herself repeatedly. Not a chance.

On the small jump from the boat to the bank, she gripped the letter, hearing the paper crumple in her fist. Unfortunately, her blinding rage seemed to have done exactly that. Blind her. At least blind her to the boxes she had stacked outside the boat. Her foot caught on one of the more decrepit scraps in the bin pile. With the rest of her body continuing forward, she was a split second away from face-planting on the ground, when she somehow caught herself.

'Crap!' she said so loudly, she caught the attention of a nearby dog walker. Under normal circumstances, she would have apologised for her outburst, but at that moment, she could focus on nothing but the rage that flooded through her. She kicked the broken box back to its original position before continuing to march down the length of her boat. Less than a minute later, she was storming onto the neighbouring vessel, where the door was already ajar, almost as if he had been waiting for her. The minute she was down the steps, she waved the letter in the air.

'What the hell is this?'

The inside of the narrowboat looked even more glorious than it had on her previous uninvited visit. The curtains were now open, allowing the sunlight to stream in in wide beams, illuminating everything it fell upon. Not that she had the time or inclination to admire anything at that exact moment.

Her still-nameless neighbour was sitting at the breakfast bar, a steaming cappuccino by his side as he worked away on his laptop. Judging by the exquisite smell, the drink had come straight from the expensive coffee machine, and a pang of jealousy momentarily interrupted her fury.

Although it was short-lived.

'Did you hear me?' she said in what was as close to a shout as she ever managed. 'I said, what the hell is this?'

Despite her grand entrance, her neighbour continued to tap away at his laptop, not even bothering to turn his head until a full ten seconds later when he swivelled slowly around on his barstool so that he was facing her.

'Is something wrong?'

Daisy had seen red more than once in her life. She had seen red with inept office managers who delegated every task, not because of their excessive workload, but because they didn't know how to do their job properly. She had seen red while driving, when idiots would cut her up, not even thinking about their own safety, let alone the safety of other people on the road. And of course she had seen red with Paul after what he had done to her. But this, this man's arrogance took her fury to an entirely new level as the blood pounded in her ears.

'You know exactly what's wrong,' she said, waving the letter in his face. 'What the hell is this? You're threatening me with a fine?'

Still maintaining eye contact, he picked up his coffee and took a long, drawn-out sip from his mug. 'I think you will find it is the waterways that are threatening you with a fine.'

'And you just happened to work for them?' Daisy responded. 'Pathetic. This is absolutely pathetic.' Locking her eyes on him, she lifted the letter up to head height. 'Well, this is what I think of your letter.'

Maintaining her gaze, she tore it into half a dozen pieces then let them drop to the floor by her feet. A feeling of satisfaction bubbled within her. A feeling that lasted until he was on his feet and standing in front of her.

'Thank you for that display, but the only thing pathetic here is you. The rules of the waterways are there to keep people safe. Do you know how many accidents happen in this lock every year? Do you? Do you know how many people have seriously injured themselves on these waterways?'

She felt like she was a child being called out by a teacher in front of the class. In front of a class where she didn't even know the subject.

'No, of course I don't.'

'Well I do. There were zero accidents on this area of the canal this year. And last year. And the year before. Do you know why that is?'

He was so close to her, she could practically feel the heat of his breath on her skin.

'Letters like this, I suppose,' she said, looking down at the floor.

'You're too right. It's letters like that. You people come here thinking you can just buy a canal boat and that it'll be an easy fixer upper. A way to make more money. Well, living on the water comes with its risks.' Daisy opened her mouth to respond but he wasn't done yet. 'And it's not you I'm worried about. It's other people. This is people's way of life. Their livelihoods. One of your boxes could send a teenager flying off his bike into the water. One piece of plastic could fall into the waterways and clog up an engine, costing the people that live here a fortune to repair. I'm sorry, but it's not my fault that you didn't do your research before you bought this boat. Or that it's a little more effort than you thought having to clear out somebody else's belongings. But those belongings were someone else's life, their history, and even ignoring the hazards you've created, that person deserves a bit more respect than you dumping their life outside on a path.'

Speechlessness wasn't something that afflicted Daisy very often, but this time she had been stunned to silence. Her heart was pounding in her chest as she racked her brain for a suitable comeback to spit back at this annoyingly attractive man. But her tongue was moving uselessly in her mouth, her brain struggling to form on any fixed idea.

'I wasn't just chucking everything away,' she said finally. 'I was trying to make some space so I could sort things. I was going to bring everything that wasn't rubbish back in when I'd done that. And as for everything else you said, I think it's you that needs to do some research. I didn't buy this boat as an easy fixer upper, as you called it. It was left to me. By my grandfather.' She was on a roll now. 'All those things I took outside, they're part of my history, too. My grandfather and possibly even my father's. So I'm sorry I don't know all your rules, but don't you dare judge when you know nothing about me. Because you know nothing about me at all.'

Angry, heated tears pricked her eyes, and to make matters even worse, he appeared to be looking at her with pity. Actual pity. No, she wasn't going to do this. She refused to. With a sharp intake of breath, she swivelled on the spot before she could let a single tear escape.

As she marched back to the boat, she picked up one of the boxes she had placed on the pathway and began the task of loading the boat back up again.

12

To make the morning even worse, Daisy was hungry. And Daisy did not do well when she was hungry. She was always the person at the office whose top drawer was filled with emergency biscuits. But that morning, she hadn't even considered bringing anything. She should definitely have bought snacks, she thought, as she loaded the boxes back into the boat. Or at least had a decent breakfast. Something that would give her enough energy to do all this lugging about. For a moment, she considered getting in the car and going in search of the nearest coffee shop, but who knew what fines would be waiting for her when she got back?

Despite her anger, her plan remained the same: to move the full boxes back to the boat and deal with the empty ones later. There had to be a large bin somewhere. After all, what did people who live here do with their waste? Annoyingly, she knew exactly who could tell her where she could dispose of all her rubbish. But there was no way she was going to ask him.

Whether it was the lack of food, or the fact she had already been moving boxes for the best part of two and a half hours, or just her annoyed state of mind, every single box felt five times heavier than it had when she was lifting it out of the boat. And to make matters worse, a light drizzle was dampening the cardboard, making it far trickier to get a hold on.

'For crying out loud!' she said as one of the boxes slipped in her hand. This one was full, and judging by the rattling noises within it, the contents were breakable. Thankfully, it didn't hit the ground, although that had nothing to do with her reflexes and more the fact that another pair of hands had grabbed it from the other side. Across the sodden cardboard, a pair of dark-brown eyes looked at her.

'I think we may have got off to a bad start,' he said. His voice was undeniably apologetic. Guilt-ridden even, but Daisy didn't move. 'Perhaps if you would allow me to introduce myself,' he continued. 'My name is Theo, and I am your new next-door neighbour.'

Given how they were both holding the box, Daisy had no choice but to keep looking at him. Her grip on the cardboard was still too slippery to pull it out of his grasp and what she really needed to do was put it down and get a proper hold on it. But any movement, other than marching straight back into her boat, would make it look like she wanted to talk to him. And she didn't. She wanted nothing to do with him.

She took a step forward, only for the box to slip out of her hands entirely. Her stomach lurched as, for a split second, it looked as if it was about to plummet to the ground. But before the box could fall, Theo had shifted his posture and grabbed it from beneath.

'That was close,' he said as he stood up. A small smile twitched on his lips. A smile that Daisy did not reciprocate.

'If you're expecting a thank you, then you sorely misjudged the situation,' she said instead.

'I'm sorry. I genuinely mean that. Summer months can be

pretty hard on the canal. Stag dos cost us a lot of money last year, people crashing into boats and things like that. It was stressful for everyone. I tend to be a bit wary of strangers around here.'

'And me, here on my own, emptying boxes looked like a stag do to you?' There was no way she was accepting that as an apology.

'Please can we start again? You're Fred's granddaughter, right? People around here have a lot of great things to say about your grandad.'

'Well, I'm not one of them,' she said bluntly. 'I never knew the guy. Now, if you'll excuse me, I need to get all of this back inside. The last thing I want to be is hit with another fine from the waterways committee.'

This time, she ensured her grip was firm as she tugged sharply and pulled the box out of his hands, before sidestepping him to take the steps down into the *September Rose*.

When she reached the inside of her boat, her eyes were once again brimming with tears. What was it with this idiot? First, he thought he could treat her like she was vermin because he was worried she was going to upset his precious waterways, and then he was trying to cosy up to her, just because her grandad was some big shot on the canal? She hated people like that. People who only wanted to be around you if they thought they could gain something from the friendship. She'd been around enough people like that in her life. She was done with it. Besides, she had too much work to get on with to waste time thinking about him.

Outside, the drizzle continued and was getting harder. Each box she brought back into the boat was slightly damper than the last. Fully clearing it out had given her the space she needed to reorganise everything. And even though three-quarters of the contents came back inside, she stacked them neatly, giving her a lot more room.

Having lived in a rented property since she left home, Daisy had never had the opportunity to do places up as she would have liked. Even now, having lived in the same apartment for nearly three years, she was hesitant to hammer any holes in the walls, to put pictures up. Then again, what pictures was she going to put up? She was hardly going to pay for someone else's art when there were boxes of her own stored away in her mother's attic. But she didn't think about that. She liked to think about art and painting even less than she like to think about Paul.

But now, she was looking around the *September Rose*, and this empty canvas that was hers to do with whatever she wanted. Light blue would be perfect, she thought, considering the position of the boat on the water. But light blue was ordinary. And Theo's boat was light blue, she remembered with an involuntary grit of her teeth. Maybe she would try something different. Like yellow. Or purple.

Lavender. The thought lit up in her mind. She could paint her boat lavender. The lavender boat on Wildflower Lock. It was so beautiful. She smiled at the thought of it, only for her face to drop at the realisation that she was still a very long way away from painting. For starters, all the peeling stuff would need to be stripped. And the old appliances taken out, although she still hadn't figured out how she was going to pay for replacements.

Still imagining the fixtures and fittings, Daisy moved through into the main cabin and started to rearrange the plastic tubs. Most of what she was moving seemed to be letters. Judging by the number, her grandad had had a thing for the old-fashioned form of correspondence, and she couldn't help but feel enamoured by that. She couldn't remember the last time she had written a letter, unless you counted birthday cards, and she was pretty bad at doing those.

Following a hunch, she discovered that the double bed pulled up to provide even more storage where she found – unsurprisingly – that the space beneath was filled with yet more boxes. Daisy was about to close it again, when her eyes caught sight of a label hidden in the shadows.

'What the...'

She pushed the mattress higher. Though it wasn't heavy, it was awkward to lift, and she was balancing a large chunk of weight on her shoulder. As she leant in to see the label more closely, Daisy blinked, a sudden chill causing the hairs on the back of her neck to rise. A thick lump formed in her throat.

There, written in black ink on a white label, stuck to a box, was her name. Daisy May.

13

Daisy had no idea how long she sat there. She had pulled the large, plastic box out from under the bed, pushed the bed back down, and placed the box with her name in front of her. But that was as far as she'd got. She hadn't managed to lift the lid yet, let alone look inside and find out what was there.

Daisy May. She had seen her name written thousands of times in her life. She had written it thousands of times too. Of course she had. It was her name. But then maybe it was somebody else's name too. This was her paternal grandfather's boat, after all. Perhaps she had been named after a family friend and whatever was contained within this box had nothing to do with her. Perhaps Daisy May was the name of another boat. It certainly sounded like it could be. Perhaps, she thought, when she plucked up enough courage, she would open it up, and find it full of manuals and service histories. Of course, she wouldn't know until she opened the box. Right now, she was having a great deal of difficulty doing that.

Her hands hovered by the clasps on the side. She had just braced herself with a deep breath in when her phone buzzed in her pocket. The sudden noise jolted her and when she saw the name flashed up on the screen, her stomach tied itself into a tight knot.

Mum.

Guilt coiled within her.

Daisy had deliberately kept all thoughts of her mother pushed to the back of her mind for the entire day. Thankfully, keeping busy with all the clearing had meant she barely had time to think of her. But there was no avoiding it now. She would have to answer. If she didn't, Pippa would think there was something wrong, and she'd keep on ringing till Daisy answered. She knew that from experience.

'Hi, Mum.' She tried to keep her voice as level as possible. 'Everything okay?'

'Hi, Daisy bear, I was just calling to see what time you were coming over. Farah asked if I wanted to pop round for a cup of tea, and I wanted to check you weren't already on your way over. You know how she likes to chat. Daisy? Daisy, love, are you still there?'

Daisy blinked. She felt as if she had disappeared the entire time Pippa had been speaking.

'Sorry? Sorry, Mum, I'm not sure what happened there. Yes. Yes, I'm still here. What was it you just said?'

'Are you sure you're all right, love? You don't sound quite right.'

The windows at the back of the boat were open, but barely a breeze was filtering through. Sweat beaded on the back of Daisy's neck.

'Yes, yes, sorry. I'm fine. I was just writing a message to Claire, that's all. Tell me what it was you said again.'

A short pause preceded her mother's answer. 'I wanted to know if you were on your way round. Farah asked me to pop round for a cup of tea and a natter. You know, Farah over the road.'

'No. I mean, no, I'm not on my way round. Yes, I know Farah. Yes, you've got time. Go to Farah's.'

'Are you sure you're all right?'

The sweating was getting worse. Talking to her mother while her damn name stared at her from a plastic box with almost more than she could take.

'I'm sorry. You just called me right in the middle of something. I'll... I'll be round later. I'll just let myself in. It's not a problem. I'll speak to you later, okay?'

She hung up the phone.

Twenty-four years. That was how long her mum had looked after her, and for twenty-two of those, they had been on their own. Never had Daisy kept something like this a secret. But it was better in the long run, wasn't it? She wiped the back of her neck with her hand. Of course it was.

She rubbed her hands together as if she were warming up for some sporting misadventure. This damn box. How much time had she wasted looking at it already? Far too much, considering how much work there was still left to do.

'Just open the damn thing,' she said. Then, without a moment to second guess herself, she whipped off the lid.

She frowned at the contents. The box appeared to be full of letters. Sealed, unopened letters. A trembling started in her chest, but almost immediately, it spread further down to her hands.

'Please be about a boat,' she whispered, almost in a prayer.

She reached into the centre of the box and pulled out an envelope at random.

Daisy May,
4 Chestnut Avenue.

Her heart lurched as a gasp flew from her lips. It was her address. The same house that her mother was expecting her to visit that afternoon. Heat was building behind her eyes as tears attempted to force their way up her throat, but it wasn't the sight of her name and address on the envelope that caused the response. No, it was the line that was struck through her name. And the words written beneath it. In her mother's handwriting.

Return to sender.

One after another, she pulled the envelopes out of the box, not considering how ordered and neatly stacked they had been as she tossed them out and over the bare mattress of the bed. *Return to sender. Return to sender*. There had to be fifty different-sized envelopes. Possibly even a hundred, of various sizes and colours, and each of them said the same thing. Each of them scribbled over in her mother's hand.

When she was certain they were all addressed to her, Daisy started checking the dates on the postage stamps: 2004, 2008, 2015, 2011. Most years had more than one, although none went past 2016. What had happened that made her grandfather suddenly stop sending these letters to her? Had he just given up when he realised she was never going to read them? It felt like a strange time to give up.

Daisy was holding a small pile from the latest year when it hit her like a hammer. Gasping, she dropped the envelopes back on to the bed and her hands flew up to her mouth. There was a reason there were no letters past 2016, and it wasn't because her grandfather had stopped writing.

It was because her grandfather hadn't written them at all. These were from her father.

14

Daisy sat motionless in the fading light. The evenings were lengthening, having just passed the spring equinox, which was a good, really. Had it been any earlier in the year, it would have been pitch black already, and she wouldn't have been able to see a thing.

Her dad had written to her. She didn't need to open the letters to know that. She could feel it in her bones. He had tried to make contact, not just once or twice, but all these times. He had tried to be a part of her life.

A stab of anger struck as she thought about all those times growing up when she had seen her friends' dads scooping them up in their arms, and she would ask her mother about her father. Why he didn't want to see her. Whether she had done something wrong. What had made him leave.

'We're better off without him.' That was what Pippa had always said. 'We wouldn't want a man like that in our life, anyway.' But the way she had spoken always made it sound like Daisy hadn't had a choice. Her father had left them and didn't want any part in her life. That was what she had grown up believing. After all, that was what Pippa had said often enough. But why would he have sent her all these letters if he didn't want anything to do with her? Daisy's head was spinning with questions she didn't have answers to, and the only way to find them out was to open the letters.

'All this rubbish out here' The muffled voice of an elderly woman reached Daisy's ears. 'It's an absolute disgrace. I've got a good mind to call the council.'

'Crap, the rubbish.' Daisy snapped out of the moment. She'd completely forgotten about all the boxes she was supposed to have moved by now. Gathering the envelopes into her arms, she tried to shove them back into the box, but they continued to spill out of the edges. She pulled some out again, only to change her mind and leave them as they were. She would deal with the rubbish first. Then come back to the letters. They would still be here when she came back.

She took the steps out of the boat two at a time, but when she landed on the bank, she discovered Theo had beaten her to it.

'Before you start, I just got side-tracked. Something happened.'

'I wasn't going to start anything,' he said. 'In fact, I've come back to help you out. I realise I was a bit harsh when I spoke before. I thought this might help speed things up a bit.' With a nod of his head, he gestured to the side, where he had already filled up a wheelbarrow with some of the broken cardboard boxes and unwanted scraps of paper. 'I assumed this was the rubbish pile as you took everything else inside. I was just going to wheel it down to the bin. You'll want to get yourself a wheelbarrow. They're a godsend. Of course, you can always borrow mine if you need it.'

Given the fact Daisy had been readying herself for another fight, she was more than a little taken aback by this change of attitude. Was he being nice? He certainly sounded like he was being nice, but she didn't have the mental capacity to deal with that right now. Not when he had repeatedly humiliated her. Pushing past him, she grabbed another handful of boxes, threw them into the top of the wheelbarrow and grabbed the handles.

'Are the bins this way?' she said, gesturing with her chin.

'Just on the other side of the green shed. I can show you if you want?'

'It's fine, I'm sure I can find my way,' she said, and began to wheel the rubbish down the path.

Thankfully, it wasn't too long a walk and, with a fair bit of cramming, it took only six trips to get the pathway empty. After her first trip, Theo disappeared back into his boat and didn't reappear.

After she'd finished the job, the dark was well and truly settling in. The sun glowed low on the horizon, casting the sky a range of pinks and orange. Inside the boat, it was almost impossible to see anything at all.

'Okay, electricity switches. Where are you?' she mused, seeing several bulbs dotted along the ceiling. How to get them working was another matter. She tried the light switches. And the breaker box, which she found in the kitchen, but to no avail. After nearly tripping up twice, she knew she was left with two choices. She could either give up and go home. Or she could knock next door and ask Theo for help. Really, there was only one answer.

Before she left, there was one thing she needed to do. She wasn't going to be leaving empty-handed.

With her phone propped on the window ledge as a torch, it took her a solid five minutes to fit all the letters back into the box, and even when she had managed it, she found it was far too heavy to carry any distance. Deflated, but not defeated, she decided to take a few home with her then, with the intention of coming back in the morning, and reading through the rest. She picked a selection of different dates, dropped the envelopes into her handbag, then locked up the *September Rose* and headed back to the car.

Daisy didn't start the ignition as quickly as she had intended to.

Her eyes moved constantly to her handbag, where the corners of the envelopes peeked out. Would it really be safe for her to drive home when she was so distracted? Perhaps if she opened one, just to check it really was written by her father, it would put her mind at rest. It certainly couldn't make her feel any worse than she already did. Her hand was poised above her handbag, ready to pull out the first envelope, when her phone buzzed. Pippa. Again.

She answered on autopilot.

'Mum.'

'Daisy, dear. Is everything all right? I thought you'd be here by now. I put a shepherd's pie in the oven.' Her mother's voice grated down the line.

'Actually, Mum, I don't think I'm gonna make it to you tonight.' Daisy could hear the crack in her tone.

'Is everything all right, love? You really don't sound okay at all. Do you want me to pop round?'

'No, no. Everything is fine. I just... It's just been a bit of a manic day. I'll ring you tomorrow.'

And without waiting for a reply, she hung up. It was now or never, Daisy thought. She needed to read those letters.

15

Dear Daisy, happy sixth birthday. Love Dad.

Dear Daisy, happy eighth birthday, love Dad.

Dearest Daisy, Merry Christmas, I hope Father Christmas brought you everything you asked him for.

Dear Daisy, Daisy, Daisy…

The first three envelopes contained two birthday cards and one Christmas card, and she read them over and over again. The handwriting was identical in each, with a little heart above the I in her name, the same way she had drawn it when she was in primary school. The fourth envelope was a little thicker than the others. It was dated 2015 and she stared at it for a good while longer, before she plucked up the courage to open it. She had just slipped her finger into the well-stuck seam when a knock on the car window made her jump out of her skin.

'We're closing up the car park,' said a woman in a high-vis jacket and beanie hat. 'If you're leaving, you better go now or you'll be trapped in for the night.'

'Sorry, yes, I'm going now,' she said, her heart pounding.

'All right, you better get going then.'

Daisy waited for the car park assistant to take a step back before she started the engine and drove out of Wildflower Lock.

The entire way home, she was on autopilot, stopping at traffic lights and turning at junctions without feeling like she was present, and when she turned into her road, it almost came as a shock that she was there.

Upstairs in the flat, she dropped onto the sofa, not even bothering to remove her shoes as she opened the fourth envelope. Once again, there was a birthday card inside, but this time, a piece of lined paper had been folded and slipped into the centre.

Her hands were trembling as she flattened it out and read the words.

Dear Daisy,

It's been a long time since I've seen you. So long that I sometimes worry you might not have any memories of me at all. I hope that's not the case, because for me, those years with you were the happiest of my life. I want you to know that I think about you. I think about you every day and wish I could have got the chance to know the amazing young lady I am certain you've become. I hope you're happy. I hope you're living the life of your dreams. And if you're not, you should know, it's not too late to start now.

Love you always,

Dad.

Daisy dropped the envelope onto the seat beside her, feeling tears roll down her cheeks. It didn't make sense. All these birthday cards never received. All these words from her father that she had never been allowed to read. When he'd died, she had thought he had forgotten her, or at least wanted nothing to do with her. But these letters didn't sound like that at all.

With a surge of energy, she picked up her phone and swiped onto the recently called list, where 'Mum' was at the top. Yet rather than pressing the dial button, she simply stared at the screen. Why would her mother keep this from her? Why would she return every letter her father had sent and foil every attempt at communication? There had to be a reason. Pippa had given everything to ensure that Daisy had had every opportunity in life. And even when Daisy messed those opportunities up – as she often did – Pippa had still been there. Supporting her. Loving her. It just didn't make sense that she would hide all this unless she had a very good reason. The problem was, there was no way Daisy would find out what that reason was unless she asked her.

She glanced out the window before checking the time on her phone. It was only just gone eight-thirty, but it felt closer to midnight. Her arms and legs were aching from all the lifting and carrying, while her head was throbbing. Even if her mother would open up about the past, Daisy was too tired to hold an actual conversation, let alone one this serious. And so she gathered up the cards and the letter, dragged herself to the bedroom and was asleep before her head even touched the pillow.

When she woke the next morning, Daisy felt as if she had barely slept. As always, the aromas of freshly baked pastries fill the room, although she was almost immune to it now. There was a crick in her neck, and her head pounded, compounded by banging from the bakery below. She squeezed her eyes shut and willed herself back to sleep for a moment before the reality of what she had learnt the night before struck her.

She needed to see her mother.

Daisy made the journey from her flat to her mother's house in a record twenty minutes. Normally, she would have been pleased to make such good time, but this wasn't a normal visit and for once, she wished there had been more red lights or traffic jams to delay her a little.

Pippa had grown up on the east coast of England, but had moved to London when she was in her early twenties for work, wanting to try her hand in the big city restaurants. Though Daisy knew her opinion was biased, she had always thought Pippa's food was easily good enough to grace the menu in a Michelin-starred restaurant. Yet after a few years working in fine dining, Pippa had grown tired of the stress and the long hours, choosing instead work at a small café just a fifteen-minute walk from her house in Edmonton.

As Daisy stood outside the front door of the two-up, two-down terraced house, she considered what she should do. Her front door key was the same one she had been given when she was eleven years old and until now, she had always used it without hesitation. But this time, her hand hovered by her side.

She knew that if she asked Bex or Claire for their opinion, they would tell her to confront her mother outright about the letters. To demand answers. But then they would weigh in with their opinions about the boat, and her keeping it hidden from Pippa. She knew her mother better than anyone. If she went in there, guns blazing, Pippa would clam up and refuse to say anything at all. That was the way her mother always acted when she didn't like the way a conversation was going. It could take days, if not weeks, to get answers. So as much as it pained her, Daisy knew she was going to have to be a little sneakier, for now at least.

And so, steeling herself with a deep breath, she slipped the key into the door and let herself in.

16

The house smelt identical to how it had when Daisy had lived there. The aroma of home-baked meals melded into the bricks of the wall. Her mother's perfume, floral and light, with undertones of woodiness, was the same she had worn when Daisy was at school. Although the scents of the house stayed the same, the decor had changed dramatically since the early years of Daisy's childhood. In the past five years, her mother had fitted a new carpet, bought a new sofa and gone through two new sets of curtains in the living room alone. All the bedrooms had been painted and the kitchen cupboards had received a dramatic overhaul the year before.

Daisy kicked off her shoes and placed them neatly on the rack. Her mum was particular about tidiness, especially when it came to things littering the floor. So, after checking the shoes were suitably straight, she hung her coat on the hook. And then her eyes fell upon the painting in the hallway.

The landscape was a blur of colours which stretched a good three feet. The blues and greys were highlighted with flecks of gold and though there were no discernible images within it, many people said the painting reminded them of the sky after a storm. Daisy must have asked her mother to move that picture several dozen times. At one point, she had even bought a replacement picture to go up and hung it there herself. But the moment she had left home, the replacement was gone, and the original was back in its place. Now she had given up asking.

'This painting was the first time we knew you had something really special,' Pippa would say each time Daisy asked her to take it down. 'Even if you're not painting any more, it doesn't change the fact that my daughter is exceptionally talented and I like to be reminded of that.'

Usually, when she came into the house, she just avoided looking in that direction, but that morning, her eyes lingered on the brushstrokes. To her, the painting was crass. Mediocre. Certainly not her best work. But then, she didn't like to think about her best work either. Not given how good she could have become had things not turned out so badly.

'Daisy, dear, is that you? I wasn't expecting you. Is everything okay?'

Pippa trundled down the steep staircase, which had been great to slide down when Daisy was young. Now she looked at them and wondered when they would start getting difficult for her mother to climb. Not that she'd ever say that to Pippa, of course. She wasn't even fifty and showed no signs of slowing whatsoever. But just occasionally, Daisy would like it if her mother thought about the future. And the fact that living in a house like this, with a near-vertical staircase, wouldn't be practical in fifteen or twenty years' time.

'Sorry, it's not a bad time, is it?' she said, her heart racing unnaturally.

'Of course it's not a bad time,' Pippa said, wrapping her arms around Daisy in a tight squeeze that lingered a fraction longer than normal. 'I was worried about you. You sounded off on the phone yesterday.'

'Just busy, that's all,' she lied.

A deep furrow formed between Pippa's brows. 'It's not this job, is it? I thought you said you liked this one. That hasn't changed, has it? Because you said the money was nice and stable.'

'No, there's nothing wrong with the job, Mum.'

'Good. Because, you know, I was thinking, this could be the one for you. Secretarial work. I was talking to Farah about it. She said you can make quite a career from it now. And that there are plenty of part-time jobs going in that field too. You know, if you wanted time to pursue... other things.'

Daisy could already feel a lecture creeping towards her. For someone who always seemed so relaxed, Pippa was very good at lectures.

'I can't stay for long,' she said, aware that time was slipping away, and she had not yet made any attempt to find any answers to her questions. 'I'm meeting Bex and Claire.'

'Are you doing anything nice?'

At this, Daisy's mouth opened, only to close again. The comment about seeing her friends had come out entirely by accident and had left her with a question she couldn't answer. 'Oh... Amelia's got some sort of competition... Gymnastics or something. I can't remember. Claire asked us if we wanted to watch.'

'That sounds nice.' Without needing to say any more, they walked into the kitchen, where her mum flicked on the kettle. 'I'm always jealous of you girls. You know it's so lovely how supportive you are of one another.'

'It is,' Daisy said, wanting to shift the conversation back to the direction she had planned. 'Afterwards, we thought we might go for a walk somewhere. Maybe a pub lunch. There's this nice new place that's opened up by a lock apparently.'

Daisy had intended to watch her mother for any tell-tale twitches or signs, but she had timed the comment badly and Pippa was currently at the fridge, taking the milk out with her back facing her.

'That does sound like a nice day,' she agreed.

Daisy gritted her teeth; she was going to need to go in a little stronger to get any answers.

'Have you ever thought about living on a boat?' she said as her mother poured the milk. Pippa froze, the milk still flowing into her mug.

'Live on a boat?' she said, catching the drink before it overflowed. 'Why would you say something like that?'

'It's quite popular,' she replied, her heart pounding. The lie sounded so damn fake to her ears, but she was going to see it through. 'Lots of people are downsizing to them. Particularly from the city. You know, saving rent, a simpler way of life.'

Her mother scoffed. 'A simple way of life? Dealing with a pump-out toilet and nosey neighbours who can moor up next to you in the middle of the night? No, I can't imagine anything worse. Never had any desire to do that at all.'

She laughed as she talked, as if the whole thing was a joke, but Daisy could see the tension flicker around her eyes. And the way she was holding the mugs was causing the liquid to ripple on the surface. Not to mention the comment about the pump-out toilet. Daisy didn't even know what that was, but it was obvious her mum knew far more about canal boats than she was letting on. After taking her tea, Daisy changed the subject, as if canals and boats had just been a passing commentary. They talked a little about Bex and Claire, and about how the owner of the café Pippa worked at wanted them to do themed lunches and how Farah's hip operation had been shifted again. When the drinks were finished, Daisy kissed her mother on the cheek and lifted her bag from the floor.

'You'll be around again for tea later in the week?' Pippa said.

'Of course,' Daisy said. 'I'm sure we'll have lots to catch up on.'

17

At Wildflower Lock, Daisy had a surprise waiting for her.

'What are you doing here?' she asked as she reached the gate to the canal to find Claire standing there looking somewhat lost. 'I thought you had to look after Amelia this weekend?'

'I did, but I thought Bex had come down with you yesterday. I spoke to her last night on the phone. She said she'd had to work. You should've told me. I would have sorted something.'

It was then Daisy noticed Amelia behind her, standing against the wall. At seven years old, she could talk for an equal length about fairies and golden retrievers as she could about the different layers of the sea and what wildlife could be found there.

'Is she gonna be okay here? I don't know how child friendly the boat is.'

'She'll be fine. We've got colouring, we've got card games, and when all of that fails, we've got a tablet and headphones. So tell me, where do we start with the cleaning?'

'Actually, can I just ask you about something first?'

Thirty minutes later and Amelia was on the tablet while Daisy filled Claire in about the letters and birthday cards, not to mention her mother's evasive response when she surreptitiously brought up canal boats.

'I can't believe you didn't throw the letters in her face,' Claire said, as Daisy predicted she would. 'How could you not say anything? I don't understand why you didn't come right out and say it: did you send my birthday cards back to my dad each time he sent them? You're being this calm about it. I'd be furious.'

'I'm not calm,' Daisy admitted. 'But there's got to be more to it, surely? Whatever kind of man my father was, he must have done something pretty damn awful for my mother to let me have no contact whatsoever, right?'

'Well, if that's what you think, then maybe you are better off not knowing.'

'Exactly, and the sooner I can get this boat done and sold, the better.'

Given the bombshell the first box in the bedroom had given Daisy, she'd shut the door on that part of the boat and focused her efforts on the rest of the space. And while she busied herself emptying kitchen cupboards of tins of soup and corned beef that were five years past their best before date, Claire got to work with a broom. With most of the floor clear, she could get into the corners and collect piles of cobwebs and dust that would put any haunted house to shame.

While the *September Rose* was still a long way from being a luxury home, its potential was becoming clearer and clearer.

'I think I'd actually quite like to spend the night on a boat,' Claire said as she stepped back and observed their work. It might have been a throwaway comment, but for Daisy, it sparked an idea of exactly what they should do the following weekend.

'Okay, you're on,' she said.

* * *

At work the next week, Daisy had a hard time focusing. Normally, her job didn't require too much concentration. Answering the telephone and responding to emails meant it was the type of job in which you just had to go with the flow. And normally she enjoyed that, but with her mind so fixated on the boat and the letters, it was hard to focus on much else.

On the Monday, she put a phone call through to the wrong office, and on Tuesday, she replied to the same email twice, although thankfully nobody at the job other than her and the client would know that. Still, it wasn't good. She liked her job and she wanted to keep this one. If she kept making silly mistakes, eventually people would start noticing. It was just hard to think about anything other than the boat and all the other things that went with it.

Tuesday evening, Daisy took her first trip to the hardware store. Although she still wasn't 100 per cent sure what tools she needed. She had spent hours researching paints for the outside of the boat, which had led down the rabbit hole of dry docks and the fact she would need to get her boat out of the water to paint the underside at some point. Still, there were plenty of jobs inside the boat she could do, and she figured someone at the hardware store would be able to point her in the direction of a decent toolkit to get her started. Though as she stepped into the shop it wasn't a member of staff she found herself faced with. At least, not a member of staff from the hardware store.

'Amanda?' Daisy said, suddenly questioning who she was seeing. It certainly looked like her line manager, only rather than wearing a power suit with killer heels, she was dressed in dungarees with an oversized hoodie.

'Daisy, what a surprise.'

It was. The fact Daisy didn't socialise with colleagues outside of work meant she knew very little about their lives, but judging by the masses of wooden planks and plasterboard filling Amanda's trolly, she was not a novice at DIY.

'Looks like you're building something big there,' Daisy said, feeling the awkward sensation that came with the need to make small talk. It wasn't that she didn't like Amanda. She just hated situations like this, where forced conversation was near imperative. Thankfully, her line manager smiled softly.

'I'm putting up a stud wall, if you can believe it. The twins have had enough of sharing and Lynn and I have had enough of them arguing.'

Twins, Daisy thought. She didn't even know that Amanda had children, yet before she responded, Amanda was talking again.

'What about you? Is this one of your normal hangouts after work?'

Daisy chuckled briefly. She tended to keep her private life separate from work, but they weren't at the office, and Amanda had already given her an insight into her life outside of the job.

'Can I show you something really quickly? As long as you're not busy?'

'Trust me, anything to give me an extra five minutes from listening to the twins argue is welcome. You think it'll get better when their older, but honestly, it's worse. With mine at least.'

After rummaging in her bag, Daisy pulled out her phone, and quickly flicked to the photographs she had taken the previous weekend. She hadn't really looked at the pictures as she was taking them. They were more for reference than anything else, before and after, but now, looking at them, she felt a deep sense of nostalgia. There was something about the way the roof curved, and those large windows. It really did have a naturally homely feeling about it.

'This is the *September Rose*. My grandfather, who I didn't even know really, left her to me.'

Amanda's eyes widened. 'Wow. Lynn and I spent one of our first dates on a narrow boat. And we spent a week on holiday on one, over in Warwickshire, a couple of years after we were married. Honestly, the number of times I tried to convince her we should pack up our lives and move into one.'

'Could you honestly do that?' Daisy said, thinking about her mother's comments about pump-out toilets. 'Could you really live on a boat?'

'I don't think I could do it now,' Amanda replied. 'And I don't think the boys would take too kindly to it either, with exams coming up. But if I was your age, maybe when Lynn and I first got married. Why not? I think it would've been an adventure. Though it looks like you've got a lot of work ahead of you before she's liveable.'

'I know. But I feel like it's gonna be worth it. I mean, I probably won't keep her. I'm sure I won't, but she is pretty special, right?'

Amanda kept her eyes on the screen for a moment longer, before turning back to her, smiling.

'Make sure you show me some photos when you're done. I'd love to see what she looks like. And perhaps you can take us out for a trip on her in the summer? Assuming you haven't sold her by then, of course.'

'That sounds great,' Daisy said, then with a nod towards the aisles behind, bid her manager farewell. She had tools to buy.

18

Wednesday evening, Daisy headed straight to Wildflower Lock. She hadn't planned on going up there, having initially decided to do the boat up on weekends only, but the day had been filled with clear skies and bright sunshine, and as such, she found herself wanting to make the most of the lengthening evenings. Besides, she assumed going on a weekday evening would mean it was quieter. She assumed wrong.

Where have all these people come from? she wondered, as she took the turning into Wildflower Lock car park.

It was worse than the weekend before, when she had first visited with Bex. Cars were practically queueing to get a space. Once again, the paddleboarders and kayakers were out in their droves, although 90 per cent of the people were dog walkers. Dog walkers, it appeared, loved Wildflower Lock.

Due to the lack of space, Daisy had to park up the other end of the parking field, an even longer walk from *September Rose*. Not that it bothered her. The walk allowed her a chance to spot dragonflies and moorhens hidden in the rushes. She hadn't decided exactly what she was going to do yet. There were still all the boxes in the bedroom that needed addressing, and the ones she had sorted in the living area, filled with winter jumpers and fishing gear which needed taking to a charity shop somewhere, too. Then again, maybe it would be useful to make an inventory of everything in the boat that was salvageable.

She had stepped onto the back deck and was considering how difficult it would be to rip out the entire kitchen and start again, when a voice called out from behind. 'Daisy? Daisy May?'

She turned on the spot. A split second of confusion at first, which passed almost immediately at the sight of the woman standing in front of her.

'Auntie Bethany!' she said, and immediately leapt from the boat.

Auntie Bethany was not an aunt. The tall, elegant lady before her, who was currently holding a lead attached to a similarly tall and elegant dog, had taken Daisy's mother under her wing when she had moved to London. For a large portion of Daisy's life, she had treated Bethany's house as if it were an extension of her own, raiding the fridge when she was hungry, scattering her toys all over the carpets and occasionally using it as a place to watch horror films Pippa would never have approved of. But then, just before Daisy's father had died, Bethany had left the rat race and headed to the country. That was the last she had seen of her.

'It's been years. How have you been? And who's this?' Daisy said, reaching down to stroke the dog.

'This is Pom-Pom,' Bethany replied. 'My granddaughter wanted to name her.'

'She's gorgeous,' Daisy said as the dog's tail beat hard against her leg. She wasn't great with dog breeds, but if she had to guess, she'd say Pom-Pom was one of those Lurcher or Greyhound types.

'What about you?' Bethany said, her question causing Daisy to straighten up and stop giving the dog so much fuss. 'I can't believe it. You've hardly changed. Are you still painting? I assume you went to art college like you always dreamt of doing.'

Daisy felt her smile tighten.

'That didn't quite work out as well as I'd hoped,' she said, wanting to change the subject as quickly as possible. 'But Mum's still living in London, and still at the same house, would you believe?'

'And I bet she's working in the same café too, isn't she?'

'Of course.'

'She's kept that place afloat for far too long. I hope they know how lucky they are to have her. You know, it's been such a long time since we've spoken, but you know what it's like. Life gets in the way and before you know it, ten years have passed.'

Daisy could see the sadness in her eyes as she said this.

'We've all let it happen,' she said, trying not to let the silence become awkward. 'You said you have grandchildren now?'

'Three, if you can believe it. And all of them are unfathomably gorgeous. What about you? What are you doing here, standing on a boat, of all places?'

Daisy's pulse flicked up. She had been so excited about seeing her old friend she had forgotten what it would mean for Bethany to see her. Suddenly, she felt grateful that Bethany and Pippa had fallen out of contact.

'Oh, I'm not up to much. Just enjoying the weather, you know? I thought about maybe trying paddleboarding, actually. With a friend. It's a friend's boat. Well, a friend of a friend.' Daisy could feel herself digging a hole, but Bethany didn't seem to notice.

'My son-in-law loves paddleboarding. He comes down here quite a lot. You never know, you might bump into him.'

The conversation was making her more and more nervous. She gestured down to the dog. 'You should probably give Pom-Pom her walk. I'll send Mum your love.'

'It's been lovely to see you, too. Try not to fall off the paddle-board. The sun might be out, but the canal is still freezing at this time of year.'

'I'll remember that.' Daisy smiled.

A moment later, Bethany and Pom-Pom trotted away, and Daisy let out a long sigh of relief.

She was still leaning against the *September Rose*, waiting for her heart rate to go back to normal, when Theo appeared out the door of his boat. Daisy wasn't going to make any attempt to speak to him. In fact, it was the exact impetus she needed to get moving, but before she could, Theo spoke.

'I didn't expect you to be back here today,' he said. 'But I'm glad you are.'

'You are?' Her voice hitched at the unexpectedly pleasant greeting.

'I've got the prices for next year's mooring fees. Fred kept his payments up to date, even when he couldn't get down here, so you're covered for the next six months, but after that, it's going to be up to you to pay them. I've got your letter in my boat, if you hang on for a sec.'

'Mooring fees?' Now Theo had mentioned them, it seemed an obvious thing to need. Otherwise, you could have anybody parking up wherever they liked. Although that was the whole point of having a boat, wasn't it? The freedom to go where you wanted.

As Theo climbed down the steps into his boat to fetch the letter, Daisy had another peer through the window. The immaculate state in which he kept his boat felt at odds to his grungy look. But not in an unattractive way. If anything, it made him more attractive.

She shut the thought down immediately. No, no way. He may be above average when it came to looks, but that didn't make a man attractive. She had already seen what he was like when he got in a mood. She wanted nothing to do with a guy like that. Or any guy, for that matter.

'Here you go,' he said, reappearing and handing her the letter. 'This is assuming you want the same mooring, obviously. Fred always had this place, as far as I'm aware, and you probably won't find a better deal than this, but it's up to you, of course. I won't be offended if you want to move.'

Was that a joke? She couldn't tell, and she wasn't really in the mood to find out.

'Thank you.' She took the envelope before turning around and walking towards the *September Rose*. She'd already ripped it open before she reached the deck and had slipped the paper out before she could put one foot on the boat. Her hand covered her mouth as she stifled a gasp. The paper was headed with the waterway's logo, and there were a few other details including dates and mooring length, but there was only one thing on the page that was holding Daisy's attention. A number. A very big number.

19

'Seven thousand pounds.' It didn't matter how many times she said it out loud, it didn't make the number any smaller. 'Seven thousand pounds. That's how much mooring fees are for a year.'

'But Theo said you didn't have to pay those right now, didn't he? He said they're not due yet.'

After the shock of the letter, Daisy had struggled to get anything done on the boat. She even thought about going back to Theo and asking if there was an extra zero on the end by mistake, but a quick internet search told her that it was probably correct. So after an hour of shifting boxes from one side of the living area to the other, she had given up and headed home, ringing Bex en route in the hope she'd be able to pop over for a drink at some point in the evening. As it happened, her best friend was there, waiting outside the bakery by the time Daisy arrived at the flat. Thankfully, she brought some beers with her this time, as well as the wine.

'Seven thousand pounds. That's nearly a quarter of my wage. I thought boating life was meant to be cheap?'

Bex took the letter from Daisy's hand and scanned through it.

'Look, it says here it doesn't have to be paid until September.

You're all up to date until then. Maybe it's possible to see if you can pay it monthly after that.'

'That's still nearly six hundred pounds a month,' she replied, rather impressed by the speed of her mental maths.

Daisy sighed. She might have spare cash for takeaways, shopping trips, and the occasional designer handbag, but in some parts of the country, six hundred pounds a month was rent on another flat.

'No, this is good,' she said, slurping back a mouthful of craft ale. 'I've got a deadline now. The boat needs to be ready to sell by the time the mooring fees are due. September.'

It was Bex's turn to do some mental maths, although it wasn't particularly difficult, especially considering her job. 'September? That means you've got six months. Six months to completely renovate a boat.'

'A six-berth wide beam,' Daisy said, slipping in some of the terminology she'd learnt over the past two weeks. 'And it's not the entire boat I need to renovate. The bathroom is fine.'

'It's still a lot of work. You don't even know anything about renovating houses. Let alone houses that are on the water.'

Daisy thought it through. Six months. That might sound like a long time. Especially when it came to holding down a job. But with all the tasks she needed to do on the boat, and with only weekends and after work to do them, it did feel somewhat daunting.

'Well, I guess we better pull our fingers out then,' she said, straightening her back.

'What exactly do you mean by "we"?' Bex replied.

* * *

Daisy was genuinely excited. Today was going to be a good day. No, it was going to be a great day. Ian had agreed to have Amelia all weekend, and Bex and Claire had dug out some old sleeping bags and blow-up mattresses. The three of them were going to spend the night aboard the boat.

'Did everyone pack extra socks and jogging bottoms? I have no idea how cold it is going to get, and I do not want any of you blaming me for this,' she said as they loaded the back of the car. Despite the fact they were only driving for an hour, and only staying one night on the boat, the boot of the car was rammed full. A large amount of that was food – crisps, chocolate and a large stash from the bakery – not to mention wine and beer. Bex had bought her Bluetooth speakers, and Claire had made a special, first-night-on-the-boat playlist. But along with the fun things, there were also more practical items. Metal tools for stripping paint, buckets, sponges and a large packet of industrial-sized bin bags. The idea was to get the boat as clean as it could be before they started painting the inside and replacing the fixtures. Then she would need to get it to wherever the nearest dry dock was to get the outside done.

'You should ask Theo to give you a driving lesson,' Bex said as they drove away, the radio blasting. 'It could be a nice chance for you to get to know each other. Almost like a date.'

Daisy gave her friend a withering scowl.

'You have to drop this, you know. I have told you I will date again when I am ready. And even if I was ready, which I'm not, Theo is so not my type.'

'I just think you've built this up into something more than it is. I'm not saying you have to get married, but you've not been on a single date since you split up with Paul. Don't you think that's weird?'

'Lots of people don't feel comfortable dating after a breakup.' Daisy could hear her voice rising.

'But it's been two and a half years.'

That was it. She'd had enough. They'd not driven very far, but Daisy flicked on her indicators and pulled in sharply to the side of the road.

'Let's get this clear; we are not talking about Paul this weekend,' she said, enunciating her words so firmly, she was nearly spitting. 'We are not talking about me dating this weekend. We are not talking about Theo and whether he's single or whether he's my type. We're not talking about what my type is. We are not talking about anything other than how we get this boat up to selling standard ASAP. Is that clear? Because if it's not, then you should get out now.'

In the rear-view mirror, Daisy could see Claire shrink into her seat, but deep down, Daisy suspected she thought exactly the same as Bex when it came to Daisy's love life. She just had the sense not to talk about it in front of her.

'We just want you to be happy, that's all,' Bex said quietly. 'You're so great, but you shut yourself off to everybody. I mean it. When was the last time you did anything with anybody new? Went for a cup of coffee with a colleague, or asked somebody at the gym if they want to go for a smoothie?'

'Since when did I go to the gym?' Daisy replied. 'And my workplace isn't like that. I don't know why you're making a fuss. I don't need new people. I'm happy with my life as it is.'

'Are you really? Because sometimes I think it's like your life stopped moving when he left you.'

Something was corkscrewing, tightening, inside Daisy's chest, although she refused to show it.

'I don't need a man to make me happy. I don't need to swipe right on idiot guys on dating apps to make me feel like I'm living. I don't comment to you about how you're dating too many guys or how you've been positive that at least the last five are the one, despite the fact we can all tell they're idiots. I'm just supportive. You know? Like you said, I don't have many friends. It would be a shame to lose one of them.'

They were harsh words, but it wasn't the first time she had spoken to Bex like that, or vice versa. The fact was, they were more like sisters. And just like sisters, they knew exactly how to rub each other up the wrong way.

'I'm sorry. You know I love you,' Bex said, leaning across the gear stick and wrapping her arms around her.

'I love you too,' Daisy huffed.

The pair stayed like that, locked in an embrace for another minute, until a cough from the backseat brought them back to the moment.

As they broke apart, Claire's head appeared through the gap between the two front car seats.

'As lovely and emotional as that bonding moment was,' she said, 'is there any chance we can get going? This is the first child-free weekend I've had in about three months, and I'd prefer it if I didn't spend most of the time stuck in a car.'

20

'Another rubbish bag coming through.'

'Where are we putting old VHSs? There are loads of them.'

'Unless they look like they're valuable, bin them,' Daisy replied.

The day had gone by in a blur. As mundane as clearing out Fred's old belongings had been before when she was on her own, this was fun. Everything went for a vote with a two-to-one majority deciding whether things should stay or be binned. Two-thirds of the boxes Daisy had kept for further inspection turned out to be full of junk, like old VHS machines and magazines from the nineties. By 5 p.m. the contents of the boat had been whittled down to five large boxes, not including the one with the birthday cards, which Daisy was still avoiding.

Two of these were full of coats and clothes that, while utterly unfashionable, appeared to be in good nick, and she reasoned that a charity shop, or somewhere, might be able to make good use of them. The other two boxes she wasn't so sure about. There were various tools, which may have been of use to somebody, and other knick-knacks, from binoculars to reels of wire. Along with that, there were still a few cupboards that needed emptying, including the space underneath the bunk beds and a hidden compartment in the steps that was filled with tools.

'Daisy, come and check this out,' Claire yelled.

'One minute. I want to finish clearing these steps out first,' she called back. She was currently on her knees, digging her hands into a matt of cobwebs, showing a massive degree of bravery.

'No, you need to come now. You need to come and see this.'

The urgency in her friend's voice piqued her interest. Wiping her hands on her jeans, she pushed herself on to her feet before heading through to the back of the boat.

Both her friends were standing peculiarly straight beside a large, plastic box while grinning from ear to ear.

'What, what is it? What have you found? Is it something valuable? Is it a suitcase full of cash? Please tell me you've found a suitcase full of cash.'

'You need to see for yourself,' Bex said.

'It's better than money,' Claire added.

'Better than money?'

'Okay, maybe that is a bit of an oversell. But it does feel like fate.'

Now Daisy really was confused. This boat was throwing her one curveball and then another, but none of it had felt much like fate. Still grinning, her friends stepped aside, giving Daisy room to see inside the box.

'There's loads of it.' Claire was unable to contain her excitement. 'And this isn't all of it either. The bedside cabinet is full too. You know better than me what it is, but it looks like there are water colours, acrylics. Loads of paper. Watercolour paper is expensive, right? I remember you saying that before.'

Daisy was only half listening. She had reached into the box and pulled out a small cloth cylinder which was tightly held together by a strip of leather. Even before she undid the buckle and rolled it out, she knew exactly what she was going to find in there.

'These are even nicer than the ones I had for art college,' she whispered as she ran a finger along the length of one of the items. She dreaded to think how much they cost, but they'd been stored in absolutely perfect condition. Fine-tip paint brushes, with barely any evidence of use. And, like Claire said, there were loads.

Daisy found another two roll-bags of brushes, all different sizes and shapes, but all of equal quality. If these belonged to Fred, then they really did have more in common than she had thought. She could just imagine herself sitting out on the front deck of the boat in the summer mornings, stroking her brush across the paper. Then again, there was plenty to paint now, in springtime, and it might be even better in winter. She loved painting moody scenes. Maybe she could position the boat somewhere when a storm was coming in, and paint as the rain drummed on the roof above.

'Daisy? Earth to Daisy?'

She snapped her head back to her friends.

'Oh,' she said, suddenly aware that she had drifted off entirely. She glanced down at her hands. The brushes that only moments ago felt full of hope and optimism were now weighing her down. Heavy in her palm. 'Yeah, good, fine.' She dropped the brushes back into the box. 'We should probably make a sell pile for them.'

The girls looked at each other before returning their gaze to Daisy.

'Maybe we'll put them in a "keep for now" pile,' Claire said diplomatically. 'I mean, if you don't want them, Amelia would love them.'

'Great. Great. But we should carry on. I reckon we can get another hour in before it's too dark to work.'

And with a feeling heavy in her chest, Daisy headed back to beneath the stairs where she'd been clearing out the cobwebs.

Two hours later, work for the day was officially over.

'I can't believe you got the electricity to work.' The women were huddled on the floor, eating cold quiches and couscous salad.

'It really wasn't that hard,' Claire replied. 'Did you actually look for a plug socket outside?'

'Why would I have looked outside? I was inside,' Daisy replied, and the three of them burst into laughter. While Daisy's inability to think beyond the boat may have been the initial source of the laughter, the sheer exhaustion and two bottles of wine they had drunk between the three of them definitely contributed to its continuation.

'Turn this song up! Turn this song up!'

Claire was on her feet. 'You must remember this song. They played it all the time when we were in sixth form. Wave your arms.'

Within moments, Bex was on her feet too, bouncing up and down while Claire bellowed out the wrong words a full tone flat.

'Please, please stop,' Daisy heaved, hardly able to breathe through the laughter.

'No, you need to get up and dance. I've never danced on a boat before. I've never danced on a boat!' At that, Claire began hoisting herself up on to the kitchen counter, only to discover there was nowhere near enough headroom to stand and dropped back down.

'You should not be allowed a child when you're this irresponsible,' Bex commented while trying to stop her from toppling forward.

'I'm not this irresponsible when I have the child with me,' Claire replied indignantly. 'Daisy, stop being so boring. Dance with me. Dance with me!'

Groaning, Daisy pulled herself up to her feet. 'All right, I'm dancing. I'm dancing, but then we're getting our sleeping bags out and going to sleep.'

'As long as it's not a good song on next,' Claire replied. 'If it's a good song, we have to keep dancing.'

21

Daisy's head hurt. Although on brief contemplation, it wasn't just her head, and it didn't just hurt. It pounded. It throbbed like someone had hammered nails into her temples and the base of her skull. Her throat was parched and tasted like she had chewed a loaf of dry, mouldy bread. And her bones. Surely her bones shouldn't ache as much as they did. She was only twenty-four, but she felt like she was seventy-four. Trying to steady the queasiness that had gripped her, she took a deep breath in through her nose, only to regret it as a wave of nausea struck.

'Oh my God, I think I'm going to be sick.' Speaking didn't help either; her own voice was so loud, it made everything else worse. And she wasn't the only one who thought so.

'Why are you shouting?' Claire groaned, her head hidden inside the sleeping bag. 'Why is everything so loud? Why is the floor moving? Tell the floor to stop moving.'

From the middle of the room, Bex let out a loud yawn before stretching her arms above her.

'That was a good night,' she said, making Daisy groan. Her chirpiness was enough to cause another wave of nausea. 'Although

I didn't realise what complete lightweights you two are. You know you were asleep before midnight.'

'Daisy, stop her shouting.' Claire's voice was a low hiss. 'I cannot be held responsible for my actions if she does not stop shouting.'

Daisy wanted to reply that she was 100 per cent on Claire's side on this matter. Only talking was proving difficult. Her mouth could move, and her brain could just about pull thoughts together, but the task of linking the pair of them was proving more difficult. On the plus side, she had managed to change into her pyjamas before she fell asleep. Not that she could remember doing so. And judging by the dark wine stain on the top of her moon and stars nightshirt, even getting ready for bed hadn't been enough to stop her drinking. Cradling her head, she let out another long groan.

'I remember singing,' she finally managed. 'Claire, you're a terrible singer.'

'And you've only just remembered that?' Bex replied. 'You, on the other hand, are still infuriatingly talented. That painting you did last night was amazing.'

'The what?'

The shock of Bex's words caused Daisy's eyes to spring open. 'What do you mean, my painting? I don't paint any more.'

'But you did last night. Don't you remember? You painted a boat.'

Daisy squeezed her eyes shut again as she tried to recall the events of the previous night. She remembered laughing at Claire's singing. She also remembered Claire getting Bex's phone to see if Theo was on any of the three hundred dating apps she subscribed to. He wasn't, although Daisy could recall being slightly disappointed by this, not that she mentioned it to the girls. She couldn't remember the painting, though. She would definitely have remembered that, wouldn't she?

Letting her head drop back down, she assumed the comment was merely an attempt to wind her up, but then Claire's next words disturbed the peace of that thought.

'Wow. This really is great. I had forgotten how good you were.'

Whatever game they were both playing, Daisy had had enough. She leapt to her feet, only to regret the action. All the blood rushed from her head and she swayed from side to side, as if the boat was out on the open sea, not firmly moored to a stable towpath. With the dizziness still rolling through her, she reached out and grabbed the side of the boat, breathing in for a few moments to steady herself. Only when her head had stopped spinning did she blink her eyes open again, before taking one, then another tentative footstep, over towards the countertop where Claire was standing.

A lump formed in her throat. It wasn't a large picture – she had torn a piece of paper from one of the A4 pads – and it was a long way from her best work. The drunkenness showed in the wonkiness of her lines, and the poor blending of the watercolours in the sky. But it was a painting of a boat. She had painted for the first time in years. The first time since she had walked out of art college and vowed never again to do something so ridiculous as dream. All those years and she had barely done so much as doodle in the corner of a notebook. And yet, here it was. A full painting. And the girls were right: it wasn't bad.

'Maybe you should put it up?' Bex said quietly. Daisy stepped back, shaking her head.

'I guess I just wanted to see if these paints still worked, or whether they'd dried out.' The excuse sounded weak, even to her. Then, on noting the watercolour palette still open on the kitchen counter, she added, 'We should probably put all that stuff away now too.'

She had at least washed up the paintbrushes and laid them out to dry. Even inebriation couldn't break that habit.

Twisting her back away from the painting, she turned to the windows, as yet undecided as to whether she was going to head back to her bed and bury her head under the pillow or open the curtains to let in more light and force herself to wake up. But instead, she remained exactly where she was, frowning at the sight in front of her.

At first, she thought it was just her eyes playing tricks on her, or it was a manner in which the light was reflecting as it shone through the glass, but as she took a step closer, she noticed a strange shadow, as if something was stuck to the outside of the window.

Stepping forward, she whipped the curtain open.

'What are you trying to do to me!' Claire cried, but Daisy didn't draw them back. She was staring at the piece of paper that was most definitely stuck to her window, a very familiar envelope.

'He has to be joking.'

22

While there was a fairly good chance the pit in Daisy's stomach was caused by the overindulgence in alcohol, something about the letter told her it wasn't good.

'Is everything okay?' Bex asked, as she boiled the tiny travel kettle they had brought with them, but Daisy didn't stop to reply. She walked outside slowly, taking the steps tentatively to try to lessen the wobble. When she reached the window, she pulled the envelope off. And withdrew the letter from inside.

'He has to be kidding.' She didn't read the entirety of the letter, but she saw more than enough to get her blood pumping. She stumbled backwards with her first clenched. There was no way this was acceptable. Absolutely no way.

'Daisy?' Bex called again. 'Is everything all right?'

Once again, Daisy ignored her, and rather than heading back into the boat, she marched down the length of the *September Rose*, barely pausing for breath, and headed towards the neighbouring boat. She stepped onto the rear deck and hammered her fists against the glass pane of the door.

'I know this was you,' she yelled, her voice loud enough to

make her own ears ring. 'You might as well open up now. I'm not going anywhere.'

She hammered again. And again.

'Is something up?'

The voice came from behind, causing Daisy to spin around on the spot and nearly lose her balance. Somehow, she righted herself just in time. There, standing on the riverbank, was Theo.

Waving the paper in her hand, Daisy took two strides up the bank towards him.

'You know exactly what's wrong,' she said. 'This.' She waved the paper in front of his face, forcing him to take a step back. Frown lines formed across his forehead.

'Am I supposed to know what this is?'

She would not have thought it possible beforehand, but his complete and utter nonchalance caused her anger to reach an entirely new level.

'Don't play innocent with me. I know it's you. I know this was you.'

While keeping his feet planted in exactly the same spot, Theo reached out and plucked the piece of paper from between her fingers. Slowly, he scanned down the white page. The furrows in his brow lessened slightly, only to be replaced by the smallest twitch on the corner of his lips.

'I take it you and your friends had a good night?' He smirked.

'It's just petty, you know that? Your behaviour is petty.'

Behind her, she could hear the rustle of movement. Bex had appeared on the bank, no doubt attracted by the commotion. She wasn't the only one. Several dog walkers had slowed their steps. Yet, their presence did nothing to deter Daisy.

'I get it. You don't like me. You don't want me on the canal. But I'm here, and I have as much right to be here as you. So you and your threats aren't going to work. Unreasonable noise? It's called fun, not that you'd know anything about that. So threaten me with another fine. Threaten me all you like. I'm not paying this. I'll tell whoever I need to that I am not the problem. You are. You and your vindictiveness.'

'I didn't put that there,' Theo said with a shrug.

'Oh no, of course you didn't.' Her words dripped with sarcasm.

'You can believe me or not, but it's the truth.' He handed her the back paper. 'I wasn't even here last night. I've just got back.' He glanced down to his side. Following his line of sight, Daisy noted a large duffel bag resting on the ground by his feet.

His words were perfectly simple, yet Daisy was having a hard time trying to make sense of them.

'What do you mean, you weren't here?' Her head was spinning. 'I thought you lived here?'

'And I thought you lived somewhere that wasn't here. It doesn't mean you can't spend a night somewhere else occasionally. As it happens, I was with my girlfriend at her place.'

It was all too much for Daisy to take in. Not only the fact that Theo would spend any time away from his boat, but that he had a girlfriend. His boat certainly didn't look like he had a girlfriend. At least not one that had any influence on how he decorated. Her mouth gawped as she searched for something to say, only to come up empty.

'You didn't stick this to my boat?' she said, eventually.

'I did not.'

'Which means somebody else complained?'

'Excellent deduction. Have you considered training as a detective?' This time it was his voice that was loaded with sarcasm, though Daisy barely registered it.

'So the fine on here, I'm going to actually have to pay it?'

'That's how fines generally work, although... Can I have a look at that again?'

Given how much Daisy had already humiliated herself, she didn't see what could be lost by letting Theo scan the letter a second time. Not that there was much to see. It was the same headed paper he had used. The same typeface. And a single line squiggly signature that didn't look like a single letter in the alphabet, let alone a full name. Not to Daisy, at least. Although, rather than reading it as she expected him to do, Theo held the paper up to his nose and took a long inhale.

'You've upset Yvonne,' he said. 'Here, take a sniff.'

Daisy was 100 per cent sure that he was just winding her up. Trying to make her look even more like an idiot than she already did. But what the hell? She held the paper against her nose and took a long, deep sniff.

'Smoke?' she said, questioning her own sanity. 'Flowery smoke?'

'Incense sticks. Yvonne loves the things, which is pretty terrifying considering she lives in a wooden home. It's Yvonne you've upset. You must've really been going for it. She's normally pretty easy-going.'

'Yvonne?' The name didn't ring any bells, but then again, why would it? It wasn't like Daisy was on first-name terms with anyone other than Theo.

'The good thing is,' he continued, 'is that she is fairly reasonable. I'm sure if you tell her you didn't realise there were timing rules to making noise—'

'There are rules on what hours I can make noise?' Daisy said, her jaw dropping.

'That kind of comment will do it, and promise it'll never happen again. I'm sure she'll drop the complaint. But be wary of making the same mistake again. She doesn't suffer fools.'

Daisy let out a long sigh. Apologising to people was hard at the best of times, so doing it to a complete stranger was her idea of a nightmare. Yet at that moment she couldn't see another option, except paying the fine, and she really didn't want to do that.

'Which boat?' She groaned.

'The *Ariadne*.' Theo pointed in the direction of the boat with all the constellations. It was the same boat she had seen moving on the water during her first visit to the lock, though now it was fixed to a mooring. A mooring on the other side of the water, that was close enough to hear the all the noise they had made. 'I definitely advise buttering her up. Cakes, flowers, whatever gifts you can think of. She loves a bit of flattery and grovelling.'

Great, Daisy thought, so not only was she now being forced to grovel, but she was also probably going to have to purchase a gift, too. Although how the heck she was going to do that on a canal which didn't even have a coffee shop was beyond her. She certainly wasn't in a fit state to drive anywhere.

'Well, if that's all you need me for, I'd quite like to get on my boat now,' Theo said.

It was then that Daisy realised she was blocking his way. She also hadn't apologised for the fact she had come around, guns blazing, blaming him for something he hadn't done.

Feeling a flush of colour rise to her cheeks, she sidestepped, giving him the room to pass, before turning up the path towards the *September Rose*.

'Oh, and Daisy?' Theo's voice caused her to stop.

'Yes?' she said, wondering what else he could possibly say to make her feel any worse.

'Great pyjamas.'

23

Back on the boat, Claire was busy rifling through her bag in search of painkillers with one hand, brushing her teeth with her other, while simultaneously slipping her feet into her trainers.

'I'm really sorry to do this to you,' she said when Daisy came back in. 'But Ian is coming to pick me up. His mum's had a funny turn. He needs to go to the hospital and doesn't want Amelia to see her gran like that.'

'Oh, no. That's okay. I get it,' Daisy said. 'I hope she's all right.'

'I hope so too. Maybe she'll listen to us when we say she needs to slow down now.'

'I should get going too,' Bex said, appearing from the back of the boat, fully dressed, with a sweatband around her head. 'Are you still okay with taking my bag?'

'You're going too?' Daisy was somewhat confused by her friends' sudden departures.

'I've got to go training for the marathon, remember? We were talking about it last night. How I need to do a 35 km run. That'll take me to the train station. Remember, I showed you on the map?

And you said you could take all my stuff back home for me to pick up in the week.'

Of course, Daisy knew Bex was running a marathon soon, just because Bex was always doing something like that, but she definitely didn't remember seeing a map or Bex mentioning she was going to be running home from the canal. That felt like something she should be able to recall, but then again, she didn't remember painting the picture of the boat or being loud enough to warrant a complaint slapped on the side of her boat.

'Why don't you head back too?' Claire suggested, resting her hand on Daisy's shoulder. 'We got loads done yesterday. Look at the place. It's really starting to come together.'

'Really coming together' was probably a little optimistic. Particularly given the empty beer and wine bottles that littered the floor. But Daisy could see what Claire meant. The boat certainly looked more saleable than when Daisy had first seen it. But at this point, she could also see how much more potential there was. Fixing the cupboards. Some paint work and re-upholstery. Then she would have something really worth putting on the market.

As she glanced out the window, her eyes fell on the *Ariadne*, with its beautiful paintwork. Was having fun a bit late in the night really that big of a deal? Probably not. But the fact was, she had obviously upset this woman enough for her to come out of her home in the middle of night and that in itself was deserving of an apology.

'It's fine. I've got a few things I need to do.'

When Ian showed up fifteen minutes later, with Amelia in tow, Daisy readied herself to say goodbye.

'Are you sure you don't want to leave now, too?' Claire asked again. 'The last thing you want to do is exhaust yourself. You do still have a full-time job, you know.'

'It's fine, honestly. I'll probably just do an hour more. Make sure all these cupboards are empty, that sort of thing.'

'And throw in an apology or two?' Bex said. 'You were pretty harsh on the poor guy.'

'Well, what goes around, comes around,' Daisy said bluntly.

She had no intention of apologising to Theo any more than she already had. After all, if he hadn't been so quick off the mark last time, she would never have jumped to the conclusion that he was the one to blame.

'Thank you, guys, for all your help,' she said, pulling them both in for one last hug. 'And perhaps the next time you come, we'll be able to take her out on the water.'

'We will be there for that.'

Thirty minutes later, Daisy had an up-to-date itinerary of all the things that needed replacing. As well as easy aesthetic alterations that could be done. The wooden slats beneath the sofa were completely destroyed, probably broken by the weight of all the boxes that were put upon them. Of the twenty-eight cupboard doors within the small area, seventeen of them needed some sort of repair or other. The remaining eleven weren't exactly attractive. The bedside tables in the main cabin, however, appeared to be in good nick and the bunk beds that Claire and Bex had fallen drunkenly asleep on were also made of sturdy stuff and didn't appear set to crumble any time soon.

With the inventory taken, Daisy worked on the windows, using a mixture of glass cleaner and elbow grease, and it was remarkable the difference it made. Fairly soon, she realised she'd spent two hours working, and not even ventured close to offering this woman Yvonne the apology she undoubtedly deserved.

As she paused to open a packet of crisps, Daisy's eyes fell on the painting. Had she really done that last night? She'd been in a state where she couldn't even remember the lyrics of songs she had known since she was a child, yet she had still managed to paint. The passion was still there, she knew, as she looked at the paintbrushes drying on the sideboard. It had probably never gone. That urge to pick up a paintbrush and swill it round in the water, to blend colours and spread them out on canvas. To add shadows and texture and make an entire world on a flat piece of paper. She knew she missed it, of course. But she hadn't realised quite how much until now. Painting had been part of her. It had been the cement in her very bones. But there was just too much pain associated with that time. Too much pain and too much failure. Still, it wouldn't take much to turn the watercolour from the night before from distinctly average to not too bad at all.

Staring at the painting, she noted with her artist's eye areas where she hadn't got the shadows quite right. Some places just needed to be a little darker, and the sky could do with a touch more cerulean.

Before she could give herself time to think, she filled up a mug with water and pulled out a stool by the breakfast bar. As her friends had pointed out to her, watercolour paper of this quality wasn't cheap. And it would be a shame to waste it on such a mediocre piece of art. With her mind set on making just a few minor tweaks, Daisy May sat down to properly paint for the first time in three years.

24

Only when Daisy's stomach growled did she realise how long she had been sitting there, absorbed in the refinement of the painting. Blinking, she leant back in her chair and observed her handiwork, only to find herself pleasantly surprised. It had taken a little time to mix the exact shades she needed. Given all the time she had spent away, she was well out of practice, losing some of that skill of blending pigment with just the right volume of water to create the tones she wanted. But it hadn't taken long to get back into the rhythm. And once she had started, there was no stopping her.

At first she worked as planned, adding thin shadows around the hull and waterline of the boat. But then she carried on, wanting to add a bit more depth to the background. She'd taken her inspiration from a weeping willow tree, which hung on the opposite side of the canal. She had always found painting images of nature so relaxing. And this was no different, though there were some issues that always arose with painting objects outside, like the way the light constantly changed, as clouds shifted in front of the sun. Still, she did the best she could.

After a while, the background was looking more detailed than the foreground, so then it was back to the boat, adding in delicate lines around the windows and texture on the deck, along with the reflections on the glass windows. By the time she sat back and observed her work, a flicker of pride ignited within, only to be replaced immediately by pained regret. She could've been so good. If life had just turned out a little differently.

Lifting her head from the paper, she let her gaze drift to outside to where the *Ariadne* remained patiently on the other side of the canal.

For a second, her eyes wavered between the boat and the painting. It wasn't flowers or cake. But it could certainly be considered a gift. Before she could second guess herself, she grabbed the piece of paper and the letter that had been stuck to her window and headed outside.

Given that the *Ariadne* was on the other side of the canal, Daisy had to cross the water to reach it, and while there was a bridge down by the car park, the quickest route by far was straight across the lock. She had already seen several people cross the thick, wooden beams, upon which there were no railings to stop you from falling into the water. Had it been any other time, she would have been perfectly confident in her ability to balance on the narrow platform. But she was still struggling with the lingering effects of her hangover, not to mention both her hands being full. As such, she took her time, placing each foot carefully in front of the other before taking the next step, until she reached the other bank, where she let out a sigh of relief. After that, it was just a short walk down to Yvonne's boat.

Theo hadn't been lying about the incense. Several of the windows on the *Ariadne* were open, and the smell wafted out heavily. Daisy wasn't even aware that people still burnt incense sticks. Scented candles, yes. And those wax melts things that appeared in every Secret Santa she had ever been part of. But incense sticks?

She hadn't seen those for years. Bracing herself against the influx of scents she was certain to face, and the tidal wave of anxiety billowing in her, she knocked on the door.

A moment passed with no reply and so she knocked again, a fraction harder. Unlike both hers and Theo's back doors, which contained glass panels, this one was solid wood, meaning there was no way to see inside and know whether anyone was there. Debating whether she should just slip the painting under the door and assume this Yvonne could work out who it came from, Daisy offered one more loud knock when a voice bellowed from inside.

'Just a minute, just a minute. Where's your patience? Making an old lady hurry. I'm coming, I'm coming.'

Great, so she really was an old lady. No wonder she complained. She probably expected them to all be in by nine-thirty, tucked up in bed with a mug of cocoa. At least that is what Daisy thought until the wooden doors open outwards.

The staggered gait and hunched back of the old lady were secondary to what Daisy noticed first. Those features were entirely obscured by the purple and pink hair that sat atop her head. Not the pastel colours you normally saw on an elderly woman, but more the type you would find on a very confident teenager. Weaved in a long plait, the vivid colours shone even more brightly against the black denim jacket the woman was wearing. For a second, Daisy felt as if she'd been transported to Woodstock, or some other famous festival from the seventies.

As a gust of incense swept out of the door, causing Daisy to cough, she remembered exactly why she was there.

'Yvonne?' she said, wondering exactly how she was going to start the apology. Both hands were full, with the letter in one and the painting in the other. She could hand them over both at the same time. That would probably be self-explanatory. Although maybe a couple of words would help too.

She tried to fix her lips into a smile, only to note the old woman's expression. Horrified was the only word Daisy could think to describe it. Not as if she had seen someone who had been a nuisance, but as if she had seen a ghost. Her eyes were white, appearing even paler against the vivid lipstick, which almost immediately disappeared as the old lady covered her mouth in a gasp. When she finally dropped her hands, there were tears in her eyes.

'Daisy May, as I live and breathe.' And then, in the most unexpected moment of the day so far, she wrapped her arms around Daisy and wept.

25

Daisy was utterly confused. One minute she was standing there running through an apology in her head, the next second, this old woman, with incredibly impressive-coloured hair, was holding her around the waist. When the woman finally broke away, she wiped the tears from her eyes.

'Oh my goodness, I don't believe it. I mean, I'd heard rumours, you know. Just rumours. I didn't believe it. I mean, why would I?' She stepped backwards, not even glancing over her shoulder, the epitome of somebody who knew their boat inside out. 'Come in, come in, come in.'

Daisy remained with her feet stuck on the deck, before tentatively lifting the letter she had found stuck to her window only hours before. But the old woman was already heading back into the boat and obviously expecting Daisy to follow. For a second, Daisy hesitated. Perhaps the woman wasn't quite in possession of all her faculties. But then, if that was the case, should she really be allowed to live on a canal boat? And that didn't explain how the woman could know her name.

Readying herself against the heavy scents of incense, Daisy stepped inside the *Ariadne*.

'I came about this?' she said, feeling the need to mention the fine again.

For the first time since she had broken the hug, the old woman turned around and faced Daisy. With a spring in her step – that was infinitely sprightlier than her movements to open the door – Yvonne reached up, took the letter from her and crumpled it in her fist. Then, with a side step into the kitchen, she pushed down the lid on the bin and dropped the letter inside.

'Oh, ignore that. I didn't know it was you. I couldn't see through the curtains, could I? Besides, it was a bad night. My hip was playing up again. I can be a little unreasonable when that happens. Ask any of them. I'll get that all sorted out.'

Daisy nodded mutely, still not sure what was going on. She'd got rid of the letter at least, although Daisy hadn't actually apologised and the painting was still in her other hand. The last thing she wanted was to have to keep it. She didn't need any reminders of what she had once been capable of.

'Well... I also bought you this,' she said, stepping inside. 'As an apology?'

As Yvonne trundled back and took the painting from her, Daisy became distracted, her attention absorbed by the magnificence of the *Ariadne*. If she had had any doubts that Yvonne was a hippie at heart, they were well and truly eradicated now. It was a clear day outside, but inside, they could've been in a fortune-teller's tent at midnight. Suddenly, the constellations painted on the outside made sense. It wasn't just a case of being pretty.

It was phenomenal in a completely over-the-top way. One wall was painted white, the other was a deep purple. Or rather, that was the base colour of the walls. It was – like Yvonne's hair – several shades of pinks, purples and blues, all covered in spirally white pinpricks, creating an illusion of a galaxy. Dreamcatchers were fixed to several of the walls and beaded curtains separated the back of the boat from the front. Crystal pillars, geodes and bowls of glittering stones were scattered on the various tables and surfaces, and every shelf was stuffed to brim with books. Some were novels, like *Jane Eyre*, and *The Curious Incident of the Dog in the Night Time*. But there were also books on travelling and music and one that Daisy spotted on natural healing remedies of European herbs. And there, with its own small table, just as Theo said, were a handful of incense sticks smouldering away.

'This is an amazing collection of... things,' she said, unable to put her finger on a more precise word for the paraphernalia in front of her.

Daisy only realised that Yvonne hadn't said a word after several minutes had passed, after she had studied in depth a brass clock formed into an almost perfect sphere. She hadn't spoken since Daisy had handed her the painting. And not only had she not spoken; she hadn't moved either. She was still standing in the same place as she had been several minutes ago.

When Daisy turned back to the old woman, she saw tears dripping down her creased cheeks.

'What is it?' she asked, suddenly fearful that she had broken some unspoken boating rule and that another complaint order was on its way. 'Is something wrong? I didn't mean to offend you.'

She couldn't see how a watercolour painting of a random canal boat could be upsetting, other than the fact it didn't fit in with the obvious aesthetics of Yvonne's boat. But it seemed a little too much to be crying over that.

'Oh, no,' Yvonne said breathlessly. 'As if you could do that. My, it just reminds me of your father. This painting reminds me so much of your father.'

The boat was stuffy and hot, and yet an icy shiver ran down Daisy's spine.

'I'm sorry?' Her throat closed, and she was desperate she had misheard. 'What did you just say?'

'It just reminds me of so much of Johnny. You know, some days I can still see him sat on that boat, paintbrush in hand. Or between his teeth half the time. Nasty habit he had, chewing those brushes.'

Dizziness – nothing to do with the heavy incense – was clouding Daisy's mind.

'You knew my father?'

'Knew Johnny? I practically raised him. And you – for a short time, mind. Your hair is a lot darker now, though. And you've lost those curls. That's a shame. They were ever such lovely curls.'

Daisy was too stunned to speak. She'd wanted to believe this woman might be under the influence of something. But there was no way she would have known Daisy and her father's name by accident.

'I'm sorry, I'm very confused,' she said, straightening her back and trying to enunciate as clearly as possible. 'Could you perhaps explain how you know my father?'

'Oh, I can do better than that, my love,' the woman said, her eyes glinting in her eyes. 'I can show you.'

26

Yvonne suggested the pair go out onto the deck, where a small, cast-iron table was set up with two chairs and yet more crystals and incense burners.

'Make yourself at home. I'll just be a minute.' And with that, she disappeared back into the boat. Despite the woman's age, Daisy heard several expletives come from inside, along with various bangs and thumps. Whatever it was Yvonne was looking for, it was well hidden. However, after a few minutes, she appeared outside on the deck, her arms filled with old, leather-bound photo albums.

'You're gonna have to bear with me a minute,' she said, dropping the albums down onto the table with a thud. 'I know I should have these dated. My Frank always told me I should date them all, not just now and then. But I know I'll find what I'm looking for in one of these. Here, you take this one. I'll look through these.'

Daisy's hand hovered above the pages. She had asked Yvonne about her father, and now here she was with a photo album, which undoubtedly contained pictures of him. But how would she know which one he was? Her mother had never had any photos to show her and the only glimpse of Fred she'd had was from the top of a staircase. Her heart was once again pounding, however the old woman had already started sweeping through the pages, tutting and shaking her head, as if she was now oblivious to her guest.

Feeling like she shouldn't sit there idly, Daisy opened the photo album. Instantly, she recognised Wildflower Lock. So much of it was still the same. Particularly the rows of purple lavender bushes, although the sheds that lined the side of the paths were in a far better state in the images than real life. She glanced at the bottom to see that Yvonne had, in fact, dated this one. 1987. The photo had originally been colour, but had faded substantially. The sky was now so whitewashed, it could all be clouds, but the boat still shone out brightly. And on the top, a family of six stood upon it, waving. A pang of sadness hit Daisy in the chest. She had never felt lacking, growing up with only her mother. After all, Pippa reminded her often enough that she and her own mother had been alone for most of their life and it had been substantially better that way. But that didn't stop Daisy wondering what it would have been like to have siblings to squabble with, and to play with on those dark winter evenings when Pippa worked and she was left with Bethany or Farah, or whichever neighbour was available.

Halfway through the photo album, Daisy hadn't seen a single photo that wasn't boat or canal related. Some photos were people standing upon the boats, others were images of locks or ducks. One particularly artistic picture showed a family of cygnets, nestled in the rushes by a riverbank. When she'd seen that one, Daisy had immediately thought how she'd like to paint it, and had to remind herself that she didn't paint any more. Last night and this morning had been an exception.

Firm in her resolution, she was about to turn to the next page when Yvonne let out a small shriek.

'Here they are,' she said, slamming her fist down on the book. 'I knew they'd be here. Now have a look at this, why don't you?'

The photo she was pointing at was older than the ones Daisy had been looking at; judging by the hairstyles and dubious patterned shirts, it was mid-seventies.

'There he is,' Yvonne said, pointing at a small child. He was sitting on top of the boat, his legs dangling off the side. If it had been nowadays, he would have needed a lifejacket on, or risk the wrath of authorities. But he was there, utterly bare chested and he couldn't have been more than three.

'You see what I mean about the curls?'

Daisy stared at the picture. Was it really her father? It could have been any small child. She squinted as if that would help her notice more details. She hadn't seen many pictures of her at the same age, given that Pippa hadn't been able to afford luxuries like a camera, being a single mum and everything, so it was hard to know if there was any resemblance between the pair of them.

'Do you have any later ones of him?' she asked. 'Any of when he was a bit older?'

Yvonne's eyes bugged from their sockets.

'Do I have any more photos of him? Almost this entire blooming photo album! And I'm pretty sure you'll see a couple of other people you recognise in there too.' On the next page, Daisy understood what she meant, as Yvonne pointed out several faces, which included her grandfather, Fred. Daisy had only met him that once, of course, but his image remained firmly in her mind.

A few pages later and her father was no longer a small child. At best guess, Daisy assumed him to be early teens.

'He was ever so tall for his age,' Yvonne said, apparently able to read Daisy's thoughts. 'I don't think he'd started secondary school in this one. No, if I remember right, this was just after his tenth birthday. You get your height from him as well, I suppose. You certainly didn't get it from your mother, did you?'

The comment caught Daisy by surprise. It was one thing

hearing about her father, but her mother? How on earth did this Yvonne know about Pippa? She wanted to ask, but Yvonne was already flicking over the next page.

'Now this is one you'll like. The day he got her. She was a beauty back in the day. Not that she couldn't be again, mind.'

Daisy stared at the photo in front of her. Yvonne was right: the boat she was looking at really was a beauty, painted a deep green with a lighter green trim.

'The *September Rose*?'

'I remember the day he first drove off in her. Proud as punch, he was. He'd worked hard, saving his pennies from as soon as he was old enough to know how to wash a boat, determined to have his own.'

'Can I?' Daisy said, reaching out to take the entire photo album. It wasn't enough just to lean over. She wanted to absorb it all.

'By all means, keep looking through. You'll find lots more in there. I remember him insisting we had plenty of photos of her. Think I got through three whole rolls of films.'

Yvonne wasn't lying.

Decades were laid out before her. Page after page of photos depicting her father on the *September Rose* in every season. He was there as a young boy, his eyes barely visible beneath an oversized scarf and hat, and then, several pages later, as an older teen wearing nothing but his swimming shorts. And in every picture, he wore the same goofy grin. It was as if he was the happiest person in the world. How was it possible that somebody who smiled like that could have forgotten about his daughter without so much as a second's thought?

Only he hadn't, she reminded herself. He had remembered her. That's why he sent all the cards.

She was about to ask if she could borrow the album for a while. Maybe take some copies of the photos. If nothing else, it would be nice to see how the *September Rose* had been decorated originally and make sure she did it justice in her refurbishment. But her fingers slipped under the next page, and she flipped it over. Once again, it was all photos of the boat and her father there at the helm. But this time, it wasn't her father she was looking at. There, standing beside him, with hair down to her waist, and thick, black eyeliner, was a short lady, barely five feet tall.

'Mum?'

Her mother was there, in the photos, with her father on the canal boat.

After everything she said. This wasn't hiding things from her. This wasn't lying by omission. She had outright lied. But that was only part of the shock that was riding through her body.

Because there, clinging to her mother, arms around her neck, was a small child with curly hair.

'I was here before? I visited Wildflower Lock?'

'Visited it?' Yvonne's voice lifted in surprise. 'You lived here. You all did.'

27

Daisy felt dizzy and nauseous and utterly confused all at once. The longer she stared at the photo, the more she could see it was her. And it wasn't just the one photo. No, there was one with her standing on the top of the *September Rose*, the same way her dad had been in a previous image. And another where she was pretending to steer with her father holding her up. On one, she was perched on her father's shoulders, while her mum was doubled over in laughter. It was the kind of photo you'd never get nowadays because someone would have deleted it due to the unflattering pose. But to Daisy, it was full of life. The way her mum could barely keep herself upright. Daisy could feel the energy and love emanating. There was one of her first birthday too, with her poised between her parents' laps, ignoring the cake in front of her as she looked up at her father. There was even one photo with her and Yvonne. She was being held, resting on the old lady's hip, not that Yvonne was old then. Although she still had the characteristically bright hair, which here, was woven into a crown with flowers.

Beside her, Yvonne had grown conspicuously quiet.

'You didn't know?'

Daisy shook her head. 'I had no idea. I just knew that he left, that was all. He left and didn't want anything to do with us. That he wasn't the type of person we wanted in our lives. That was what she told me.'

Yvonne's response was far more emphatic than Daisy would expect as she offered a throaty scoff, laden in scorn. 'Your father had his flaws, but he was a good man. A very good man. And he thought the world of you.'

'Then what happened?' Daisy asked the question more to herself than anyone else. After all, something must have caused her mother to change from being this happy to so angry, she couldn't even mention her father's name without turning red with rage. Before waiting for an answer, she turned over the page, expecting to see more family photos. And there were. There were Daisy and her father. Daisy and Fred too. There were Daisy and Fred and Johnny together in the stream, her father looking like he was about to dunk her. And another one that held her attention even longer. Daisy's second birthday.

That was what she assumed the collection of photos were, judging by the cakes and piles of presents stacked up around her. In one, she was sitting on Johnny's knee, her lips pursed as the candle flickered into a puff of smoke in front of her face. So many smiling faces greeted her from those photographs: Yvonne, her father, at least half a dozen strangers too.

But there was one face missing.

'Where's my mother in these?' she said, scanning between the faces just to double check. 'I can't see her. Was she the one taking the photos?'

She had assumed the answer would be yes, but when she looked up, Yvonne's lips were pressed in a tight line, the creased features of her face even more crumpled than before. She reached her hand across the table and placed it on Daisy's.

'It's not my place to tell you, love,' she said quietly. 'I wish it was. But it's not my place.'

A stray tear dropped from Daisy's cheek onto the photo album. She withdrew her hand to wipe it away quickly.

'I'm sorry,' she said, pushing herself to standing, only to find there was nowhere to go. She was at the end of the boat. 'I'm sorry about everything. And I'm sorry about the noise. I... I...'

'Do you want to take this?' Yvonne said, holding the photo album out to her.

Daisy shook her head. 'Perhaps later. Would that be okay? Not today, but maybe later, if that would be all right?'

'You are welcome here anytime, my love. Any time you want.'

Daisy nodded. As she squeezed past the cast-iron table, she noticed how several of the incense sticks by the back door had burnt their way down, a tilted head of ash balanced on the end, about to drop. That was exactly how she felt. Like one more heavy breath and she would collapse straight over and never recover.

She needed answers. She needed them now.

She didn't even bother going back to the *September Rose* to check she'd locked it up properly. Even if she hadn't, it wasn't like there was anything in there worth stealing except the art supplies. And maybe someone stealing them would be a good thing.

She walked as if she were on a mission, not stopping or even slowing until she reached her car. It was a miracle she could see to drive, the way the tears continued to leak down her cheeks. More than once, she considered stopping so she could regain her composure. But how was that going to happen? How was she ever going to think straight until she had spoken to her mother?

She shouldn't have waited. She should have come right out and demanded the truth when she had found those birthday cards, but she had been so worried about hurting Pippa's feelings. Pippa wasn't the only one hurting.

This time, she wasn't going to leave until she knew the truth.

Sunday traffic was busier than she expected and every red light felt like a deliberate attempt to delay her from learning about her true past. Finally, after what felt like hours, she turned onto her mother's road. The road she had grown up on. Only it didn't feel like it normally did. Normally, it felt like everything would be okay once she was there because it was her home and it had always been. But that just wasn't the truth any more.

There were no doubts this time as she took the key from her pocket and stepped inside.

'Mum?' she called, only to cut herself short as voices drifted towards her. Her chest tightened. Someone was here. Hopefully, it was someone who could read the situation well enough to know that Daisy needed some privacy with her mother. Or perhaps Pippa would see the urgency of the situation and suggest they leave.

Wiping away her tears, Daisy pinched her cheeks to regain some of the colour she was certain she had lost before slipping off her coat and shoes.

When she entered the living room, she saw that her mum was sitting in the armchair. It was the same chair she always sat in, whether she was watching TV or crocheting or pawing over some recipe that she wanted to modify for herself. The sofa that Daisy predominantly sat in was occupied.

'Auntie Bethany?' Daisy said, her stomach lurching. 'This is a surprise.'

Bethany stood up from the sofa, offering Daisy a kiss on the cheek.

'I know. You haven't seen me for nearly a decade and then twice in one weekend. But you're the reason I'm here. When I saw you, I thought how it had been far too long. Far, far too long. So I rang your mum, and she told me to pop round this afternoon. We've been having a great catch up.'

Daisy could barely move her eyes to look at her mother, and yet she could feel her gaze boring into her.

'Well, isn't that great?' She forced her lips to curl into a smile before she finally turned to look at her mother.

'Oh, yes,' Pippa said, with exactly the same forced tension around her eyes. 'We've been having a very interesting catch up. Very interesting indeed.'

28

Given how long it had been since Daisy and her mother had seen Bethany, she was thankful their old friend indeed knew them well enough to spot that something wasn't quite right. Her smile hardened as her gaze shifted between Pippa and Daisy.

'Well, it's been lovely catching up,' she said, turning around to hug Pippa. 'We mustn't leave it so long next time.'

'No, we shouldn't,' Pippa agreed, her expression momentarily softening as it shifted from Daisy to Bethany. 'It's been lovely to see you. Let me see you out.'

'I wouldn't worry about that.'

'Please, I insist.'

The two ladies exited the room, leaving Daisy alone.

Perhaps Bethany hadn't said anything about the boat to her mother, she thought optimistically, only to dismiss the thought almost immediately. That look her mother gave her was almost identical to the one she had received when she was sixteen and had snuck out with Claire to a rave, only to find Pippa waiting up on the sofa when she'd arrived home at three the next morning.

As the front door clicked closed, Daisy's nerves multiplied.

Pippa reappeared in the living room silently, her arms folded over her chest.

'Well, that was an interesting conversation,' she said. 'Bethany tells me she saw you on a boat. A boat on Wildflower Lock, no less. I assume this is something to do with your grandfather passing away?'

Daisy's jaw fell open. 'You knew? You knew he had died, and you didn't say anything?'

'What does it matter to you? You didn't know him. I didn't realise he'd be so stupid as to leave you something. Just tell me it wasn't that bloody boat.'

Daisy looked at her mother, aghast. It was as if she barely recognised the woman standing in front of her. Her silence was all Pippa needed to assume she was right.

'So he did? And you've been lying to me, sneaking around behind my back—'

'Me? You're accusing me of lying to you? Don't get me started.'

'Whatever people have been telling you—'

'People? What people do you mean, Mother? Do you mean Yvonne? Because she's the only person I've spoken to at the lock who knew Grandad, but you know what? It turns out she knew you, too. And while we're on the subject of lying, I guess our address was just scribbled out by accident on these?'

From her bag, she withdrew a handful of the cards that had been returned to sender, and tossed them at her mother.

'You said he didn't want to know me.'

'He didn't deserve to know you.'

'That's not the same thing and you know it. He wanted to know me. He wanted us to have a relationship. I should have had a choice in that.'

Pippa picked up a card, opened it and scanned the words written inside. Part of Daisy wanted to snatch it away from her. She didn't deserve to see what it said, but she stood there firmly and waited for Pippa's reply.

'It's not that simple,' she said finally.

'Why don't you try to explain it to me, then?' Daisy's posture mirrored her mother's exactly, with her hands folded across her chest. 'Why don't we start with the fact that I used to live on a boat?'

'Yvonne.' Pippa muttered the name so quietly under her breath that Daisy could barely hear it, but she did, and she pounced.

'Obviously, I asked Yvonne why you cut my father from my life, but she said it wasn't her story to tell. Still, I reckon if I go back and push... if I tell her I tried to ask you, but you refused to tell me, then she'll tell me everything. Including why you were missing from all the photos around my second birthday. So it's up to you, Mum. Are you going to tell me or not?'

In all her life, Daisy had never spoken to her mother in this manner. Never had she issued an ultimatum that could result in the entire breakdown of their relationship. But she had never had a reason to before.

With her arms still crossed, she tilted her chin a little and looked up. She was prepared to walk away. To walk out of her mother's life if that was what it took, until she told her the truth about her past.

A stony, impenetrable and painful silence twisted between them. Daisy lifted her foot, ready to turn around and leave, when Pippa spoke.

'I think I should fix us both a drink.'

29

Daisy had never seen Pippa pour herself such a large measure of gin, nor stare at it so intently, although that wasn't what concerned her the most. What concerned her was the way Pippa's hand trembled as she opened her mouth to speak, only to close it again several times.

'How much do you know?' she said, eventually. 'What did Yvonne tell you?'

'Honestly? Not much. That I lived on the boat. Dad loved me. That he was a good man – according to her, at least. But something obviously went wrong.' Hoping to prompt something more, Daisy carried on. 'You looked happy. In the photographs of you and Dad. You look so happy. What happened?'

Her mother's skin was so pale, it was near translucent, and in the space of this conversation, she seemed to have aged at least a decade. A flicker of guilt burnt inside. Daisy didn't want to make her mother feel like this, but then she'd had twenty-four years and chosen not to tell the truth. That, in her opinion, was more than enough time to prepare.

'I met your dad when I was young, like you and Paul.'

'How young?'

'I was thirteen the first time I saw him. He didn't go to the same school as me, but his father had a boat moored up at Wildflower Lock. This little thing. Not like the September Rose. Beautiful though I used to walk past it on my way to school. The first day, the first conversation... That was it. We were hooked. I didn't see any future other than with your dad. We waited until he'd saved up enough money to buy the boat and then we got married. We had a honeymoon on the *September Rose*, would you believe it? We went all over the country. Six months travelling. The thing is, the honeymoon never really ended.'

The remark confused Daisy. Wasn't that a good thing? Didn't people refer to the honeymoon phase as a sign the relationship was going well? Apparently not, according to her mother.

'I don't understand,' she said, at which her mother took a long, drawn-out sip of her gin, followed closely by another.

'I had dreams too,' Pippa continued. 'Your father had known that when he proposed. Supported them too. At least that's what he said. Maybe he would've done if—'

Whatever it was she was going to say, Pippa cut herself short.

'What is it? What happened?'

'I don't want you to take this the wrong way, love. I really don't. You're the best thing that's ever happened in my life. Without a doubt. But you weren't exactly planned. I hadn't even known I was pregnant until I was four months in, and I'd been so busy applying for all these different internships...'

'To do what?' Daisy asked, increasingly feeling like she knew her mother less and less. 'I thought you'd always wanted to cook?'

'Oh, I have, my love. Always. But I had big dreams, like you and your art. And having you...' Her gaze drifted away, as if Daisy wasn't even there. 'It had always been Paris for me. I'd always wanted to go, not just to see the Eiffel Tower, you understand, but for the food. They can teach you so much about food, the French. An opportunity came up to spend a year learning from the best. You were only a baby, but I thought Johnny would be okay with it. I thought he might even enjoy it. There are boats in Paris, after all. Sure, he would have had to learn the language, but it would have been an adventure for all of us. But he wouldn't come. It didn't seem to matter to him how much this meant to me, or how much I needed it... I needed me again. I supported him in his dream, living on that boat. Packing up and travelling the country, away from all my family and friends, but when it came to me, he wasn't willing to do the same.'

Daisy could hear the pain in her mother's voice. The anger she felt at her father having betrayed her like that, but there were still more answers she needed.

'So what did you do?'

Once again, silence fell between the pair of them, and Daisy already knew that whatever her mother was going to say, she wasn't going to like it. She could feel her breath growing shallower and shallower. Her heart knocking against her ribs. She wanted to stop. She wanted to tell Pippa that it was okay. She didn't want to know. It didn't matter. They could just go back to how things were before and forget she ever found out about the boat and the photos and the stack of returned mail. But she couldn't do that.

'You need to understand, I wasn't well,' Pippa said quietly. 'I didn't realise at the time what it was. Things like that weren't talked about back then. And I don't want you to think that I ever blamed you for how I felt. Not for one second. But I needed it. I needed to do it for me.'

Daisy already knew what her mother had done. She could see it there in her face, in every tear that weaved down her cheek, but she needed to hear the words. She needed to hear them come out of her mother's mouth. Her mum, who she had believed and trusted and would've sworn blind had never lied to her in all her life. She needed to hear her say it.

Finally, sniffing back the tears, Pippa looked her in the eye.

'I left you. I left both of you when you were only a baby and I went to Paris.'

30

It felt as though the air had been sucked clean out of the room. A breath fixed in Daisy's lungs, unable to escape. Her hands were trembling as she blinked repeatedly, trying to make sense of what her mother had just told her.

'You went to Paris anyway? You left me? When I was a baby?'

'You were eighteen months,' Pippa replied. She was once again staring at her drink, unable to even lift her gaze to face her. 'I think... I think I did it to test Johnny – to start with, at least. I thought there was no way he'd let me stay there on my own. No way he'd manage without me.'

'Manage? Do you mean manage looking after me?'

Pippa nodded, and another minute of silence passed. A minute of them both swallowing back tears, and thousands of unspoken words. More than once, Daisy considered standing up and leaving. She had heard enough. She knew her mother had lied over and over again, and that was all the justification she needed to walk out of the front door and not look back. But she couldn't leave yet. She still needed to know more. After all, if Pippa was the one who had walked out, then why was her father the one who had been cut out of her life? It didn't make sense.

'I take it he managed,' Daisy said when she finally found a voice again. 'He raised me by himself?'

'I think he would agree it would be a stretch to say *by himself*. He had half the canal babysitting you. But he managed. He managed as if I'd never even been there. Which I suppose was true in a way. I hadn't been there. Not in the way I was supposed to be. I could fake it, of course. Turn it on when I needed to and make it look like I was in control.'

'And what about me? Did I even fit into your thoughts?' Daisy didn't bother to hide the bitterness in her voice.

'I knew it was a mistake. I knew that. The first week, when Johnny didn't come running after me, begging for my forgiveness, I realised I'd made a mistake. But I'd put all my savings into my dream. Into putting down a deposit on a scabby little flat on the outskirts of Paris. And you have to remember, you get your stubbornness from me.'

Her lips parted, as if she were attempting to smile, but the gesture never made it quite that far.

'I came back the day of your second birthday,' she said. 'I saw you there on the *September Rose*. I watched Yvonne taking photos and your father holding you over the edge of the boat by your ankles, and you screaming with laughter. I don't think there's ever been a happier child in the entire world.'

This time a smile formed on Pippa's face, but Daisy didn't have the time for sentiment.

'So what happened then? You just took me back and built a web of lies about my father? Used the next twenty-two years to turn him into the villain of the story?'

'I thought about leaving you again,' Pippa said matter-of-factly, her eyes bloodshot from all the tears. 'I saw how happy you were there with him and I thought that maybe you'd be better off without me. But I couldn't do it. When I saw how much you'd grown, and realised how much I'd missed out on, all I cared about was never missing another second. That's all I wanted. I wanted to go back in time. I wanted it to be as if nothing had changed.'

'But he wouldn't have it? He wouldn't have you back?'

'That's what that family of his would have liked. Fred, and the rest of them on the canal. They tried to turn him against me. I know they did.'

'I think you turned them against you yourself when you abandoned your daughter.'

'I didn't abandon you.' Pippa's voice rose for the first time since she had started talking. 'I rang you every night. Every penny I had went on telephone calls to you. Listening to you gabbling away trying to say my name. I didn't abandon you. I just needed to find me.'

Bit by bit, things were starting to fill in. But there were still too many blanks. Too many gaps that didn't yet make sense. More question she had to ask.

'I still don't understand why he wasn't in my life. If you wanted to be with him, why did you keep him from me? Was it jealousy? Were you mad at him?'

'You really think I'd be that petty?' Pippa said, true hurt and anguish clouding her face.

'Then why?'

'Why do you think? To protect you.'

31

Never had Daisy's heart remained lodged in her throat as long as it had done that day. From the moment she had woken, to finding the fine on her window, from meeting Yvonne to sitting there in her mother's living room, hearing about a childhood she couldn't have dreamt of, her body had been wrought with tension, a constant, unending stream of adrenaline coursing through her veins. Her only respite those few hours of painting, and any calm she had felt from that had well and truly gone.

'I waited until the party had ended before I saw you. God, it hurt waiting that long. I thought my heart was going to burst, being that close to you and not being able to touch you. Johnny had just tucked you up in bed when I finally plucked up the courage to step inside the boat. "I wasn't sure we'd see you again," he said to me. Those were his first words. That he wasn't sure he'd see me again. Broke my heart almost as much as leaving you. Because how could he think that? How could he think for one moment that I'd not come back to you? To both of you.'

'I think it's a pretty fair assumption, Mum. You left him. You left us both.'

'This is why I didn't want to tell you,' she replied, with just a hint of motherly impatience. 'Because I knew you wouldn't understand. I knew you'd take his side.'

'So far, you're not giving me any reason not to. You left, and then you kept him from me. If there is a villain in the story, Mother, it's you.'

Pippa shook her head. 'Do you think I cut him out just like that? That I'd separate you from your father if there wasn't a reason?'

'Right now, I'm still waiting to hear what it is,' she said. 'What on earth could he have done that was worse than what you did?'

Pippa sighed and looked at her knees before biting down on her bottom lip.

'I moved back into that boat. Or, at least, I tried to. But the way they all looked at me. All those sideways glances. Conversations falling silent whenever I passed. Every one of them knew what I had done, and they were judging me for it the entire time. I'm not saying I didn't deserve it.' She raised her hands defensively, as if preparing for Daisy's attack. 'I know what I did was wrong, but I deserved a second chance, didn't I? That's what I thought you did when people made a mistake – gave them a second chance. So I asked him. I told him I needed to move away from the canal. Away from Wildflower Lock. I needed a chance to start over properly. And he agreed. He said he was okay with that. So a couple of weeks later, I got offered a job. A good job, in a nice restaurant, and it came with a flat. It was perfect. Everything was sorted. I accepted the position. They were expecting me to start, and then he changed his mind.'

'He didn't want to leave the boat?'

'He'd been offered a job too, he told me. A job I hadn't even known he'd applied for. It was a travelling position, working up and down the waterways, surveying locks or something like that. A different mooring nearly every night. I told him it was no life for you. He said it would be an adventure. But the year I'd been gone, the only children you'd mixed with were a couple of children living on the river too, and they were all three times your age. It wasn't enough. You needed to have children your own age and stability.

'Of course, he threw that word, "stability", right back in my face. I begged him. I tried to make him understand that I knew what I'd done was wrong. Explained that I'd been ill and that I was feeling better now. But he refused to listen. So I gave him an ultimatum. You take that job, and Daisy will be out of your life. He didn't believe me when I said it, but then why should he have done? I don't think I believed it myself.'

'What happened then?'

'I took you to spend the night with my mum. I told Johnny I hoped we could talk about things the following morning. But then the morning came, I went down to the river... Your father and the *September Rose* were gone. He'd left us.'

Daisy rubbed her temples, her thumbs moving in small circular motions, trying to deal with the throbbing that was developing.

'You cut him out of my life for leaving? When that's exactly what you did to me? You punished him when you expected him to forgive you? That's just hypocrisy, Mother.'

'I know. I know that. I do. But it's not that simple. I told myself as long as he came back and saw sense, like I did, I'd forgive him. I'd give us another chance. But he didn't call, Daisy. Not one telephone call for an entire month. Your heart was broken. I know I have a hefty piece of the blame to shoulder here, but he raised you and then just dropped you. So, when that month passed, and I'd heard nothing from him, I moved.'

'What do you mean, you moved?'

'Exactly that. I found another job, packed up our belongings, and left. We came here. To this house. My mum gave me a deposit. A down-payment so I could get a mortgage and that was it.'

Daisy's head was pounding, her throat coarse and dry as she struggled to think.

'But the birthday cards. He knew where we lived?'

At this, Pippa scowled, her nostrils flattening as she took a sharp breath inward.

'That's the reason I didn't want you seeing him. The reason I couldn't have him in your life.' She sighed a long and laboured breath before she carried on. 'I should've known that he'd find out eventually where we were. We'd been living here about six months when there was a knock on the door. And in my gut, I knew it was him. You just know sometimes, don't you? But the man who turned up... I'd never seen him like it. Oh, he'd enjoyed a drink in the past. We both had. But this was different. It reminded me of my dad.'

Pippa had never mentioned her father before. Not once. She had raised Daisy alone, just as her mother had raised her. They were women raising women alone. No men needed.

'Maybe in my heart, part of me knew your father wasn't the same,' she continued. 'But I couldn't take that risk. I couldn't. I knew what having a drunk as a father does to a child. I lived through that. And I couldn't let you live through it, too. Your father knew what I had gone through. He knew the things I had seen. And so the fact he would turn up on my doorstep, in that state...'

Pippa shuddered, and for the first time since she had arrived at the house, Daisy felt the slightest pang of sympathy. What her mother had done wasn't right. It was a long way from fair, but at least now it made a little sense.

'I'm sorry, my love. There aren't enough apologies in the world to right what I did. What I did to you then, and what I did after, hiding him from you. But I only did what I thought was best. You understand, don't you? Please tell me you understand that?'

She was pleading now, her wide, bloodshot eyes once again filled with tears, but Daisy couldn't move. She was frozen to the spot, shaking her head in disbelief.

'I need some time,' she said finally.

32

There was too much to make sense of. Too many conflicting emotions. Pippa's childhood and the trauma she had suffered weighed heavily on Daisy's mind. As did the fact that her mother had suffered so greatly after Daisy's birth. Obviously, Pippa had needed support, but was that really an excuse? So many years had passed. How would she not have at least checked in on Johnny, even if only to confirm her worst suspicions and discover that he had turned into the violent drunk she feared? She had cut him from both their lives out of fear and Daisy was the one who had paid for it.

Swallowing back the tears, she started her car and began the drive towards her flat, though as she approached the mini roundabout, she hesitated. She had so many memories of herself and her mother there. Her mother helping her move in, never once questioning her decision to pack up her dream and take a job in an office. Beautiful meals and cakes her mother had cooked for her to celebrate new jobs and birthdays. The flat was filled with tokens of her past. A false past of her mother's construction. She needed to go somewhere else.

And so she drove to the only place she could think of.

* * *

Wildflower Lock was a very different site at night time. The public car park was closed, and so Daisy parked up on the verge nearby and walked along the narrow pathway. There were no paddle-boarders now. No kayakers or dog walkers chattering away, filling the air with their laughter. The only sounds came from the gentle lapping of the water as it flowed slowly through the canal, bull-frogs, and the rustling of birds making their roosts. There were far more stars out here, she noticed as she glanced up at the sky. Stars her father must have looked at a thousand times from this very same place. Probably thinking about her. Thinking about the times they had together. All the mistakes he had made that meant she was cut from his life.

When she reached the *September Rose*, she climbed on the back deck and dug her hand into her bag for her keys.

'Where the hell are you?' she said as she pushed aside her wallet and packets of tissues in search of the small keyring. She had no idea when her bag had become so filled with junk, but it felt as though there were a thousand receipts and crumpled pieces of paper in there, not to mention the odd lipstick and compact mirror. Basically, everything other than her keys. After a minute of rummaging, she finally found them tucked in the corner of one of the pockets. She picked them up between her fingers and pulled them out of her bag, only for them to slip out of her hand and onto the deck.

'For crying out loud,' she shouted and slammed her fist against the doorjamb of the boat. 'Can't you cut me some slack?'

It was taking every bit of restraint not to scream aloud. Instead, she covered her face with her hands and crumpled to the cold, wooden deck. It was difficult to know how long she sat there, hands around her knees, the chill of the spring evening causing goose-bumps on her arms. She didn't think about how loud her crying must be as she leant against the cabin and sobbed. Or the fact that there would even be anybody there to hear her. But she was still lost in her tears when a voice cut through the darkness.

'I don't suppose there's anything I can do to help, is there?'

Wiping her eyes, Daisy placed her hand on the ground beside her, ready to stand up, when her fingers touched something cold and metallic. The keys.

'Of course,' she muttered to herself, before standing upright and turning to face Theo.

Even in the dusky light, she could see the concern etched in his expression. Concern that looked pretty genuine.

'Don't worry, I'm not planning on breaking any canal rules,' she said. 'Just a bad day, that's all.'

'Do you want to talk about it? Or alternatively, not talk and just eat? I've put some food in the oven. More than I can eat on my own.'

'You don't have to do that.'

'I know I don't.' His pause lingered, as if there was more he wanted to say. It didn't take long for her to find out what that was. 'I spoke to Yvonne today.'

'Oh.'

Though she wouldn't have thought it possible, the weight in Daisy's stomach sank even further still.

'She showed me the painting you did for her. That's an impressive gift you've got there.'

'Maybe once. Not any more, though.'

'You could've fooled me.'

Daisy waited, expecting him to say something more about

Yvonne or about her father. About her life on Wildflower Lock that she had never known about. But he didn't.

'I'd better head inside,' he said. 'I don't want my focaccia to burn.'

'You made focaccia?' Daisy said in surprise.

'I did. Olives and sun-dried tomato focaccia, to be exact. And it's not so bad, even if I say so myself. You're welcome to try some. I've got a cold beer in the fridge too.'

Daisy considered it for a moment. Today had been a crappy day on so many levels, and now a man she barely knew was offering her kindness. She took a breath in, ready to refuse him, her mind now on autopilot, only to hear her voice speak.

'Bread and beer sound great.'

33

Daisy should have guessed that when Theo said he had a beer in the fridge, he didn't mean a can of Red Stripe, or a bottle of Corona.

'A buddy of mine makes all these artisan beers,' he said, opening up the fridge, and displaying dozens of brown bottles, all with handwritten labels. 'They're great, but he gives them to me quicker than I can drink them. It's nice to have someone to share them with. Take your pick.'

'Surely you've got your girlfriend to drink with,' Daisy said, only realising too late how rude the comment sounded.

Thankfully, Theo smiled.

'She's more of a Pinot girl,' he replied. 'Go grab yourself a seat. I'll get the bread out of the oven.'

His boat had an ingenious layout, she thought as she watched him move around to the oven. Even more ingenious than she had thought when she first saw the place. Several racks were fixed to the walls, housing a variety of kitchen utensils, all hung vertically for easy access. There was a full-size oven, microwave, and obviously the coffee machine. As Theo opened the oven door, the aroma of freshly baked bread filled the space. Instantly, Daisy's mouth started watering. It was then she realised she had eaten nothing that day. Not at all. That morning, she'd felt too hungover. Then she'd been at Yvonne's, and after that her mind had been far too occupied with thoughts of her mother and father to even consider getting something to eat. As such, she was more than a little disappointed when Theo next spoke.

'We should probably give it a few minutes to cool down.'

Daisy's stomach growled in annoyance, though it was quickly settled as Theo fetched two glasses and gestured towards the ales.

'Have you chosen which you want?'

'I'll let you decide for me,' she said.

After a brief deliberation, Theo flicked the top off two of the bottles and handed one over.

'So I'm guessing you don't want to talk about it?' Theo said. 'Whatever it was that had you hammering your head against the boat. You should probably know it's going to take more than that to make a dent in it.'

'She's already got plenty of dents on her, or haven't you noticed?'

'Is that what it was? Frustration about the boat? Because I know it looks like a lot of work, but honestly, you'll be amazed how quickly these things come together when you really start working on them.'

Daisy smiled gratefully at his attempt to cheer her up.

'No, it wasn't the boat. Well, not directly.' She paused, contemplating whether she should carry on with what she was saying. After the briefest contemplation, she decided there was nothing to lose. After all, Theo was obviously close to Yvonne. She had probably said something already. 'Did you know that my father used to live here? On Wildflower Lock?'

Theo's eyes shifted downwards as he dipped his chin in a nod.

'I did. I don't know what happened, though. Fred used to talk about him, but I wasn't here for that long before Fred started to struggle to get down to the boat. I know your grandfather missed him. A lot.'

'It was a heart attack,' Daisy said before she could stop herself. 'He was only forty-two. Fit and healthy, apparently. I don't know, I never knew him. But that's what people said at his funeral. They were surprised.'

Theo appeared to study her for a moment, taking a sip of his drink. 'So you never knew him, but you still went to his funeral? Wow. That says something about you.'

'Something good, or something bad?'

Theo let out a small chuckle. It was amazing how his eyes twinkled when he smiled. She'd never spotted that before, but then, they'd never had a conversation which involved either of them smiling before now.

'I think to go to the funeral of your father, when you don't even know him, is a brave thing to do.'

'Yeah, well, I wanted to know something about the man who never wanted to have anything to do with me,' she replied, taking another long sip from her drink, and praying it wasn't too alcoholic. After all, she still had to drive home. 'But it turns out I was wrong about that. I was wrong about a lot of things.' She paused, her eyes falling to the wooden planks beneath her feet. The dark wood was far deeper than on her boat, but she liked it. She liked being here. There was something easy about this place, this home on the water. Perhaps even Theo himself.

'Turns out that I lived here on Wildflower Lock too,' she said, suddenly overwhelmed with the urge to tell somebody.

'And you never knew?'

'I never knew a lot of it. I never knew my mum ran away to Paris, leaving me when I was a baby. I never knew that my dad sent me a birthday card and Christmas card every year until he died, but my mother immediately returned them to sender. I didn't know that my mum had postnatal depression, or an alcoholic father. I didn't know any of these things. And I kind of wish I still didn't.'

Immediately, she regretted speaking. She was saying too much. Theo was staring at her, but the twinkle in his eyes had been replaced by a penetrating gaze that made her feel more and more conspicuous by the second.

'I'm sorry. I shouldn't have unburdened. You don't want to hear this.' She stood up, ready to move. But Theo was there, his hand on his shoulder.

'Sit yourself down,' he said softly. 'And I'll bring the bread over. And while I'm at it, I've got a couple more of these.' He lifted the bottle of beer. 'By the sound of things, you could do with more than one.'

Considering how much Daisy avoided socialising with strangers, the conversation between her and Theo never stopped. They moved seamlessly from one topic to another, discussing everything from the name of the flowers Daisy had spotted on the towpaths, to the fact that neither of them knew any songs currently in the charts. She was amazed how easy it all felt. She was also amazed at how good the bread was.

'You should sell this,' she said, as she polished off her first sizeable slice.

Theo laughed. 'I'm not sure I have the time to do that. What with the full-time job and everything.'

'I don't even know what you do,' Daisy said, realising she knew so little about this man upon whom she had imposed.

'I'm a linesman,' he said, in a manner that implied that she was meant to know what that meant. From the confusion on her face, he quickly gathered she didn't. 'I'm in charge of this section of the canals. Making sure the banks are kept clean, cutting the rushes.

Checking the lock's in working order. That sort of thing. It's the same job Fred had, before his arthritis got so bad that he couldn't live out here any longer.'

'I never knew that. About Fred being a linesman, or the arthritis, or any of it, really. There's so much about my family I don't know.'

'I don't think you're alone in that,' Theo replied. 'That's the thing about families, isn't it? They all have secrets. Things they don't want others to know. They're just human, after all. We all are.'

Daisy picked up her beer, only to find it empty, and placed it back down on the coffee table in front of her. Of course, her mother was only human, and made human errors, but it was Daisy's life those errors had impacted. Didn't that make some kind of difference?

'Here, let me get you another of those.' Theo stood up. 'And I've got some salmon in the fridge if you're still hungry. Home smoked.'

'You smoke your own salmon?' Daisy asked before realising that of course he did. 'I don't want to eat you out of house and home,' she added quickly.

'You won't be. Like I said, it's nice having someone to share this with.'

It was the second time he had made that comment, almost wistfully. Yet this time, Daisy wasn't willing to let it go quite so easily.

'What about your girlfriend? I'm sure she enjoys being waited upon like this.'

He chuckled. 'Heather definitely likes being waited upon. It's more the boat that she has an issue with.'

'Really?'

'She's more into five-star hotels and luxury beach resorts.'

'That works for you?'

'Strangely, it does. Or at least it always has done. We've been together for a long time. Since we were fourteen. Back then, I didn't really have any interest in boats, let alone living on one. It's fair to say she's been flexible enough with my life choices for me to try to be accepting of hers.'

It was a big statement. That flexibility and compromise was certainly something Daisy and Paul had been missing.

'So what happened? With the boats, I mean. How did you end up living here?'

Lifting the glass to his lips, Theo gazed around, as if this was his first time viewing the space, before he turned back to look at her.

'I needed a job. I'd finished school and had no idea what I wanted to do with my life and my mother, being the hard-nosed, but very supportive woman she was, said she didn't mind what I did, but I wasn't lounging about all day so I needed to find a job. And I saw an advert for a trainee linesman. I'll be honest, I thought I was applying to work on a football pitch.'

Daisy nearly spat out her beer with laughter.

'You're not serious?'

'Oh, I'm deadly serious. Anyway, I got the job and started work. The guys I worked with said if I lasted the first winter, I'd be hooked. And what do you know, they were right. A couple of years into the job, someone was selling this boat on the cheap. The name seemed too fitting: *Narrow Escape*. That's what it felt like I'd had: a narrow escape from real life. So I bought her and did all the work myself.'

Daisy had been admiring the workmanship in the boat since she the moment she had first stepped on it, but now she was seeing it with an entirely different light. Theo had made it all with his bare hands.

She dropped her drink onto the table with slightly more force than she anticipated.

'You should do this as a job. You should do up boats. They'd sell for a fortune.'

He smiled almost sympathetically.

'It's difficult. I love doing it. But these are personal spaces. Each boat has its own characteristics and you need time to examine that. To explore that.' He may have wanted to say more on the matter, to tell her about how he had unearthed the characteristics of his own boat, but Daisy had something else on her mind.

'You can help me? You could help me sort out the *September Rose*! I don't have a lot of money, but I'm sure I could scrape together a bit. Then pay you properly after we sell it.'

'I'm not gonna take money off you, Daisy.'

'I'll split the profit. Twenty-eighty. Or more. Say what you want.'

'I would help you anyway. All you have to do is ask. That's the way things work out here on the lock.'

'Oh.'

A flush of embarrassment flooded her cheeks. After how well the evening had gone, one minute was all it had taken to mess it up. Yet Theo remained looking perfectly relaxed.

'I will help you,' he said. 'Free of charge, but I need to know a bit more about you first.'

'More about me?' She raised her eyebrows at the comment. 'Did you not just hear when I poured out everything about my parents? About my mother leaving me to go off to Paris, then taking me away from my father?'

'I was here. I heard all that, but that wasn't about you. You told me about them. I want to know about you. Your painting, for starters. It's phenomenal, yet you don't like to talk about it. At all.'

'There's nothing to talk about.'

'See, you've done it again. But that's my deal. I would like to know why you are so reluctant to talk about painting. You do that, and I will help you with the *September Rose*.'

34

Daisy held the bottle in her hand, the cold chilling her skin as she contemplated the weight of what Theo had asked her. She didn't talk about that period of her life, or her life generally, because it reminded her of what a failure she was. Most of her friends had careers or successful relationships or houses they owned. In some cases, like Claire, they had all three and a child to boot. Then again, if anybody had asked her before today, she would have said that she didn't paint at all and that she trusted her mother explicitly, without any exceptions. A lot of things had changed over the course of a day. Maybe opening up about her past would be another of those.

She took a deep breath and started before she could chicken out. 'I had a high school sweetheart,' she started, only to change her mind and head further back. 'Actually, we were together before then. We were boyfriend and girlfriend in primary school, if you can believe that. Not that we ever did anything other than hold hands and line up next to one another in the lunch queue, but you get it. When we went into secondary school, it became an actual relationship. He was my first kiss, my first love, my first everything.'

Deep sadness swelled within. She had learnt long ago that it was impossible to even think about her childhood without thinking of Paul. He had been ingrained in her life, right from the very start. Her best friend. Her shadow. And that was how she had always assumed it would be. It wasn't right to say he was her first love. He was her only love.

'We never had bust ups or arguments. There was none of the teenage drama that you normally get. We were just in sync with each other. I honestly thought we would be together forever. Marriage, kids, the entire world.'

'And this is somehow related to your painting?' Theo said, as Daisy took a breath. 'I don't mean to interrupt or anything, it's just I was hoping to hear why you gave up on such an incredible talent, and I feel like I might be about to slip into an episode of *Dawson's Creek*.'

'*Dawson's Creek*? How retro are you?' She was grateful for the sudden injection of humour. 'I'm getting there. Just give me a second.'

She paused again, though only briefly, as she stemmed the deep aches that came with thinking about this time in her life. So many years and yet the pain was still there. Maybe that was because she had never wanted to move on from it. Not really. After all, it was the only evidence of their love she had.

'Paul was going to work for his dad's business as a mechanic. It was always planned that way. He knew every make of car before he could do his two times table. He could name the parts of an engine before we were in secondary school. There was never any doubt what he would do. I, on the other hand, liked to draw. No, I loved to draw. Which is why I applied to study art, at Brighton.'

Theo looked at her quizzically. 'I take it that's a good place. I'm sorry, I don't know that much about art, studying it or anything.'

'Yes, one of the best. It was a miracle I even got in.'

'Why would you say that?' Theo interrupted her train of thought. 'That's obviously not the case. I've seen how talented you are.'

'There are a lot of talented people,' she countered. 'Luck definitely played a part.'

At this, Theo stiffened slightly. 'I don't like that. I don't like the way you put yourself down. Maybe luck did play a small part, but you make your own luck too. People don't get lucky without putting in the work first.'

'Perhaps.'

'Also,' he continued, 'I might be off the mark here, but I'm getting a distinct feeling that this Paul guy is going to turn out to be a complete dick.'

At this, Daisy choked out a laugh, causing beer to rise up her nose. Bex and Claire would like this guy. Somehow, he was making talking about Paul a slightly less torturous experience. That was a near miracle.

'Paul may have turned out to be a dick, yes,' she replied, still smiling, although it was dipping rapidly. 'He thought that the distance was going to be too much of an issue. And he didn't think much of me doing art. That doesn't mean he didn't think I was good; he just couldn't see how I was going to earn money drawing pictures.'

'And what about you? What did you think? What did you want to do?'

She stared at the bottle in her hand, wondering if she was actually going to say it. After all, her childhood dream was something she hadn't even allowed herself to think about for years.

'I always wanted to illustrate my own children's stories. Paint bright, colourful pictures, full of crazy scenarios, bring characters to life. Probably with animals. I loved painting animals, the cartoon type, not realistic. I imagined illustrating books about animals getting themselves into adventures. That type of thing.' She silenced herself. It was a dream she rarely let escape her lips, even to the girls. She sucked out a breath and forced herself back into the moment.

Silence bloomed between them. Silence that probably would have formed into something more melancholy, had Theo not been there, ready to break it.

'So, Paul the Dick— Prick, that works better, right? Paul the Prick, he didn't want you to go?'

'He couldn't see how it would help us in the future. Getting into debt when we should have been saving for a wedding or to get on the property ladder. That had always been our plan, after all.'

'So you just didn't go?'

'I just didn't go,' she said flatly. 'I rejected the offer and got a job working as a chambermaid in a hotel. And I hated every minute of it. On my feet all day, clearing up other people's mess. I was miserable.'

She recalled the days so clearly, traipsing up and down staircases, her feet and back throbbing as she hunched over, arms ladened with piles of sheets.

'Is that why you guys called it a day?' Theo said, his questioning ensuring Daisy stayed on track with her story. 'You broke up because you were miserable and hated your job?'

After finishing her mouthful of beer, Daisy scoffed. 'Oh, I wish I had seen sense then. I mean, he knew how miserable I was, but he was happy that I'd stayed close to him. We were together for the next two years, all while he completed his training to be a mechanic. Then, when he was fully qualified, he got offered a job in Aberdeen.'

'Aberdeen? Why there?'

'He had cousins up there, I think.' She tried to make it sound as if she could only half remember. 'So that was it. He still didn't think that the long-distance thing would work, though. And he didn't give me the option to follow. It was time we expanded our horizons. Those were the words he used: "Expand our horizons". That's how he told me it was over.'

Her teeth ground together at the memory. It was the way Paul had been so relaxed about it. As if he were giving her this opportunity for a whole new life by pulling the rug from beneath her feet.

'So what did you do then? Is that when you moved to London?' Apparently, Theo was still not done with his questioning, although this one was the worst one yet. Because this was where Daisy had to admit that giving up on her dreams hadn't been Paul's fault at all. It had been hers.

She shook her head in response to his question.

'No, I was twenty, nearly twenty-one by this point. And I was still living with Mum. I'd saved up all the money from the chambermaid job. Some of it was earmarked for a house, but the truth was, I'd really saved it for our wedding. I'd even picked out the colour of the bridesmaid dresses. I was so certain that we were going to be together. So when Paul moved, I decided to do what I always wanted. I reapplied to art college. I wanted to see it through and fulfil those dreams of becoming an illustrator.' She paused, swallowing back the tightness that was clamping her chest, hoping that Theo might say something to ease the dull ache she could feel building, but he remained silent. Looking at her, as if he were utterly transfixed by her words. And so she pasted a false smile on her face and carried on.

'I got accepted onto the same course as the one I'd applied to before. The one I dreamt of. But from the moment I got there, I felt so out of place.' She was struggling to find a way to explain those feelings she had tried to suppress for so long. 'I was older than everyone there. Only by a couple of years, but the difference between eighteen and twenty-one felt enormous. And I was out of practice. I'd been working full time in a job which had sucked all the life from me and I hadn't had the energy to pick up a paint-brush for years. At least, that's what I told myself. I got accepted on paintings I'd done back at school, and faced with all these fresh, eager students, I felt like I was constantly playing catch up. It cost me a fortune – the rent, the fees – and I tried to stick it out. I managed one term, but I knew I was never going to make it. So just before Christmas, I quit. I skipped my lectures one day, applied for a temping agency in London, and took the first job they offered me. And that's it.'

The heavy weight she knew she would feel at recounting this time of her life pushed down into her ribs.

'I've been moving from one job to the next ever since, and I've never really settled. I get bored. Pick holes. Either find a reason to quit, or for them to get rid of me. I love my flat and everything, but over the last couple of years, I've decided that perhaps I'm just not meant to settle anywhere, really.'

Theo looked across the narrow width from his seat to hers, his expression motionless.

'I'm so sorry. I'm sorry for the things with your dad and your mum. I'm so sorry you gave up on your dream like that. But you know it's not too late, right? You're an incredible artist. I've seen what you can do.'

'I don't know. I'm not even sure my heart's in it any more.'

'Trust me, looking at that painting, your heart is definitely in it. You just need to have the courage to go for it.'

His eyes were staring so intently now that a nervous tingling was starting to spread through her. A nervousness that she hadn't felt in a long time. Swallowing back a lump in her throat, she stood up and placed her drink on the table. 'I've chewed your ear off for far too long. I should get home.'

Theo stood up, too. In such a small space, their bodies were surprisingly close together.

'You're not thinking about driving, are you?'

'I've only had two of those,' she said, indicating the brown bottles.

'Exactly. You've had two of those. They're 9 per cent each.'

'9 per cent?'

'As an estimate. A conservative one. Damien, the friend who made this, once brewed an IPA that was fourteen. No idea how he did that.'

Suddenly, Daisy's loose tongue made a lot more sense. She must have consumed at least five units. Way too much for her to even consider driving home.

'I'm so sorry,' Theo said. 'I wouldn't have offered you them of I'd known you were planning on going home. I thought you were staying on the *September Rose* again. Like last night.'

Daisy nodded, her head still swimming. Consuming the equivalent of half a bottle of wine, with only focaccia and a small piece of smoked salmon to line her stomach, wasn't her wisest decision.

'I'm sorry,' she said, feeling as if the boat was growing smaller and smaller by the second. 'It's fine. I can sleep in the boat. Of course I can. I'll just have to get up early to go to work.'

Theo didn't look convinced. 'Do you need anything? Is it warm enough? I've got plenty of spare blankets and pillows.'

'It's fine. My sleeping bag is still there.'

'You're sure?' he asked. 'Let me walk you home at least.'

All the way to the back of her boat, Theo remained a step behind her, and when she reached the stern, she stopped, ready to say goodbye, but Theo got in there first.

'This has been an unexpected evening, Daisy May. A good, but unexpected evening. I've enjoyed getting to know you.'

'I'm pretty sure that next time we need to devote more of our conversation to your deep, dark secrets, rather than me divulging everything to do with my shameful past,' she replied with a smile.

'There was nothing shameful about your past at all,' Theo replied. 'Not a single thing.'

For a second they stayed there, as if there was something more that should be said. A distant sense of déjà vu spread through her, only for it to hit her hard. She knew exactly what this felt like. It felt like she was on a date.

She took a step back, the palms of her hands growing sweatier and sweatier by the second. It had 100 per cent not been a date, even if there had been drinks and food and lots of talking involved. But this moment was feeling like the awkward part of the evening where they would decide if they were going to agree to see each other again, or just offer casual niceties that implied this was the end of the road. Or perhaps... perhaps even kiss. She cleared her throat, willing the thought back out of her head, wishing that he would just turn around and walk to his boat so that she could go inside. But he stayed there. Still not moving.

'Well, this is me,' she said.

He smiled, although it was a shallow one and had barely started to form when he parted his lips and said, 'Daisy May, what are your plans for tomorrow afternoon?'

35

Daisy slumped down onto the bed of the *September Rose*. If that hadn't been a rollercoaster of a weekend, she didn't know what was. Now, to top it off, she was going to have to get up an hour and a half early so she could get home in time to shower, get changed and still make it into work. Groaning, she set an alarm, then added one extra, just in case, before closing her eyes and falling straight asleep.

Blissful birdsong was the first sound she noticed. High-pitched trills, accompanied by lower, dense warbles. For a moment she lay there, her eyes closed, assuming that she was still in her dream. She wasn't sure she'd ever had a dream sound that realistic before. Slowly, she rolled over and smacked her hand hard on a side table she hadn't expected to be there. Jerking awake, she bolted up.

It took her a split second to remember the day before. Her talk with Yvonne. Her mum's confession. Memories of her night drinking with Theo, and the fact she had spent the night on the *September Rose*.

'Crap!' She shot out of bed, pulling open the curtains to be met with a bright blue sky. Her pulse rocketed. 'Please, just be a bright morning.' She grabbed her phone and furiously tapped at the screen, praying that the sun looked brighter without the smog and haze of the city. After jabbing her phone screen for a full fifteen seconds, the realisation that the battery had run out dawned on her and, as a result, neither of her alarms had buzzed to wake her up.

She reached for her trousers and hopped around on one leg as she tried to pull them on as quickly as possible.

'What the hell is the time?' she yelled, although there was no one around to answer her. When she started renovating this boat properly, the first things she was going to do was nail a clock to the wall. A big clock so she'd be aware just how much she had messed up when she overslept.

With her clothes on, she forced her feet into shoes, and stumbled up the steps on to the deck before turning around to lock the door.

'Everything okay?' She turned around to see Theo standing in front of her, two steaming mugs of coffee in his hand. 'I thought you might want a drink?'

'What time is it?' She was still fiddling with the lock and ignoring his offer entirely. 'Do you know what the time is?'

In somewhat of a balancing act, Theo twisted his wrist to look at the time on his watch, not spilling any of his coffee.

'It's eight-thirty. Just gone.'

'Crap!' Daisy's panic reached a whole new level. 'I'm going to be late.' She took one of the coffees and gulped down several steaming mouthfuls before handing the mug back to Theo.

'Thank you,' she said.

'No worries. I understand. I'll see you here whenever you knock off work. If you're still all right with that?'

Daisy wracked her brain, wondering what it was she'd forgotten. A second later, her memory flicked back to Theo's vague offer from the night before.

'Sure, sure,' she replied, not even sparing the time to even think of a valid excuse for cancelling. All that mattered was getting to work.

She ran to the car. Not that it made any difference. For the entire journey, the traffic gods were against her. She hit every red light going, got cut up at more than one junction, and even sat in a half-mile tailback because of a broken-down white van.

'There's no need to rush,' she tried to tell herself repeatedly as she reached the final turning onto her road. 'I've had a family emergency. They will understand.'

Having spent two consecutive nights aboard the *September Rose*, she couldn't even skip a shower. She rushed through the front door, pulling the post out of the letter box as she went. Post that consisted mainly of circulars, with one small, brown envelope amongst the pile. Her name and address were handwritten on the front.

Daisy stopped and frowned. The letter about the boat had come in a brown envelope. But that had been bigger, with her name typed on a sticker, not scribbled in pen like this one. Knowing that another three minutes wouldn't change anything, she opened it up and read the contents. Only to wish she hadn't.

At work, Daisy was relieved by the lack of fuss at her late appearance. In fact, no one seemed to notice her at all, which was a good thing, given how she was unable to focus on anything other than the contents of the letter. She should've seen it coming.

Her landlord was going to up her rent.

It shouldn't have come as a shock, given that she'd paid exactly the same since moving there, about 20 per cent less than the average rental flat in the area. She should've known it was going to happen at some point. And it wasn't unreasonable. The landlord had informed her that next month would be the start of an eighty pounds a week increase, in line with inflation and standard rentals in the area, also noting the fact she'd had no increase in rent before. All of that was true, but an extra three hundred and sixty pounds a month was absolutely impossible. That was an extra four thousand pounds a year. Maybe if she'd been working at the office a little longer, she could've asked for a pay rise. But she'd only been there six months. And today, after arriving late, hardly seemed like the ideal time to ask. She'd have to figure something out. Maybe go through her wardrobe and dig out some of those old shoes and clothes she'd been holding onto. People made money doing that, didn't they?

With her mind preoccupied and having missed half the day, she had nowhere near enough time to get all her work done. The stream of emails was constant, but it was nearly impossible to reply due to the arrival of clients for face-to-face appointments. And to make it even worse, her productivity was hindered further by the incessant ringing of her phone.

Ringing Daisy at work was not something Pippa had done before, but that day she hadn't stopped. No doubt she wanted to apologise again, or perhaps just check that she was okay. But given how much she had to do, Daisy just didn't have the time to talk to her. Besides, there was nothing she had to say. Not yet. She needed some time to make sense of things. So, the first dozen times her phone buzzed, she just tapped on the end call button. But by three o'clock, when she had received nearly twenty calls, she gave up.

'This is not a good time, Mum,' she said abruptly, checking to see whether any managers were within earshot.

'Daisy, I just want to you to know—'

'No. I don't want to talk to you like this. Please. I will speak to you again when I'm ready. But not now.' She dropped her head as she hung up the call. Only when she lifted it again did she see the shadow hovering in the distance.

'Everything okay?' Amanda asked.

'Sorry, yes.'

'The family emergency again?'

Daisy wasn't sure whether there was a shortness to Amanda's tone. Then again, it was Monday. Everyone was short on Monday, weren't they?

'Yes, unfortunately,' she replied.

'Well, let's hope it all gets cleared up soon.'

When the clock finally tipped to five o'clock, Daisy's whole body groaned in relief. What she wanted to do now was head home and get a proper night's sleep in a proper bed.

It was on the bus part of her journey when Daisy's thoughts slipped back to the night before. She couldn't remember the last time she had chatted to someone as easily as she had to Theo. There was an ineffable ease about him. Although her musing of their newly formed friendship was followed by a heavy groan. With all the stress of the day, she had entirely forgotten they'd arranged to meet up.

Damn. Another late night was the last thing she wanted. Under normal circumstances, she would have rung and cancelled, but she didn't have Theo's number. And she couldn't just not turn up. Not after he'd agreed to help with the *September Rose*.

Feeling like she had aged ten years in one weekend, she reached her front door and saw the bulging bag waiting for her.

One that was substantially larger than normal. It must have been a slow day at the bakery, she thought as she pulled it off the handle. Slow days were always bad news for the bakery, of course, but good news for her. And today, she considered with a smile on her face, Theo too.

36

Wildflower Lock was once again teeming with paddleboarders and dog walkers.

'Back here again?' one paddleboarder said, offering her a short wave as she passed.

'Guess I am,' she replied, not sure if she had already met this person or not.

When she reached the *Narrow Escape*, Theo was out on the deck, a book in his hand. If this was how relaxed someone looked when they worked as a linesman, perhaps she should consider the change in career, she thought, only to remember she didn't really have a career. She had a job instead.

As she approached, Theo sat up and closed his book.

'I'll be honest. I thought you might stand me up,' he said.

'I'll be honest. I thought I might stand you up too.'

Not waiting for an invitation, she stepped onto the boat.

'Here you go,' she said, handing him the plastic bag.

'What's this?'

'You have to open it to find out. I don't know. Could be croissants, could be a Bakewell tart. I live above a bakery. The guys there leave me any of the extras they don't want.'

'Nice arrangement.'

'It's a definite perk. Not that I'm sure how much longer I can stay there. My landlord's put the rent up. I found out today.'

Theo let out a thin whistle from between his teeth.

'I guess you need to get this place sorted as quickly as you can then,' he said. 'There'll be no landlord to worry about when you're living on the water. You'll just have the mooring fees. Assuming you don't want to keep moving.'

'I am not planning on living on the water,' Daisy replied. 'I'm fairly sure I told you that.'

Theo sat forward, a thin smile playing on his lips.

'You did. I remember you telling me that it was your boat to do with whatever you wanted. You were quite emphatic on the matter.'

'Well, you hadn't particularly endeared yourself to me.'

'Fair enough. I was a bit of a jerk when we first met, but I was thinking about last night. There's a reason you haven't considered living on the water yet. That's because you've never been on it.'

'What are you on about? I slept on the *Rose* two nights in a row,' she said, somewhat indignantly.

'Yes, in a mooring. You haven't been out. You haven't seen what the countryside has to offer. Which is why, this evening, Daisy May, I am going to show you all the highlights of Wildflower Lock and beyond.'

Daisy didn't move. She wasn't 100 per cent sure what Theo was saying. She waited, hoping he would clarify, but when he didn't, she was left with no choice but to ask.

'Do you mean…' She still wasn't able to finish.

'I mean today, Daisy May, I'm taking you for a drive.'

* * *

Daisy wasn't sure why she felt nervous about going on a boat.

'You really don't have to do this,' she said more than once. 'I get it. Living on the water is lovely. I suspect it's all calm and peaceful. I can tell that.'

'How about you stop talking and we get to work?' he said, stunning her into silence. 'Okay, so Wildflower Lock is behind us and Paper Mill about five miles down this way. Am I right in assuming you have never been in a lock while it's in action?'

'You'll be more right assuming I've never even seen a lock in action.'

Theo's jaw dropped.

'Okay, that's not technically true,' she said, feeling like she needed to stand up for herself. 'I've probably been in hundreds of locks. I just don't remember it. I did live on a boat, remember?'

Theo pursed his lips slightly before continuing.

'Okay, so that means this is going to be your first time casting off. Go down to the bow and untie the rope.'

'The bow?'

'The front of the boat. Down there.' He nodded to where a white rope was twisted around a metal post at the far end. 'When you've done it, come back here. I'm going to get you working.'

As disgruntled as she could've been, spending her evening doing further work, Daisy struggled to control the flutter of excitement she felt as she untied the knot and threw the rope onto the front of the boat. She headed back across the bank to jump onto the back next to Theo.

'You've untied the front... The boat's not connected at the bow at all, so now we need to get out of this mooring. I want you to pull on this rope sharply.'

The rope he was referring to was wrapped loosely around a

metal post and holding the back of the boat in place. Pulling on it didn't seem like the most sensible thing to do if they wanted to move out into the canal.

'Pull on the rope?'

'Just trust me, pull on it.'

Knowing that there was no point ignoring the person who actually knew what they were doing, Daisy gripped her hands around the rope and tugged it towards her.

'There you go. A little more, a little more,' Theo encouraged, though Daisy couldn't see anything. 'Have a look up by the bow,' he said a moment later.

It was then that she saw the effects of her work. The nose of the boat was no longer parallel to the bank of the river. But instead, it was pointing out into the centre.

'I haven't been out on the river for a couple of days, so I warmed the engine up earlier. You'll need to do the same when you take the *September Rose* out.'

Daisy laughed. 'Oh, I don't think I'm going to take her out. Remember, my aim is to get her into a saleable condition. That's it.'

'And if you want to get a decent price for her, which is likely your main purpose, you're going to need to make sure she's in good nick. People aren't gonna pay top dollar for a boat that doesn't go. All right, so I'll get us out of here, but when the riverbank clears up a little more, and we're away from all these other boats, you're gonna be the one in charge of the tiller.'

'The what?'

Theo rolled his eyes, though it didn't stop them twinkling with a smile.

'The steering, Daisy. You're going to be in charge of the steering.'

Given how slowly it felt like they were going, Daisy was

surprised that it didn't take long before the boats along the side of the canal thinned out and then disappeared altogether.

'This is beautiful,' Daisy said, her heart swelling in her chest at the view.

The scenery constantly changed. One moment, they were gliding past thick, dense trees with branches overhanging into the water. Then it was rushes, filled with moorhens, cygnets, ducks and plenty of other waterfowl Daisy didn't know the names of. There were open fields to the sides of them. Houses. Footpaths with joggers. Every time she turned her head, the view changed.

Far sooner than she would have anticipated, Theo turned to face her.

'Okay, time for you to take over.'

She looked at the long metal pole in his hand, which was connected directly to the rudder, and shook her head.

'I don't think I'm ready for that right now,' she said. 'Honestly, this is fine. Better than fine. This is great.'

'There's nothing to worry about,' Theo replied softly. 'Honestly, I'm not going to let anything happen to you.'

Daisy was about to refuse again when she was cut off by her phone ringing.

'I don't know if it's a good thing or a bad thing you've still got reception here,' Theo said, lifting an eyebrow.

After a quick rifle through her handbag, Daisy saw that once again, her mother was calling. With a firm press of her thumb, she switched the phone off and turned back to Theo.

'Do you know what? I think I might give this tiller thing a go after all.'

37

By the time they were heading back to Wildflower Lock, dusk was upon them. Never in her life had Daisy felt like she spent so much time simply staring upwards. She was enjoying watching the brushstroke clouds as they swept across the pale, rose-gold sky.

'I love this time of day,' Theo said, standing beside her, his gaze lost in the same clouds as hers.

'I find it mesmerising, the knowledge that you'll never see the same sky twice,' Daisy replied, wishing she had the words to convey what she was feeling. 'Does that make sense?'

'It does. I feel the same about the water. Canal life. Wildflower Lock isn't big, but every day it changes. The water, the clouds, the birds, the plants. No two days are the same.'

'I suspect that can get addictive,' Daisy said, more to herself than Theo, but when she brought her gaze away from the clouds she saw how he was staring straight at her. Her skin flooded with warmth. Shifting slightly, she placed her hand back on the tiller. 'So where next?'

They had gone under bridges, beside busy roads and through open fields. But without a doubt, her favourite part of the evening adventure had been her first experience of a lock. Not that she had done anything. Theo had very definitely done all the work this time, but she had watched on as the water rushed through the open paddles, raising her boat so it could join the level of the rest of the canal.

'Do you never worry that it's going to go wrong?' she asked as they slowly drove through the open lock and back towards their mooring. 'Like the water might rush in too fast and you'll sink?'

'Just take your time. River life isn't about rushing,' he replied. 'As long as you're not rushing, you'll be fine.'

As the *September Rose* came into view, Daisy was struck by a hint of sadness. Obviously, she couldn't keep Theo out all night. Especially not having accosted him the evening before, too. And there was the added fact that it would soon be dark, but she really could have spent hours on the boat.

'So, are you hooked yet?' Theo asked when they were moored up.

'I think it'll take more than one trip out for me to be hooked. But I will admit, I enjoyed it. I enjoyed it a lot.'

Following Theo's instructions, she tied the ropes around the mooring post, before stepping back to let him check her handiwork. When the *Narrow Escape* was secured, Daisy couldn't help but look at the *September Rose* with despondency. It was going to take so much time and money to fix her up properly; it was hard to know if it would be worth it. After all, it wasn't like she had cash to spare at the minute.

'I don't know how I'm going to do her up. I might be better just calling it a day, sell her for scrap and take whatever I can get.'

'You can't be serious. You've already done the hardest part: clearing out all the stuff. That's the dull bit. Everything else from this point is fun.'

'I don't think we have the same idea of fun. I've never so much as put up a shelf. There's no way I can do all this on my own.'

'I told you last night, you're not alone in this.' His hand rested on hers for a fraction of a second. Then, as if he had realised what he had done, he snatched it back.

'I... I... I should get going,' Daisy stuttered, wondering why her pulse had taken such a sudden upward surge. 'Work tomorrow.'

'Of course. I completely get it. But first, would it be possible to get your telephone number?'

Daisy swallowed, only to be hit by a spur of anger. He had a girlfriend. One he'd told her all about. And now he had the audacity to make a move.

'You're with someone,' she said.

A pink tint coloured Theo's cheeks. 'Oh... no... I didn't mean like that. At all... God, I am... No. I just meant for the boat. You know, if I find anything that might be able to help you. Or it might help to have each other's numbers if you want to let me know you're coming down; then I can check the engine and things. You'll also need someone here at the lock to have a way to contact you.'

It was Daisy's cheeks that coloured this time, and not to a light pink flush, but fluorescent red. She could feel the heat burning on her face.

'Oh. Of course. Yes, sorry. My mistake.'

'I really shouldn't invite women into my house for focaccia.' Theo laughed as he handed her his phone. When she handed it back, with the number now saved, he hesitated. 'I don't want to come across as too presumptuous or anything. But would you mind giving me one of your keys?'

'My keys?' She'd already embarrassed herself over the phone number incident, but this seemed a step too far.

'It's up to you, of course. It's just... I could get some work done on the *September Rose* before I start work. With the mornings getting light and everything, I'm up by five most days just pottering about. Only if you don't mind, that is?'

Would Daisy mind somebody helping her out, doing work on the boat for free? The answer to that was absolutely not. Or not in any normal circumstance. But something about Theo wasn't feeling entirely normal. Not for her, at least. She had opened up about her past to him in a way she had never done with anybody. Whether there was alcohol involved or not, it didn't change the fact he knew more about her than she felt comfortable with. Throw into that the ridiculous, heart racing moment that occurred simply from him touching her and her mind was a mess. Still, she needed to think objectively. Firstly, he wasn't her type. And it wasn't like she actually liked him. These emotions had simply arisen because of the trauma of everything with her mum. He had been there at the moment she needed somebody. That's all it was. And she would be a fool to refuse a gift like he was offering.

'That would be great,' she said, handing him the small keyring with all the boat's keys on. 'It's my only spare, though. So try not to lose it.'

'Great. Well, I'm not making any promises on how much I'll be able to do, but I'll see what I can make a start on during the week. Unless you're planning on coming back before next weekend?'

Daisy shook her head. After the weekend she'd just had, she didn't need any more excitement for the next few days.

'No, I'll be back at the weekend.'

'Then I'll see you then, Daisy May.'

38

Although Daisy had given Theo her telephone number, and the keys to the *September Rose*, she hadn't actually expected to hear from him. Which was why when a message pinged through on through her phone at seven-thirty on Wednesday morning, she was more than a little surprised. Although she was even more surprised by the contents of said message.

How attached are you to the side panelling?

Daisy stared at the question. Was this some kind of trap? It certainly sounded like a trick question, though she quickly decided he was serious. Theo didn't seem like the type of person who would send messages just for fun.

As Daisy considered her reply, she tried to work out which side panels he meant. The entire inside of the boat was clad with them, all different colours, in both the cabin, the kitchenette, and the living area. And none of them were particularly appealing.

Not attached

She replied.

Good. Because I've already pulled it off

A bolt of trepidation rushed through her. Perhaps giving a near stranger keys to her most valuable possession hadn't been the wisest idea. Several hours later, when another messaged pinged through, she was forced to wonder the same thing again.

'Oh wow,' she said, as she opened up the photo and stared at the image of bare, wooden walls.

Okay, that's definitely looking different.

Don't worry, I have a plan

Theo messaged, almost as if reading her mind.

And it's not going to cost you any money.

'Plans like that are definitely my favourite type,' Daisy said, still talking out loud to herself.

'More boat things?' Amanda's voice caused Daisy to jump on the spot. Her line manager was standing there, blocking the doorway. For how long she had been there, Daisy had no idea. The woman seemed to be a master of apparition.

'Yes, actually.' She handed Amanda the phone so she could see the photo. 'My neighbour is helping me do some work on it. He's not a handyman, he's a linesman, but it seems that he's great at everything. Baking, DIY. Gallantry. Although he appears to be tearing off pieces of my boat.'

'A handyman boat neighbour. Sounds like a thing of dreams,' Amanda replied, passing the phone back. 'I just wanted to know if you've written up those schedules for the Arc account? I was hoping to have them by this morning.'

'They're the next job on my list,' Daisy said. 'I was just making sure all next week's appointments were sorted before then.'

Amanda's smile was wide and showed far too many teeth for Daisy to feel comfortable.

'Well, if you could get on that,' she said, before turning her back and leaving.

With a loud sigh, Daisy made her tea and then returned to her desk to make a start on the task. It wasn't exactly a big job, but typing numbers into spreadsheets was far from her favourite thing to do and recently that had felt like it was her only job.

Immediately, she honed in on her thoughts. This is what she did, she reminded herself. She started to pick holes in her job, her employers, her work environment. She made herself dislike the place so much that it became unbearable, and then she quit. That was the habit she had got into over these last three years. But she couldn't afford that right now. Her rent was going up, and judging by the photos from Theo, the boat was even less saleable than i had been when she first got it. She needed this job. She liked thi job. She was just tired, that was all.

It wasn't only her mother's calls that Daisy had been avoidin that week. Both Claire and Bex had rung and messaged her wanting a catch up on how things were going, while apologisin for dashing off so early on Sunday morning. But Daisy hadn replied to either. She didn't feel like lying and saying that every-thing was okay, but she didn't have it in her to talk about her dad o mum just yet.

Deep down, she knew she was going to have to speak to ther both eventually, although she hadn't realised exactly how quickl that was going to happen. After a long day at work, laden wit weariness, she had just reached the bakery when she saw a bright-pink silhouette that could only be Bex by her front door.

'So, you do exist,' Bex said. 'I was starting to get worried.'

'It's Wednesday,' Daisy replied. 'I saw you on Saturday. Sunday morning, actually. We've gone longer than that without seeing each other.'

'Without seeing each other, yes. Not without messaging. In fact, the only time we've ever gone more than three days without messaging was in Year 10 when you decided that Hazel Fonda was going to be your best friend instead of me.'

'I did not do that. I was only hanging out with Hazel because you got all chummy with Katie Joynes and weren't letting me join in.'

Bex shook her head and laughed.

'Whatever. You haven't replied to my messages. Any of them. I was worried. I thought you might want to talk about it.'

Daisy looked at her door, disappointed to see there were no pastries hanging up for her. In that case, it would have to be beer instead.

'How long have you got?'

By the time Daisy had finished recounting the last three days to Bex over a takeaway pizza, she actually felt slightly calmer about the whole thing. The truth was, she knew that her mother had only made certain choices to protect her, and every time she told the story about her parents, and what Pippa had done, it had reinforced that fact.

'But you still haven't spoken to her? Not at all?'

'I don't know where I'd start.'

'But you're going to soon, right? She must be going out of her mind.'

Daisy sipped her drink, guilt once again rising within her. She tried to quash it. After all, why should she feel guilty? Her mother had been the one to bring this upon herself. Even as the thought formed, it faded.

'I'll see her at the weekend,' she said eventually. Adding quickly, 'After all, her ringing is driving me insane.'

'You could always pick up the phone?'

Daisy shook her head, then reached down to her glass to find it empty. 'I don't want to do this over the phone.'

'I get it,' Bex replied. 'And if there's any way I can help support you, you know I'm here, right?'

'Thank you.'

For a second, the old friends sat in silence. It was the type of silence in which nothing needed to be said. The type of silence you could only share with someone who knew you inside out. Although it didn't last quite as long as Daisy expected.

'So, Theo?' Bex said, unable to suppress her grin. 'Two dates in a row.'

Daisy picked up a cushion and threw it at her across the sofa.

'This is why I didn't want to say anything to you. Because I knew you'd do this. I knew you'd read more into it than is actually there.'

'He took you out on his boat.'

'To show me the canal. He is my neighbour, that's it. Possibly a friend, but nothing more. He has a girlfriend, remember?' she added slightly sullenly. 'So, even if I was interested, it's not like I'd do anything when he's seeing someone.'

Bex's jaw dropped open.

'Even if you were interested?' she repeated. 'You never say that. You never say you're interested in a guy.' Her eyes were glittering, bulging out of their sockets.

'I didn't say I was. I said even if I was, he has a girlfriend.'

'And does this girlfriend know about you? About him taking you out for trips along the river, moonlight strolls on the water?'

'It wasn't moonlight. I'm not even sure if you're allowed on the canals when it's dark. That's probably something I should know. Anyway, it doesn't matter. That's what it's like there. Everybody helps each other. It's a community. He's just being neighbourly.'

'And that's what he's doing now? Being neighbourly as he sorts out your boat? That sounds like a boyfriend job to me.'

'Or maybe he's fed up having to wake up to a view of my ugly boat each morning. I think that's more likely, don't you?'

At this point, Bex stayed silent, but it wasn't the same type of silence as before. It was the type that implied there was more she wanted to say.

'He's not even my type anyway,' Daisy added, hoping to reinforce her argument.

'I didn't think you'd dated enough guys to even have a type,' Bex quipped back. 'But I can see you with someone like him. Someone good with his hands if you know what I mean.'

Daisy shook her head and stared at her empty glass. She had no intention of drinking another beer. She was still on her best behaviour at work after her Monday morning late show. Though it shouldn't take long to get back into Amanda's good books... After all, one late morning was hardly enough to hold a grudge, was it? Besides, she wasn't even sure anyone had noticed.

She was just about to suggest that it was time to call it a day when her doorbell rang.

Glancing down, Daisy checked the time on her watch, surprised to see that it was already gone nine.

'You expecting someone?' Bex asked.

Daisy shook her head. 'You're the only person who shows up uninvited.'

The doorbell rang again, this time for even longer; whoever it was was not letting go.

'Daisy?' her mother called up from the street below. 'Daisy? It's Mum. I know you're in. I just want to talk to you. Let me in. I just want to talk.'

39

'Crap,' Daisy said. All the peace and relief that talking to Bex had given her instantly evaporated.

'What are you just sitting there for?' Bex asked. 'You said yourself you need to speak to her. You should let her in.'

'I said I needed to talk to her on my terms. I was going to talk to her this weekend. This, turning up here, ringing my phone all the ime, it's too much. Why doesn't she get that? I just need a little bit of space.'

'I think you might be overreacting.'

'Overreacting? She hid the fact that my father raised me alone while she moved to Paris. She stopped us having contact and made t seem like he wanted nothing to do with me. Did you not hear hat?'

'Okay, maybe overreacted is the wrong word.' Bex backtracked lightly. 'But would it be really the worst thing in the world to talk o her a couple of days earlier than planned? She's obviously as evastated by this as you are.'

Daisy barely considered the thought. It had taken all her ontrol to get to a point where she could even contemplate talking to her mum. She wasn't going to be forced into a conversation when she wasn't ready.

'Could you just stay quiet?' she said instead. 'I'm sure she'll give up soon.'

It was another twenty minutes before Daisy let Bex check the curtains, to discover, to Daisy's relief, that Pippa had gone.

'You need to talk to her. Soon,' Bex said, as she kissed Daisy goodbye. 'Things won't get any better if you don't.'

'I will, I promise.'

'Okay, I just don't want things to get worse, that's all.'

'They won't,' Daisy promised. And she actually believed that it was true.

* * *

Determined to make amends at work, Daisy caught the earlie train in for the rest of the week and used the extra time to make teas, schedule emails, and even headed down to the doughnu shop to keep the kitchen supplied. She also kept her phone o during office hours and, with no distractions, was completely up t date by the time four-thirty on Friday rolled around and Amand came over to invite Daisy out for drinks.

'A few of the team are going across to the Queen's Head Amanda said. 'You're welcome to join us.'

It was an offer they had made several times during Daisy's fir month at the company, but she had refused, and soon they ha stopped asking. This time, however, she wasn't so quick to dismis the offer.

'That would be great,' she said.

'Fantastic, I'll see you there.'

The minute Amanda left, Daisy regretted her choice. She never been to the Queen's Head, but it was close, which meant was going to be London prices. Central London prices. Which meant two pints were probably equal to the increase in rent she was being expected to find out of nowhere. And maybe they did rounds. If they did rounds, there was no way she was going to be able to afford things.

She was debating whether she should try to give a believable excuse – like the fact that Theo had messaged and needed her to go to the boat – or just bail. After all, there were enough people going that they probably wouldn't notice she was missing.

Even when she had packed up her things and was heading out of the building and onto the street, Daisy was still deliberating what to do, and was so lost in her thoughts, she didn't even notice a woman had stepped out in front of her until they almost collided.

'Mum?' Daisy said, as confused by the sight of her mother as the near collision. 'What are you doing here?'

'What do you mean, what am I doing? You won't pick up my calls You won't answer my texts.'

Never had Daisy seen her mother in such a state. Her skin was sallow, her cheeks drawn in, and she was trembling as if she hadn't eaten a single thing since Daisy had last seen her.

'This is my workplace,' Daisy said, equally mortified by Pippa's state as she was the fact her mother would show up here. She wasn't even aware her mother knew where she worked. Glancing over her shoulder, she saw the building's elevator opening. Amanda and several of the other managers stepped out. 'You shouldn't be here.'

'You turned off your phone. You won't answer the door to me. What options did you leave me with?'

'Mum, I'm not doing this here in the street. I'm not doing it now. Please, you have to leave.'

She was still staring in disbelief when Amanda sidled up beside her.

'Is everything okay? Daisy?'

'Everything will be fine. I just need a minute,' she said, aware of people slowing their pace as they walked, watching the scene unfold. 'Mum, not here. Not now. You need to go.' She softened her voice further still. 'I'll come over on Sunday. We'll talk then, I promise. But you need to leave now.'

Daisy's breath trembled in her lungs as she prayed her mother would hear her and leave. But she didn't know what she would do. This person standing in front of her was like a stranger. Silent tears dripped down Daisy's face as, without another word, Pippa turned around and disappeared into the crowd.

The second she was gone, Daisy expelled the air in her lungs in one long gasp. All the watchers on had scuttled away, no doubt disappointed by the lack of drama, although one person remained beside her. Amanda.

'Family drama?' she said before Daisy could get a word in.

'I'm so sorry, Amanda. I don't know what got into her. It won't ever happen again. I promise.' She waited for the reprimand, clenching her muscles against the inevitable firing or official warning she was certain would come. But Amanda smiled.

'You're out of the office. And it's out of work hours, so it's really not any of my business. To be honest, I'm kind of relieved. You have no idea how many staff we've had using the term "family emergency" as an excuse for not setting their alarm.'

'It really was—' Daisy said, overlooking the fact her own alarm had failed to go off. But Amanda raised her hand before she could continue.

'I get it. I do. Nobody's family is straightforward. I learnt that long ago. Just don't bring it into work, all right?'

Daisy nodded her head rapidly.

'Absolutely. It won't happen again. I'm so sorry.'

Amanda dipped her head slowly, indicating that the conversation was nearly over, although when Daisy moved to leave, she spoke again.

'I don't know what she's done, but every person is fighting a thousand battles you can't see. Remember that. Intentions matter. No matter the outcome, intentions matter.'

Daisy decided to skip the pub, and when she reached home, briefly considered her Friday night plans. A few weeks ago, they would've involved Bex, a cocktail bar and dancing until the early hours. But she didn't feel like that right now. The idea of battling for ten minutes just to get a drink had never sounded less appealing. Besides, Bex had messaged something about being unavailable, which almost always meant a date. But that was fine. Daisy needed to do other things, too.

She had already messaged Theo to say she was heading down to Wildflower Lock that evening, but as she headed back out of her front door, jeans and trainers on, she knew there was somewhere else she needed to be.

40

She didn't use the key this time, but knocked on the door and waited. Her heart knocked faster and faster with every passing second. Daisy had never felt anxious coming to this house before. It had been her safe place. The place where she could unequivocally be herself. But that had changed now.

Pippa opened the door, only to step back at the sight of her, her eyes filling with tears as she spoke.

'I'm so sorry, my love. I wasn't thinking. I was just so worried. I was so worried about everything I've done.'

'It's okay, Mum,' Daisy said, stepping forward and wrapping her arms around her mother. 'It's all okay.'

They didn't even bother to close the front door; they just stood together, Pippa's head on her chest, her sobs stifled by the fabric of Daisy's top. Never, in her life, had she embraced her mother like this. Finally, when they broke apart, Daisy had a proper look at the state of the hallway.

'Mum? What happened?'

Post was piled up by the door, with shoes scattered on the carpet. And a quick glance told Daisy the mess wasn't confined to where they were standing. Her mother had been so house proud. Daisy had never seen it in such a state.

'I thought I'd lost you, my love.' Pippa spoke in broken gasps. 'I thought you'd never forgive me. I thought you'd never speak to me again.'

Daisy bit down on her lip, piecing together what to say next. She didn't want to knock her mother down but she couldn't make her think everything was all right when it wasn't.

'Forgiveness is going to take some time,' she said honestly. 'I've got a lot I need to get my head around. But that doesn't mean I don't understand why you did what you did. I may not think it was the right decision – I'm pretty sure it wasn't – but I understand what you were scared of. So I'm going to try. I'm going to try to remember that, while I work on forgiving you.'

Pippa sniffed, wiping her tears with the back of her hand.

'Would you like to stay for tea? I need to have a bit of a clear up, I know. I've not done any shopping this week, but we could get a akeaway. We could go to that place you like. You know the one that does the falafel?'

'Actually, I've already arranged to meet someone.'

Pippa nodded, but Daisy could see the tears welling again in her eyes. Worried that her mother would slip backwards the moment she left, Daisy added, 'but one day next week? I'm free any ay. You can choose.'

'Monday? Would that be okay? I can cook. I can make the lamb agine you always like.'

'That sounds nice.' As she turned her back to open the door, ippa went in for another hug. This time, Daisy felt rigid beneath er mother's grip. She had meant every word she said, about trying remember Pippa's reasons for her behaviour, but the bit about rgiveness had been equally true. It wasn't going to happen in a eek. One lamb tagine would not erase years of lies.

As gently as she could, she prised her mother away from her, then opened the front door.

'Look after yourself, Mum,' she said. 'I'll see you soon.'

* * *

As much as she was against lying to her mother, particularly now, she hadn't actually arranged to meet Theo that evening, though she had messaged to let him know she was coming to the boat. For his part, he had replied with a short but self-explanatory smiley-face emoji. So it wasn't a total lie.

She parked her car and as she walked down the edge of the canal to the *September Rose*, the sense of relief she felt was entirely unexpected. Almost as unexpected as the scene she faced. Her boat. Or at least what she thought was hers. The entire roof was lost under planks of wood, and several more were propped up on the side, blocking the windows.

'Theo?' she called, standing between the *Narrow Escape* an *September Rose*, assuming he would be in one of them.

'Hey,' he said, appearing a minute later on the deck of her boat.

'Someone seems to have turned the roof of my boat into scrapyard. Do you know anything about that?'

Grinning sheepishly, he brushed the dust from his knees an hands. Those grubby trousers with stains and rips really di suit him.

'Sorry, I forgot you were coming down. I thought I'd get all th sorted before you got here.'

'What is it?'

'The panelling. Among other things. One of the guys down c the river is renovating; all that stuff on the roof he was just givi away.'

'I can kind of see why,' Daisy replied.

'Oh ye of little imagination. There are some great finds in there.'

Given how pleased he was with the haul, Daisy took a step back to get a clear view of what he had collected.

'I'm going to be honest. It looks like a lot of broken wooden planks to me.'

Theo cocked his head in mock annoyance. 'Well, if all you've come down here to do is throw insults at the free labour you're getting, I should probably get going.'

'I'm sorry,' Daisy said, genuinely meaning it. 'Can I come in and see what you've done?'

'Absolutely.'

It felt strange that Daisy was following Theo into her own boat, but given how many tools and screws were on the floor, it was a good job she did. As expected, the side panels were now gone, but what was less expected was the gaping hole where one of her windows had been, and the large patch of floorboard that had been stripped up.

One thing was certain. She couldn't sell it as it was.

'So, this is all a work in progress, right?' she said optimistically.

Theo picked up some of the tools from the floor and placed them on the worktop. 'Like I said, I wasn't expecting you. Now, do you want the good news or the bad news first?'

'How about you tell me the good news is that there is no bad news? I could live with that.'

Something about the way his face lit up when he laughed made her feel like everything was going to be fine.

'Not going to do that, I'm afraid, but there is a lot more good news than bad news.'

'Fine, give me the good new first, along with an explanation of why that windowpane is out.'

'The window is not something to worry about. I'll replace the glass before you go. Some of the wood was warping around the frame. It wasn't a big deal, but the last thing you want is for it to start leaking. As for the good things, the boat is actually in a lot better nick than I thought. I've given the engine house a check over, and it looks okay. Heats up all right too, though we won't know how she runs until we take her out. Basically, from what I can tell, most of the repairs are cosmetic.' Despite the upbeat way he spoke, Daisy couldn't ignore the niggling feeling that came with the knowledge there was more to come.

'Which brings us to the bad news?'

'Yes.' He gave a deep breath out. 'I spoke to Yvonne, who thinks the last time the boat was blacked was coming up five years ago.'

'And that's not good?'

'Eighteen months to two years is a good benchmark. Some people leave it longer, but five years is really the maximum time you want to stretch it.'

'Okay.' Daisy wished she had a piece of paper to write things down. 'So is that it? That's the main bit of bad news?'

'That and your water tank.'

Daisy's stomach sank, although it didn't come as much of a shock. She had deliberately not tried any of the taps for fear of what kind of sludge may ooze out of them. Even when she and the girls had stayed the night on the boats, they had brought bottled water to drink, and opted to use the hedgerows and fields when nature called, rather than risking the toilet on the *September Rose*. Unfortunately, her hope of living in denial was now over.

'It's probably best if I show you,' he said.

Feeling her bank account emptying with every step, Daisy followed Theo to the back of the boat, to the well deck, as he had referred to it. Only when he got there, there wasn't a deck at all. The wood had been lifted back and was currently propped against the side of the wall, exposing whatever it was that lived beneath.

'After you,' Theo said, gesturing towards it in a manner that implied he wanted her to look inside. Holding her breath, Daisy peered down the gap.

'You're going to need this,' Theo said, handing her a torch.

As she shone a light around the inside of the tank, it took her a second to make sense of what she was seeing. The sides of the tank were covered in a brown-red sludge, lumpy in places, still oozing and dripping in others. But it was the items on the bottom of the tank that had her most confused.

'Are those nappies?'

'Yup. They work a treat, soaking up water you can't scoop out. You'll still need to give it a week or so to dry out properly, then you can get on with fixing it up.'

To Daisy's untrained eye, it seemed impossible that anything in this state could be fixed up, although she didn't say such a thing aloud. The fact that Theo had taken up her floorboards, and even ventured to clear out the tank, went beyond the limits of any friends. And she didn't even consider them proper friends.

'I've had a bit of a dig about, and structurally, it's sound. Totally salvageable, it's just not been taken care of. Once you've got in there with a chisel and a wire brush, you can repaint it, and it will be good to go.'

'Get in there with a chisel?' Daisy said, hoping that she had misheard. It wasn't the chisel that was an issue, only the tight space. 'You want me to get in the water tank? Inside that water tank?'

'Assuming you want it to be useable. Yes.'

She clenched her jaw, wishing there was another way out of this.

'This is where I wish I had the money to pay someone else to do it,' she muttered half to herself.

'Actually,' Theo said, with a sudden brightness in his voice. 'I was thinking about that. About a way for you to earn some extra money.'

'You did?'

'Your paintings.'

'What about them?'

'You should sell them.'

The chuckle which exploded from Daisy's lips was far sadder and bitter than she had anticipated.

'I don't think anyone would buy anything I painted. And I don't even know what I can paint any more.'

'What do you mean? Sell pictures of the boats. Like the one you did for Yvonne.'

For a second, she wondered if he was actually winding her up. If he was, it was a sure-fire way to ensure a very swift ending to their burgeoning friendship.

'Are you serious?'

'I am deadly serious. I saw that painting again today. Trust me, I've seen far worse hanging on people's walls.'

'Well, that's a backhanded compliment if ever I heard one.'

He blushed. 'I didn't mean it to be backhanded. I promise, it was definitely a compliment. What have you got to lose? You've got all the kit, right? Why not give it a go?'

Silence hung in the air, as it became apparent that Theo's question was not rhetorical. Unfortunately, she didn't have an answer.

'I'll think about it,' she said, and stepped back from the well deck into the main part of the boat. 'So if I can't attack the water tank until it's dried out, I guess you should tell me what to work on now.'

41

'He's essentially a boyfriend,' Bex said. 'And it's perfect timing, too. We can go on double dates. You and Theo, me and Newton.'

'Newton?'

'I met him online last week. I'm sure I told you. I think he could be the one.'

Daisy pressed her lips together and forced herself to bite her tongue. If she had a pound for every time Bex thought she had found the one, she would be able to pay someone to do the boat up for her. But she wasn't going to get into that now.

'Theo is not "essentially a boyfriend". He's just my neighbour. And as I keep telling you—'

'If you tell me he's got a girlfriend again, I'm going to ignore you. Where was she this weekend? You were with him from dusk till dawn, doing up your boat – just like a couple would do, I might add. You've never even seen her.'

'You've already said that. Several times.'

'That's because it's true and the point needs reinforcing. They can't be that serious if they don't even see each other on the weekends.'

'Or they're secure enough in their relationship that they don't feel the need to live in each other's pockets. If you must know, she was away working. And Theo spoke to her several times while I was there.'

What Daisy didn't add was exactly how awkward it had been for her each time Heather rang, the way the shrill tone would cut through the conversation and Theo would apologise as he took the phone outside for some privacy.

Or at least the illusion of privacy. Given that he remained on the bank, directly outside the *September Rose*, where the windows were still open to let the paint dry, Daisy could hear everything they said. She wasn't deliberately listening in. Or at least she was trying not to listen. She couldn't help but feel a twitch of some-thing tight and ugly when he hung up with the words, 'I love you. Though once again, that wasn't something she was going t mention to Bex.

'They sounded very loved up,' she said, hoping that would b enough to stop any further pestering. 'I heard him tell her severa times how much he missed her and how much he was lookin forward to her coming home.'

'Of course he said that. He's hardly gonna say he was bus crushing on the girl from the boat next door, was he?'

Daisy took a deep breath in. There was no getting away from i Bex was not going to let this go. Not unless she had somethin juicier to discuss. For a second, she considered asking abo Newton, but that would still be talking about a relationship an she knew that Bex would absolutely find a way to circle it bac around to her. Thankfully, there was one another thing s genuinely wanted to discuss.

'So, I've arranged to see Mum tomorrow.'

'That's good. Really good. It feels wrong, you two not speakin You know she only did what she did because she loves you. S thought it was for the best.'

'I know. I know that. I just wish... I wish I could've found out the truth earlier. Dad raised me by himself, only for a little while, but he did. There are photos of it, and we looked happy. He never stopped thinking about me. It's hard to let go of that. It's hard not to look at her and think about the relationship I never had with my father, because she kept that from me.'

'I get it,' Bex said, the pointed humour from earlier gone. 'I can come with you if you want. Offer some moral support? Or be referee if that's needed.'

It was a sweet offer and one Daisy knew Bex meant, but she needed to rebuild this relationship by herself, one step at a time.

'Thanks, but I think it's best I go alone.'

'Fair enough. Where are you meeting? Is she making lamb tagine? I don't suppose you could bring me back a doggy bag if she is, could you?'

Daisy laughed, grateful for both her friend's support and her ability to lighten any situation.

'She did offer, but I thought we should try for more neutral ground. We're meeting at a restaurant. I thought that way, it would be easier to talk.'

'That sounds like a good idea. Though I really fancied some lamb tagine.'

Bex laughed, and Daisy thumped her lightly on her shoulder, though she was unable to stop the grin from crossing her face.

'Do you want to talk about it?' Bex asked eventually, once the laughter had died down, replaced with a more serious tone. 'Practice what you want to say to her. That type of thing.'

'Thank you,' Daisy said. 'But I've gone through the conversation a thousand times in my head already. I'd rather stop thinking about it if I'm honest.'

'Fair enough. So, if talking about Theo is banned and you don't want to talk about your mum, does that mean we're allowed to talk about the fact you've brought all the painting gear back off the boat?'

She gestured to the corner of the room where Daisy had stacked the various boxes. Bringing it all back to the flat – the paints and brushes and all the other painting paraphernalia – had been a split-second decision, but there was something incredibly comforting about having artist's gear back in her house.

Although that was something she wasn't planning on telling Bex just yet.

So instead she said, 'Why don't you tell me about Newton?'

42

Unlike normal Mondays, which dragged by at an impossibly slow pace, this one rushed by, every hour faster than the previous one. As Daisy found herself walking to the restaurant to see her mum, she couldn't help but think she needed more time to prepare.

She stopped outside the door and hesitated. She could send a message. Say she needed more time. As bad as she would feel, no one could make her go inside. But that wasn't fair. So she stepped into the white-walled room filled with dark-blue tables and scoured the space.

There, in the corner, she spotted her mother, an open bottle of wine with two glasses in front of her.

'I wasn't sure you'd come,' Pippa said, jumping to her feet.

'Of course I was going to come,' she replied, not mentioning her momentary wobble outside.

Pippa had dressed in her smartest clothes. Not to mention jewellery. She looked as though she had put on every single item Daisy had ever given her, from the silver bangle that she'd had engraved for her mother's fortieth, to a pair of gold earring she had bought her when she was still living at home years ago. It was almost as if Pippa had wanted to remind Daisy of all the good times they'd shared. All the times when Daisy had loved her enough to spend her money on gifts.

With Pippa standing at barely five feet, Daisy remembered what it was like when she was finally taller than her mother – although she was only in Year 8 at the time – and how she had loved being the one who could now give the big hugs. But there were no hugs now. In a manner far more formal than usual, Daisy kissed her mother on both cheeks before they sat down.

'A friend from one of my training courses runs this place,' Pippa said. 'I'm looking forward to seeing what it's like. To be honest, I always found him a little pretentious, but that doesn't mean the food will be.'

Daisy was only half listening. Instead, she was looking at the prices on the menu in front of her.

'Is everything all right, love?' Pippa said with a hint of worry. 'If you don't like the look of anything, we can go somewhere else.'

'Oh, no. The food looks lovely.' She forced herself to smile. 'It's just a bit more expensive than I thought.'

'Well, I can pay. Is everything all right with money? It's not like you to worry about the price of a meal. Have you lost your job? What happened? I thought you liked it there.'

Daisy's automatic response was to assure her mother everything was fine, but she pulled back that answer and said the truth instead.

'The job is good. I've just got a lot going on, that's all. My landlord put my rent up, by a lot. And there's still work to do on the *Rose*. Spare cash is limited, that's all.'

Pippa chewed briefly on her thumbnail, her eyes darting down to the table and back up again before she spoke.

'So, you're going to sell her then? You're going to sell the boat?'

'That's the most sensible thing to do,' Daisy said. 'Even if wanted a boat, it's far bigger than I would need. There are people on the lock with families in the same size berth as this one.'

'So you've met others,' Pippa said, keeping her tone even. 'The people that live on the lock. Are you getting to know them?'

'Not really,' Daisy replied honestly. 'Theo has the boat next door to me. He's been helping me renovate. Well, he's done most of the work so far. And I've met Yvonne, obviously, I told you that. But that's it, really.'

A small pause filled the space between them. There were questions her mother wanted to ask her, that much was obvious. Probably about Yvonne and how much she'd told Daisy about her dad, out instead of asking about this, Pippa went a different route.

'So this Theo, is he old?'

Daisy had to smile. Sometimes her mother was as subtle s Bex.

'A couple of years older than me, perhaps. He lives on the river ull time. He took me out actually, on the *Narrow Escape*. That's his oat.'

'I bet it was beautiful at this time of the year,' Pippa said, almost istfully. 'All the ducklings are about. Trees in blossom. Spring was robably my favourite time. Particularly when you're out in the untryside, all the lambs bleating and the calves jumping about.'

Daisy hadn't planned on talking about the boat, or the canal, ainly because she thought her mother wouldn't want to. But now at Pippa had brought it up, it seemed like a wasted opportunity t to ask the questions that had been filling her mind since eeting Yvonne. Unfortunately, that was the exact time that the aitress came to their table.

'Are you ready for me to take your order?'

Daisy wasn't ready. Not at all.

'I think we might need a few minutes,' she said, willing the man away before her mother changed her mind and no longer wanted to talk about the boat. Thankfully, the waitress took the hint and offered a strained smiled before disappearing.

'So you lived on the river full-time?' Daisy said, taking a sip from her wine as she tried to imagine her mother anywhere other than their two-up two-down. 'How did you find it?'

'All my friends thought I was barking when I first moved there,' Pippa started, that same wistful look remaining. 'I didn't think anything of it, though. Not really. It was this time of year. May. That was when I moved in. It gave me a couple of months to settle in before the summer. A boat is a good place to be in the summer when you're young. I'm sure it's changed a bit now, but back then you could jump straight into the water and go swimming, no matter where you moored up. We used to have this little barbecue on the deck where we cooked up fish your dad caught. Obviously, was the one that cooked it.'

It was the first time Daisy had ever heard her mother speak about her father without animosity and she wanted to ask more But at the same time, she was worried that her speaking woul break the spell and her mum would clam up like she always dic Thankfully, Pippa remained lost in her old life and so Daisy sippe slowly at her wine and savoured the moment.

'Autumn has its charms on the water too,' Pippa continue 'There's something special about seeing the world change fro your view on the boat. Seeing those leaves turn yellow to orang then brown before dropping from the trees altogether. Tho long sunsets, where the sky was so bright, it would look like was on fire. I remember those well. But winter…' Pippa carri on, looking at Daisy with the slightest glint in her eye. 'Oh, th first winter, I thought that was it for me and your father. Wint was hard. Inside was lovely and snug, mind. Probably too snu because when you left the boat and had to venture outside She paused and shuddered, as if she could still feel the cold fro all those winters ago seeping into her bones. 'Every time you had to step outside, there was nothing to protect you from that howling wind. God, it was freezing, filling up the tanks with water, checking the bilge pump, emptying your pump-out. Sometimes I thought I was going to lose a bloody finger from frostbite.'

Daisy wasn't sure which surprised her more: the fact that her mother had just sworn, or the fact she talked so easily about life on the canal. She waited, not daring to speak, hoping that there was more to come, but when a minute had passed, Daisy knew she would have to keep the conversation going.

'My neighbour Theo, he works as a linesman,' she said. 'When he went for the job, they told him that if he lasted the winter, he'd be hooked.'

'Let me guess: when the winter passed and the spring came round, he bought himself a boat?'

'I think that's pretty much what happened.'

Her mum smiled. 'Well, it's a way of life.'

A silence spread around them. Not awkward like it had been before, but contemplative. They had not even ordered their food, and yet already, Pippa had offered Daisy a window into her past. It only seemed fair that Daisy told her something, too.

'I know about the painting. How Dad used to do it too.'

Pippa's gaze shifted down to her glass, although when she looked back up, Daisy was surprised to find she was smiling.

'Oh, he could paint. Nowhere near as good as you, mind. But he loved it. Painting, the water and you. Those were his three loves in life. That's what everyone would say.'

There was so much missing in those words. So much pain in her mother's past. Pain Daisy wished she could wipe clean.

'I thought you might want to know. I've been thinking. Thinking about maybe doing some painting again too.'

For a moment, Daisy wondered if she had made the right choice telling her mother. Particularly given her previous words.

However, rather than replying, Pippa reached across the table and took her hands in her own. When she looked at her, her eyes were glistening with tears.

'I think that sounds like a wonderful idea, my love. A wonderful idea indeed.'

43

Daisy May's heart was in her mouth as she stood on the stern of the *September Rose*, Theo by her side.

'It's a big day today. Are you ready?' he asked.

'No, not in the slightest,'

'Trust me, you're going to love it.'

Daisy wished she could agree. All night, her stomach had been in knots, and at best she couldn't have got more than two or three hours of sleep. Every time she closed her eyes, images floated to the top of her mind. Although floating was probably the wrong word to use, given that almost all the situations she had conjured up consisted of the *September Rose* sinking irretrievably to the bottom of a very deep canal.

'I just think we should wait. Maybe the nightmares I had were a sign?'

'Stop being such a pessimist. I've checked her engine. She's going to be fine. We're only going to go a short way. We need to see if we can drive her to the marina to get her hull blacked, and so you can sort that water tank out, which you've been putting off cleaning. The only way we're going to know is if we actually give it a go.'

Daisy puffed out her cheeks and let out a long breath of air. She had, admittedly, put off cleaning the water tank, partially in the hope that Theo would relent and do it himself, although she knew what a terrible person that made her. But it was one thing going into a small hole with a torch and a chisel in the safety of the dry dock, and another doing it when you knew you were only a couple of inches away from being submerged in water. But Theo was right. Time was running out to get the boat sold before the mooring fees were due, so the sooner she could get everything done, the better.

'Okay, but I'm keeping my eyes closed.'

'You're ridiculous. But fine.'

The engine was already rumbling away beneath them. They weren't quite ready to leave yet, but apparently boat engines weren't like cars. They needed to be warmed up first. At least when they hadn't been out on the water for a while. And the *September Rose* had not been out for a very long time.

'Here goes.'

Despite saying she couldn't watch, Daisy's eyes were primed as Theo pushed the throttle of the boat into forward. A loud chugging noise spluttered behind them.

'That doesn't sound good.'

'It's completely fine. We're just going to take it easy.'

How was it possible that standing still could get her hear beating so fast, Daisy wondered as she gripped the railing. He knuckles were white, and her clench only tightened as Theo pushed the throttle forward a little further, all while swinging th tiller away from him.

'How does it feel?' she asked, every part of her tensed as sh waited for a bang, or a crash, or to just start sinking unexpectedl but instead, they were moving. Moving slowly down the cana towards Wildflower Lock.

'She feels good,' Theo replied, a hint of surprise inflecting his voice. 'You want to have a go?'

'No,' Daisy responded automatically.

'You drove the *Narrow Escape…*'

'Not by the lock. Not when there were other boats around.'

'It's fine. I'm here. I'm not going to let you hit something. You should be the one driving her. She's your boat.'

Daisy hesitated for a minute longer. Just enough time for Theo to badger her a little more.

'Honestly, with the speed we're going, you could have a head-on collision and you're not going to damage much except the buttons. Go on, you know you want to.'

The strange thing was, Daisy really did want to. Unbeknownst o her, she had at some point stopped gripping the rail, and now er hands were itching to take over the steering.

'Fine, go on then,' she said, and with her heart hammering, she laced her hand on the long, metal pole of the tiller. There was less esistance from the water than she expected. More control, and less ear, too. Perhaps it was because of Theo standing so close beside er, but it didn't take long until her heart rate was almost normal. r as normal as she expected it to get, given what she was doing.

As they glided past Yvonne's boat, a strange heat built in her eart. Her dad would have done this too. He would have held this xact tiller on this exact boat and driven it towards Wildflower ock. Did he feel this at peace, she wondered, before chuckling wardly.

Of course he did. That was why he stayed on the boat. That was hy he didn't leave when Pippa asked him to. Because this was here he belonged. And she couldn't help but feel that part of her longed here, too.

Neither of them spoke as Daisy continued to steer the boat, not that there was much steering involved. On the occasions they approached a slight bend, Theo's hand appeared close behind hers, guiding the steering, only to drop away again when they were back on a straight stretch. It reminded Daisy of the silence she could share with Bex and Claire. Or even her mum. There was no need to say anything. They were fine like this. Better than fine.

The blissful silence continued for a while longer until Theo broke it clearing his throat.

'Okay, while I know she's your boat, and you're obviously a natura at this, I figure you don't want to try to go under a bridge yet, do you?'

A curved, cast-iron footbridge came into view in front of them.

'You think I'm a natural?'

'Well, you're certainly not terrible. But I still don't think yo want to test that assumption on a bridge. Particularly not this one It can just get a bit shallow near the banks. And you get lots o boats coming from the other direction.'

Driving past stationary boats had been one thing, but Dais wasn't ready to try moving ones.

'She's all yours,' she said, and took a seat on one of the benche She had given it a good, yet painstaking, sand down, but what really needed was a lick of paint. Of course, she'd have to decid what colour she wanted the boat to be first. Part of her wanted stick to the colours her father had chosen, the greens and cream but why, when she wasn't even going to keep it? The best thing do would be to pick the more popular colours, although for som reason that idea didn't make her feel great.

A little way after the bridge, in a wide area of the river, Th turned the boat around and they began the drive back. Daisy did take the tiller again. She was sure Theo wouldn't have minded, b she was too lost in her thoughts. Too busy imagining what it wou be like to keep the boat. Even if it was just for holidays. But wh was the point of that? The only way she could really afford to keep it was if she lived on it full time, and she couldn't possibly imagine doing that. Could she?

Back on dry land, Theo offered her a very firm high five.

'I'd say that was a success, wouldn't you?'

'I'd say it was definitely more successful than I expected,' she conceded.

'So no more nightmares?'

'Oh, I'll be having nightmares about this boat for years.' She laughed.

'Well, now that you know she's water worthy, we should book into the dry dock. I'll schedule some time off work to help you.'

'You don't have to do that.'

'I know I don't. I want to. And maybe while the boat's out of the water, you can show me some of the paintings you've been working on?'

He raised his eyebrows. It was only a slight movement, but in Daisy's eyes, it shifted his level of attractiveness from undeniably cute to outright irresistible. The thought of seeing Theo in such a manner, and so openly admitting it to herself, was enough to make her jump nearly a foot backward.

'Are you all right?' Theo asked, looking notably concerned.

'Yes, yes, I'm good. I just remembered. I'd arranged to meet Claire this evening. But… yes, thank you. Thank you again for today.' She stretched out her hand to shake his, as if this was some formal meeting. 'Right. I need to go.'

She turned as quickly as possible, hoping to hide the fact that her face was fluorescent pink, and only when she had reached the other end of the *Narrow Escape* did she turn back.

'I'll text you,' she yelled before turning back and quickening her pace further still.

She reached the car and dropped her head onto the steering wheel.

'Oh, Daisy,' she said to herself. 'What have you got yourself into?'

44

Daisy May did not have enough hours in the day. Three months ago, life consisted of work, her two best friends and her mother, while her downtime was spent watching horror films, interspersed with occasional shopping trips and nights out as Bex's wing-woman. Now, weekly shopping trips involved looking at different types of waterproof paint and insulation, and downtime was well and truly a thing of the past. How she had ever thought she was busy before the *September Rose* was a mystery.

Of course, there was the added factor she was trying to squeeze painting into her time too. As much as she wished she could push the idea back to the recesses of her mind, she couldn't. Painting was part of her. Maybe she wouldn't set the world alight with something modern or spark an entire new movement with her unique style, but that didn't mean she shouldn't keep going, and maybe earn a bit of money on the side to help deal with the rising rent. Little by little, she had been growing more confident. In fact, she was surprised how quickly she had got back into the swing of things.

'I forgot how incredible you are,' Bex said as she sifted through the section of paintings Daisy had left out on her dining room table. 'These should be in a shop. No, scrap that. These should be in an art gallery. A freakin' big gallery.'

'Thanks,' Daisy said, taking the painting from her hand and replacing it with a beer. 'That's what Mum said when I showed her last week. But you're both biased.'

'Your mum came over? That's good. How are things between you two?'

It was a question that didn't have a simple answer. They were making progress, but she knew enough about life to know progress was never linear. Some days, it would feel like nothing had changed. She and Pippa would be chatting away on the phone about work or Claire or one of the neighbours, and then something would be said – normally about the boat – and her mother's attitude would change entirely. Not since their first dinner together had she spoken so freely about her times on the canals, no matter how much Daisy wished she would. And the more Daisy asked, the more Pippa clammed up.

'We'll get there, slowly,' Daisy said, eventually. 'But right now, I don't have time to think about that. Once we've got the *September Rose* done, I'll think about it a bit more.'

'But you're nearly there, right? You said it's going well?'

'It is. I mean, this week is the big week.'

Bex had barely taken a sip of her drink and was already lookin back through the paintings.

'I can't believe you're using a week of your annual leave to d up a boat.'

'Neither can I. But it'll be worth it. I hope. I mean, it could en up bankrupting me, but Theo doesn't think it will. He's sure th hull is in okay shape. He didn't find any leaks after we took her ou at least. But we won't know for certain until we get her out of the water.'

'Ahh, Theo. With the mystery girlfriend.'

Gripping her drink, Daisy prepared herself for what she knew was coming next.

'She's not a mystery. Her name is Heather and she travels a lot for work. That's all. He spent last weekend at hers. That's why I lidn't go and work on the boat.' Daisy realised the mistake in her wording. She tried to backtrack. 'I needed his help, that's why. Not because I wanted to see him. I don't only go to the boat when he's here. That's not what I meant.'

'No, of course not.' Bex smirked. Somehow her silence on the natter was even worse than her goading. 'So, apart from the fact hat you two are seriously crushing on each other, why is Theo lriving your boat to the marina? You've been driving her on the veekends, right? You said you went out with her last week?'

'I drove her for less than a mile. This is going to be a three-hour ip. I need to drive the car down to bring us back in the afternoon. we both go down in the boat, we'll have no way to get back.'

'That sucks.'

'I know.'

'I mean, not only are you not going on your own boat, but u're also going to miss out on three hours alone time with Theo. at must be hard.'

Somehow, Daisy didn't bite. She was gutted about not going on e *September Rose*'s first big trip, but she and Theo had talked ough the logistics, and this was the only way it worked. And no atter how much Bex tried to wind her up, the fact was, Daisy did joy Theo's company, more than she did most people, but he was r friend, and that was the way it was supposed to be. So what if d friend was objectively attractive?

Knowing that the conversation had, as it always did, focused almost solely on her, Daisy asked the one question she could guarantee would distract Bex.

'So, Newton?'

45

They had the perfect day for it. The sky was bright blue, with only a handful of the fluffiest, whitest clouds, while the air was so still that the scene around the canal looked as though it had been painted there. That didn't stop Daisy from being a bag of nerves, though. The nightmares about a sinking boat had returned, only this time, they were combined with images of them being washed out to sea.

Although it would have been quicker for Daisy to drive straight to the marina, she had woken up before six so she could head to Wildflower Lock first and bid Theo good luck.

'You'll make sure you text me with how you're doing?' she asked as she stood on the bank, taking in what she worried could be her last look at the *September Rose*. 'Perhaps when you pass through a lock? Or if you hit any delays?'

She knew she sounded like her mother, the way Pippa would worry whenever Daisy went away, but that was what she felt like.

'I will stay in touch, and I promise you, she'll make the journey fine. It's not that far.'

'It's twelve miles.'

Twelve miles didn't sound like a lot in the car or, for some, even for a run. But for the *September Rose*, who managed a stately four miles an hour, it was going to be a proper trek. But that was the closest marina with a dry dock, and getting the boat out of the water was a vital part of the renovation process.

'Trust me, she will be absolutely fine. And there's nothing like seeing her come out of the water for the first time. Then things really get exciting.'

'And by exciting, you mean I get to climb into a tiny metal box and scrub the grime off the inside of the water tank?'

Theo smirked. There was no way around it now. Daisy had taken the time off work to get these jobs done. By the end of the week, the water tank and blacked hull would be done. Not to mention a vast amount of the outside painting, too.

Theo had been true to his word in sourcing as much as possible from other boats to get the interior renovated, and Daisy was loving the eclectic look that was coming together because of it. She had been working as hard as she could, sanding down and fixing cupboards, painting floorboards. She had even fitted a new electric oven that Theo had found someone giving away online. Another month tops and the *September Rose* would be ready to go on the market. Daisy pushed the thought to the back of her mind.

'I still feel terrible that you've taken a day off work to do this for me,' Daisy said. 'You'll have to let me know how I can repay you.'

'Really, there's nothing to feel bad about. And I'm not taking time off work. The marina is still under my jurisdiction as a linesman. I need to visit it now and then. I just changed the schedule around a bit, that's all.'

'You did?'

'Did I not mention I love my job?' He smiled.

Daisy's heart throbbed with a hint of sadness. Theo talked about being a linesman like Pippa talked about cooking: as if the had found their absolute calling in life and couldn't imagine doing anything different. It was how she expected to feel when she got a job illustrating picture books. But that was just a pipe dream.

'I should let you get on,' she said, and bent down to untie the rope, when a voice called from further up the bank.

'Don't go!'

It was a yell unlike any Daisy had heard at Wildflower Lock before, but she knew the voice immediately.

Confused, she jumped onto the bank.

'Claire?' She looked over, only to see another figure marching by her friend's side. 'Bex? What are you two doing here?'

The pair were almost breathless when they reached her.

'Thank God, I thought we might be too late.'

'What are you doing?' Daisy repeated, desperately wanting to hug her friends, only to be blocked by the coffee cups in their hands.

'For starters, I find it ridiculous that there's not a café on this lock and thought there was no way that you were going to get through this stress without a decent hit of caffeine.'

She handed Daisy one of the cups. With all the adrenaline coursing through her, anything else to push her heart rate up was probably a bad idea. Still, she took a long sip.

'Good morning, ladies.' Theo stepped off the boat and injected himself into the conversation. 'Just so you're aware, I have a pretty good coffee machine on my boat, and Daisy knows she can help herself if she wants.'

'Does she now?' Bex said, coming forward and kissing him on he cheeks as if they were old friends, although they'd only met nce. 'Theo, nice to see you again. Dressed.'

'Bex, isn't it?' Theo replied. 'And you must be Claire,' he said, urning to face her.

'I'm glad that Daisy's been talking about us,' Claire said.

'Possibly as much as she talks about you.' Bex grinned.

Daisy shot her best scowl.

'You still haven't actually told us what you're doing here?' Daisy said. 'This isn't where we take her out of the water. Theo's got to take her down to the marina for that.'

'I know. I do listen,' Bex said indignantly. 'Which is why I would like your car keys.'

'My car keys?' Despite having asked several times what they were doing, Daisy still had no idea why her friends were there, nor why they could possibly want her car keys.

'I'm still insured on it, right? From our road trip up to Edinburgh?'

'Umm, yes, I think so.'

'Fabulous. Then Claire and I will drive to the marina separately. I've already arranged with the guy in the office to drop your keys with him when I get there. Then you and Theo can drive back together whenever you want.'

Daisy was having a hard time accepting that they were even there, let alone able to piece together what Bex was saying.

'But you have work?'

'No, I called in and took the morning off. Although it's such a nice day, I might take the afternoon too. They owe me anyway fo all those weekends we had to pull for the audit. Now, are you goin to get going, or do I need to push you onto that boat of yours?'

A lump formed in the base of Daisy's throat, almost as if he heart was too full to be contained within her chest. With tears i her eyes, she wrapped her arms around her two best friends.

'Hey, mind the coffee!'

46

)aisy wanted to paint everything she saw. Every minute, another haracter would come to her mind. The water vole who was scared f getting wet. The heron who wouldn't eat fish. Inspiration flowed s freely as the water beneath her. Of all the gifts her best friends ad given her over the years, this one – being able to take the *ptember Rose* all the way down to the marina – had to be one of ie best.

'Having fun?' Theo asked.

He was at the helm with the tiller in his hand, though Daisy d done her fair share of driving, too. This time, whenever they ached the locks, she didn't have to ask what to do, jumping aight onto land to close the gates behind them as soon as they re through.

'I love it,' she answered truthfully. 'I wish I didn't have to go ck to reality.'

'This is reality if you want it to be. You already own a boat. king that plunge is normally the hardest part for people.'

'I think a massive commute would be the problem for me.'

'Then find another job. Or find a mooring nearer your current job. If this is how you want to live then you can make it happen.'

The way Theo spoke made it sound so simple. Move jobs. Move moorings. But she liked her job, more than the others she'd had, at least, and could she really imagine having the *September Rose* anywhere other than Wildflower Lock? But if that was the case maybe it wasn't the boating life she loved so much as the person she was doing it with?

'It can't be long until we're there,' Daisy said, ignoring he previous thoughts. 'Are we going straight into the dry dock?'

Theo shook his head. 'It's tidal there.'

'Tidal?' Daisy knew what the word meant. She just wasn sure how it was linked to the canals they were on, given th locks.

'We go in when it's high tide,' Theo explained. 'Then when it low tide, the water goes out and we close the lock so it can't go bac in again. It's a nice easy process, actually.'

When they reached the marina, Daisy discovered that, whi the process was easy, it wasn't fast. As Theo expertly drove tl *September Rose* into the dock, Daisy realised she had no idea ho long it was between high tide and low tide.

'About six and a half hours,' Theo told her.

'What?' Daisy's jaw dropped open. 'We have to wait six hou until we can start work?'

He laughed. 'No, we have to wait until it's low tide. We can s do things inside the boat. Although, to be fair, I thought we mig want to take a bit of a break first. There's a lovely pub about a for five-minute walk away. We could go there first?'

A forty-five-minute walk to a pub wasn't something Da would have ever considered doing before, not when her car was readily available, but at that moment, she couldn't think anything she'd rather do.

After picking up her keys from the marina office, the pair walked side by side along the edge of the estuary.

'I love these days where the water looks like a mirror,' Theo said. 'It reminds me of where I grew up.'

'Where did you grow up?' Daisy asked. For all the time they spent together, she knew very little of Theo beyond his life on the canal.

'Germany, near the border with Austria, to be exact.'

'Wow, I had no idea. You don't have any accent.'

'No, I know. My parents worked out there. We moved back just before I was eight, so I don't remember much, but I remember the lakes we'd visit on the weekends. Some days the water was so still, it was a perfect mirror.'

Daisy had been abroad a fair few times in her life. Mostly with the girls or Pippa. She and Paul had been away a couple of times, too. But all the holidays were the same sort – package trips booked last minute, either to a busy city or a beach. No variation. She wouldn't have even considered going to a mountain lake, but now she thought about it, the idea was definitely appealing.

'So, if you lived in Germany, does that mean you speak German?'

'Maybe.' His lips tightened playfully, causing Daisy to bounce on her feet in delight.

'I'm so jealous! I wish I could speak another language. You need to say something. What can you say? Can you say, "My name is Theo, and I used to live in Germany"?'

'I'm not speaking German for you.'

'Please.'

'Nope, now hurry up. At the rate you're walking, the tide will have gone out and come back in again by the time we've had lunch.'

'I'm not a slow walker. I'm walking at the same pace as you.'

'Because I'm walking slowly for you. Now, if I was at my actual pace...'

The rest of the walk was spent laughing and joking. Mostly, Daisy tried to persuade Theo to say something, anything, in German, which he steadfastly refused to do. It was strange not to be talking about the boat for once, as so often, it was their sole topic of conversation. Occasionally, Daisy would stop to take a photo of a passing sailboat, or a flock of birds passing the sun and a whole storyline would swirl around in her mind as she imagined the colours and materials she would use to depict them.

When they reached the pub, they ordered at the bar before taking a seat outside.

'I was thinking about your paintings again,' Theo said, as they sipped on the ciders. 'Actually, I was talking to Heather about them.'

'You were?' This discovery surprised her far more than Daisy expected it to. She didn't know why she assumed Theo wouldn't talk to his girlfriend about her, given all the time they spent together. But then again, maybe that was the exact reason she assumed he wouldn't. Ignoring the slight stabbing behind her ribs, she forced herself to smile. 'What were you saying?'

'Well, I said that they're brilliant, obviously, and that I thought you needed to get them in a gallery. Maybe one somewhere like Camden, you know, with all the boats and the lock and everything.'

It made sense, although for once it wasn't Theo's opinion Daisy was interested in.

'And what did Heather say?' she asked, trying to sound as casual as possible.

'She suggested you try somewhere touristy outside of London. She actually suggested somewhere like Leigh-on-Sea. Do you know it?'

Daisy shook her head. The name was familiar, but not familiar enough to actually know where the place was.

'It's not far from here, really. On an estuary, so plenty of boats, although a lot aren't our type. She used to go there as a kid and said there were quite a few galleries. I mean, it might be nothing, but it might be worth checking out.'

'Thank you, I'll look into it.'

For the first time all day an awareness shifted between the pair of them, and Daisy wasn't sure whether it was from the mention of her art or the mention of Heather. Either way, she didn't like it. Thankfully, just like with Bex, she knew exactly how to get Theo talking again.

'Okay,' she said, clearing her throat and readying herself for the insightful lecture that was about to come her way. 'Let's go through my checklist of what I need to do when we get back to the boat.'

And just like that, Theo was talking again.

47

Given that this was the only afternoon Theo would be at the marina to help, Daisy was determined to make the most of him. Thankfully, Theo had the same idea.

'I'll try to get as much of this old paint off the top of the roof as possible,' he told her, holding a device that looked like it should be used to dig holes in tarmac rather than on the roof of her boat. 'Then tomorrow, once you've finished the tank, you'll need to sand it all down. You need to get that done by the end of the day because Wednesday, you have to get the base coat on the roof done so that you can do the primer on Thursday. We can put the final topcoat paint on back at the canal.'

Just listening to the list of jobs she had to get done was exhausting, but there was no way she wanted to go over schedule. The dry dock charged per day and although their fees weren't extortionate, getting the bottom of the hull blacked with waterproof paint had not only cleared out her savings, but had also taken a loan from Pippa too. A fact Daisy felt incredibly guilty about. She just kept reminding herself of how it would all be worth it in the end.

'So, have you got your head torch ready?' Theo handed her a chisel. 'It's going to be a long afternoon.'

A long afternoon was putting it mildly. While Theo worked on the roof with a machine louder than the average jet engine, Daisy was confined to the inside of the water tank, chiselling away by the light of her head torch, trying to stop her legs from cramping or her back from feeling like she had aged five decades in the space of an afternoon. In the end, she found the only way to work effectively was to set herself a timer. She worked solidly for fifteen minutes, chiselling off as much of the rusty-coloured dried sludge as she could, before allowing herself fifteen minutes of air out of the water tank, where she would check how Theo was getting on with the roof, and how the workmen were doing with the blacking.

'It's a lovely boat you two have got here,' a workman said during one of her breaks. 'Room for kids too, if that's what you've got planned.'

'Oh, it's not... Theo and I... It's my boat,' Daisy spluttered, taken by surprise by the comment. 'We're not together.'

'Ahh, the old "just good friends" line, eh? My missus and I had that going for a while there, too.'

'We really are just friends,' Theo joined.

'And not even particularly good friends,' she added, with a quick playful glower at him.

'More like passing acquaintances.'

'Who I use for manual labour.'

'That right, eh?' The workman looked like he wished he'd never asked. 'Well, I better get on with this. Need to get that first coat done today.'

Just like the canal, the marina had rules about noise and Daisy had no intention of breaking them. As such, she knew they had to finish the day's tasks by 8 p.m. and was making the most of her final thirty minutes of work time when Theo appeared on the deck above her.

'Wow, that looks fantastic.'

Still crouching down, she attempted to turn around only to realise it was going to be impossible in such a small space, and instead, stood upright so that her head was sticking out the top. From there, she shuffled the one hundred and eighty degree required to look straight at Theo.

'I think I've got most of it,' she said, trying to stretch up. Her shoulders and neck clicked several times, though it did very little to alleviate the cramping in her legs, or the throbbing in her knees. One of the first things she was going to do when she got home was ring Claire to see if Amelia had a set of kneepads she could borrow for the rest of the week, assuming the roof was going to be as tough as this was.

'You've definitely got it. I'd ask one of the guys here to have look at it tomorrow before you start painting it, but I'm sure they say it's good to go.'

Daisy shrugged her shoulders a couple of times, hoping would loosen up some of the muscles, yet all it actually did was s off a chain reaction of yawning. One yawn, then another, each o longer than the last. Instinctively, she went to cover her mouth wi her hands, only to find them rust red and covered in dust.

'Come on, it's time we got you home. You've still got to driv Theo said, reaching his hand down into the tank to help her out.

Every other time Daisy had climbed out of the water tank th day, she had done so on her own, without any help. It had take bit of practice, involving jumping upwards and flopping hers down flat on her belly in a manner similar to that of a wal launching itself onto the ice – though it worked well enough her. But at that moment, with Theo there offering his hand, neither wanted to, nor felt the need, to perform the walrus launch manoeuvre. So, she took his hand and let him heave her upwards.

As he pulled her up and out of the small opening, she felt their grip slip for a moment. The dust that covered both their palms lessened the friction, though she squeezed his hand tight, and allowed herself to be lifted further still. Everything above her knees was out of the tank when their hands slipped again. Just one inch higher was all she needed to be able to lift her leg out of the hole and onto the safety of the wooden deck and she squeezed tighter still, but it wasn't enough. She could feel herself falling. The drop would be less than a metre, but it wouldn't be an easy landing. Worst case scenario, she could end up breaking something, but even a twisted ankle would screw up her week. She couldn't afford for that to happen. She just couldn't.

With all the strength she could muster, Daisy pushed her feet against the far side of the tank and lurched forwards. Had it been one of her walrus lurches, it would have been perfect. The height she got was by far the most she had managed all day, but it wasn't like other times. This time it wasn't the flat, wooden slats of the deck in front of her. There was Theo.

The instant she moved forward, she could see what was going to happen. There was no way around it. She leapt upwards, pushing him backwards against the boat, and pinning him there with her body pressed up against his. Their eyes locked on one another.

Her lips were only inches from his.

Daisy's heart rocketed and though she couldn't be certain, she was sure she could feel his heart racing, too, pounding beneath his shirt. She was so close to him now. She could move her lips a tiny fraction. That was all in would take. She closed her eyes, imagining what it would be like to feel his lips against hers, but the instant she closed them, her eyelids sprang open again, and she jumped backwards, only narrowly missing the water tank.

'Sorry about that,' she said, horrified by her own thoughts. He had a girlfriend. What the hell had she been thinking? By contrast, Theo was standing stock still, his gaze penetratingly focused as it fixed on her. Had she not known better, she could have sworn there was a slight hint of disappointment in his eyes.

Ignoring the pulsing in her chest, Daisy brushed her clothes down and righted herself the best she could.

'We should get going,' she said. 'I've got an early start in the morning.'

48

'Well, I have to say, your dad would be very proud. Very proud indeed,' Yvonne said on Friday evening as she and Daisy watched Theo manoeuvre the *September Rose* back into her mooring at Wildflower Lock. 'You two have done a fabulous job.'

'I can't take any of the credit,' Theo said, as he cut the engine. I'm just the driver.'

'That's not true,' Daisy replied. 'You scraped all the paint off oo, remember? That was a massive job. I wouldn't have got everyhing done without you.'

There was only a hint of awkwardness in her voice. The almostiss moment – which had probably only been an almost kiss in aisy's mind – had not been mentioned and thankfully there had een more than enough to do in the days that followed to keep her istracted. Even on Friday, when they were getting the boat back to the water, there had been too much to think about to worry bout a moment that had never actually happened. So much so at she had almost convinced herself it was all in her imagination.

'Just in time for summer too,' Yvonne continued. 'Have you cided where you're going to take her? You know your grandfather had a thing for the west country. There are some lovely routes around there. Bath, Slimbridge. Beautiful places.'

Daisy shifted on the spot, trying to work out how to answer. She had assumed the old lady had known she planned on selling the boat, but obviously that wasn't the case, and it was surprisingly hard to tell her.

Then again, if it hadn't been for a massive credit card bill from getting the hull done, she would probably be happy to stay in denial.

She smiled politely.

'I've still got a way to go yet,' she said. 'I'm going to do the first top coat of paint tomorrow. I'll finish it off next weekend. Then I want to get painting the rest of the outside.'

'Next week?' Theo said. 'What about Sunday? You're not thinking of taking a day off, are you? Anyone would think you've had a tough week.' He grinned, although his question caused a flurry of nerves to sweep through her.

'Actually, I've got something else planned for Sunday,' she said.

* * *

Daisy May was genuinely nervous. So nervous. She hadn't felt thi way since those first days in art college all those years ago. Eve going for job interviews hadn't been this nerve-wracking, probab because she'd never cared about a job this much. And she care about this. She seriously cared.

Her stomach was rife with butterflies as she stepped out of h car and retrieved her portfolio from the back seat. After mu deliberation, she had taken Theo's – or rather Heather's – advi and headed to Leigh-on-Sea. Just like Theo had said, there was selection of art galleries, and the fact it was a place she never we to meant she wouldn't have to endure the embarrassment of seeing her work constantly on display.

She had left home early, hoping to arrive when the galleries first opened up, but the sunny weather had brought out visitors in droves, walking their dogs or sitting on benches by the waterfront enjoying fry ups. Rather than a stream of empty shops, she was faced with a bustling high street.

'You can do this,' she said to herself. 'Five seconds of bravery. That's all you need.'

With several galleries to choose from, she paused, trying to gure out the best place to start. As fate would have it, one of the alleries was on the water, on a barge. Perhaps that was a sign, she ought, before dismissing the idea. The fact it was on a barge eant they might be more critical of the boat she had painted.

In the end, she let logic decide for her; only one gallery did not ave customers browsing in it, and so that was the one she picked.

A bell jingled above her as she pushed the door open and epped inside. A flash of fear surged through her. In her past, she d revelled in places like this. The calm stillness of the white alls that let her shut out the rest of the world and allowed her to me in on the intricacies of the artwork. But rather than calm, the ite walls felt cold. Almost unwelcoming. She shook the feeling and pushed her shoulders back as she stepped further inside.

'Can I help you?' A man stepped out from behind an equally ite desk, on top of which sat a bright white computer. He was ssed in a crisp, white shirt, accented with striped braces, dark users and brogues, though his top button was left open, giving impression of forced casualness. 'Is there something in partic-r you're looking for?'

Daisy stepped forwards, wondering if the drumming in her st was loud enough for him to hear.

'Actually, I'm not here to buy. I'm an artist.' The word cracked in her throat as if she was a fraud, but what option was there? She could hardly say she was a one-time, drop-out artist who reall didn't think she was good enough to do this but was giving it a g anyway. She straightened her back and forced confidence into he smile. 'I was hoping you might consider displaying some of m work.'

Daisy hadn't noticed whether the man's smile had been tight lipped before she had told him why she was there, but it certainl was afterwards.

'Have you had your work exhibited anywhere else?' he asked.

'Oh yes, several times.' She hoped he wouldn't ask where. Th school art show and her mother's living room didn't give a gre impression.

'And yet you've come here, rather than returning to one those galleries?'

Daisy's heart kicked up another notch now. But this was ju like any other job interview. And she was good at job intervie Even if she wasn't she great at holding on to the jobs after she'd g them.

'I've recently taken a change in direction,' she said, offering h most genuine smile. 'The work I'm doing now is more commerci Something I thought would be suited to your gallery and the cli tele you have here.'

She sounded good. She knew she did, and the slight quirk his eyebrow confirmed it for her.

'I don't normally take unsolicited visits, but it is quiet t morning, so why don't you bring your work over here so I can t a look?'

Lifting his hand, he gestured to a table in the corner of room. Daisy hadn't noticed it before, no doubt because its w top and table legs ensured that it was completely camouflaged.

Trying to stem her trembling hands, she placed the large, black folder down and opened it up.

She started with a painting she had finished only two days beforehand, although she had been working on it for the best part of two weeks. Wildflower Lock, in all its beauty. The purple blooms, bright against the pale-blue sky, and deeper toned water. She had made an effort to pick out intricate details, like the patterns on the paintwork, and the dog shaking the water from its fur as he climbed out on the towpath. The sense of pride that she had begun to feel more and more swelled within her as she looked at the image, before turning her gaze to the curator.

'Hmm.' He looked at her, indicating that she needed to get more of her work out. Hastily, she delved into the folder, this time pulling out several paintings. Another home on the river, but this time there were no people or dogs. She had painted a sunset. Vivid pinks and oranges casting a silhouette of trees in the foreground. She also withdrew some of the other work she had been doing. Not of the lock, but her illustrations. One painting was a hedgehog, curled up in a little bowl, his pink nose and bright white eyes just visible amongst the mass of spikes. Another was of a dormouse, climbing an ear of corn. It was a type of image found frequently in shops like this, most likely to be hung on the walls of children's nurseries. Clean. Simple. Good.

The curator's movements were minuscule. A half step to the right. The tilt of his chin. And his words were even less forthcoming. Other than that initial humming noise, when he'd indicated he wished for Daisy to show him more, he didn't utter a single word until he stepped back and folded his hands across his body.

'I can see you've worked hard on these,' he said.

The fear that had been gripping Daisy all morning loosened by just a fraction.

'Yes, yes, I have. It's been a while since I exhibited anywhere.'

He nodded. 'Can I be perfectly honest with you?'

'Yes, absolutely.'

'You work isn't exactly terrible. In some ways, I'd say it's actually above average.'

Above average? The tightness was re-forming in her chest.

'But the truth is, I find it bland.'

'Bland?'

'It's derivative. Where is the soul? Where is the life? You can paint a dormouse, whoopty doo. Oh, look, a pretty canal. It's hardly pushing the artistic boundaries of life, is it?'

'I wasn't looking to push artistic boundaries,' Daisy said, her throat constricting as she spoke.

'That much is obvious. Tell me, before you stepped in here, expecting me to tarnish my walls with this mundane scribbling, did you actually look at what I sell? Did you look at the quality of what I'm offering?'

Daisy stopped. She glanced around the room. Of course she had looked, admittedly only fleetingly, as she entered, but the works in the window seemed on par with what she was doing. Perhaps a little more abstract, but certainly not as far a cry as h was making it seem.

'The truth is, I get ten of you a week who think just becaus their paint their granny's birthday cards, they've got what it takes i this world. Young upstarts thinking that it's going to be a way t earn a quick buck. That if I hang your painting on my wall, you' become the next Banksy or Jenny Saville. But it's not that simpl You have to stand out. You have to have something special. Yo have to *be* something special. And as much as it saddens me to sa to you— What did you say your name was?'

'Daisy,' she replied quietly, although she wished she hadn't.

'Well, you, Daisy,' the curator said with a sad sigh, 'do n appear to have that something special.'

49

Daisy barely even remembered packing up the paintings, zipping up the large folder and returning to the car, but she must've done so, because less than five minutes later she was sitting there, in the driver's seat, weeping.

Who the hell did he think he was? She wanted to go back and cream at him. Who the hell thought they had the right to speak to omeone like that? To make a judgement on her as a person and an rtist by looking at half a dozen paintings. He knew nothing about er. Nothing. Yet deep down in her heart, she felt like he had got it oot on. After all, she was average. Average at art, average at her b. Average at life.

Sitting there in the car, she allowed herself to wallow, when at me point all that self-loathing turned outwards. She knew this as the wrong thing to do. She had told Theo she wasn't ready. hat her art wasn't ready. It wasn't good enough. But he had ıshed. He was the one who had made her go there. He was the e that was to blame for her feeling like this. And he could bloody ell know it.

She drove with nothing but anger fuelling her. All of this was down to him. He was the one who had persuaded her to start painting again. He was the one who pushed. She hated him for it, but he was also the one she wanted to go to now, and only partly because she wanted to scream at him. Somehow, she knew that he would know the right thing to say, too. She didn't doubt that for a moment.

Her bad mood was only compounded when she reached the car park and was unable to find a space. Didn't these people have anywhere else to go? Surely there were better things they could be doing with their Sunday mornings than traipsing up and down the side of a canal. She headed out of the car park and drove half a mile up the road where she found a suitable place, before marching towards Wildflower Lock. There was no stopping to pe the dogs or smile at the paddleboarders she saw week in week out Not once did she slow her pace until the *Narrow Escape* came int view.

The first thing that caught her attention was the music. Sh and Theo would often listen to the radio while they were workin on the *September Rose*, but that was always her choice. She'd neve heard him listen to music on his own before. And if she had, sh would never have guessed that eighties pop would have been hi taste. Still, she had too much to yell at him about to worry abou his taste in music, so she continued on, jumping on the stern of th *Narrow Escape*, ready to let herself in.

It was when she grabbed the door handle that she heard th laughter coming from inside. High-pitched, unbridled fema laughter. Her heart skipped a beat. The curtains were drawn on th inside of the door, so she hopped back onto the bank and peer through the window. Theo was sitting there on his sofa a lounging across him with her legs over his lap, was a girl wi auburn hair, the owner of the free-spirited laugh. Daisy stare momentarily transfixed. She had formed an image of Heather

her mind. For some reason, frumpy had been one of the defining features. She had imagined her to be short and stout. Perhaps with wonky front teeth, or slightly squinty eyes. Of course, there was no reason why she should have imagined her in such a manner. Theo was undoubtedly an attractive man. But Heather. Heather was beautiful. Beyond beautiful. She was perfect.

All Daisy's failures felt compounded by this one moment.

She could ring her mum, she thought, but then what? Recount ow much of a failure she was? No, she couldn't do that. Claire was ith her family and she already knew that Bex was spending the ay with Newton, a relationship that actually seemed to be gaining ome legs.

For a split second, Daisy even considered calling Amanda, her anager. She just needed a moment to get away from it all. A oment to block out all this hurt and escape the realities of her e.

That's when it hit her. She knew exactly what she had to do.

50

Daisy had watched enough vlogs and YouTube tutorials to kno that five minutes of engine warming would be all the *Septemb Rose* needed. Five minutes, which would be just enough time f her to get ready to cast off. With the engine on, she got abo undoing the mid knot, where the rope was tied to the centre of t boat, then headed to the bow to undo the knot there. Lastly, s returned to the stern and unhooked most of the rope, leaving single half loop like Theo had shown her.

By that time, the engine was ready to go.

Gradually, as Daisy pulled on the rope, her pulse steady, bow of the boat began to swing outwards, a small amount at fi then further and further. A minute later, she was pointing at centre of the canal. Her flurry of excitement kicked a notch hig as she flipped the throttle from neutral into forward.

And she was off. The rush of adrenaline was more what would have expected of a rollercoaster than going at less tha mile an hour, but it was exactly what she needed. Pushing the ti hard left, she waited until she was out in the canal before she ea off and straightened up.

She breathed in excitedly as she trundled down between the boats. Several kayakers were coming towards her and a flurry of anxiety struck, but they stayed close to the bank, well out of her way and she continued on, keeping to the right, heading away from Wildflower Lock and towards the quiet of the countryside.

It was difficult to believe how natural she was finding it all, pushing to the left when she needed to go right a little and vice versa. All the practice with Theo had definitely paid off. Then again, perhaps it was in her blood. Perhaps, she thought, she could have managed the trip to the marina by herself after all.

When she passed the last of the moored boats, the bank was overtaken by tall rushes and wildlife. Out here, life felt even slower. Birds were heading to roost, and the few dog walkers that strolled along the towpaths were heading back towards the car park and home. For a few minutes she pushed on, feeling her heart rate lower, although it didn't take long before the lethargic pace with which she was moving felt ridiculous. After all, she had done the hardest part. There would be nothing wrong with going a little faster now that everything was clear, right?

Feeling a fresh rush of adrenaline, she pushed the throttle orward. The engine responded with the surge of water speeding ehind her.

'I wish this could be my life,' she said aloud, admitting the ruth she had been trying hard to ignore over the previous couple f months. Of course her father had wanted to live on the river, not tuck in some boxy flat, where the wind never reached. Who would hoose a city, surrounded by smog and noise, over this? This was hat her life was meant to be.

As she continued, Daisy allowed herself to dream of the past. o imagine her and her father, standing in this exact spot, all those ecades ago. He would probably have known all the different ecies of birds. And the names of the clouds that swept across the sky. There would have been so much she could have learnt from him, not just about boats, but about life and about herself. She was still thinking of him, imagining herself sitting upon his shoulder, when she spied the bridge ahead.

'It's fine,' she said. 'Just take it nice and slowly. You've got this.'

She reached for the throttle, ready to pull the speed back, when she spotted a boat coming from the other side of the bridge.

She had thought the *September Rose* was wide. At least, she'd been led to believe that, given she was a wide beam. But the vessel coming toward her was a monster. More a barge than a canal boat. It was at least another three feet wider and blocked almost the entire canal. How the hell was she supposed to get past it? In her state of panic, the workings of the rudder were entirely forgotten, and she pulled on the tiller in the wrong direction, pointing the *September Rose* straight into the path of the barge.

'No!' she screamed and pulled the tiller back again, but she'd gone too far. The rudder was horizontal to the boat, doing nothing to steer it. She hadn't even slowed down, Daisy realised. Any second now, she was going to crash.

In a blind panic, she pulled the throttle all the way back into reverse. The engine stuttered and stumble, slowing by just a fraction as she yanked back on the tiller, bracing herself for the crash she knew was about to come.

51

Daisy pushed herself back up onto her feet. The jolt of the crash had sent her lurching forward and her ribs throbbed from where she had caught herself on the boat. A searing pain spread out from one side. Although her main concern was for the *September Rose*, he bow of which was lost in the rushes.

'Are you all right, lass? What happened?'

The crew of the giant boat were all outside, shock and worry olouring their faces.

'I... I...' She couldn't speak. What was she going to say? That ie was an idiot taking a boat out on her own for the first time and ost control? Why the hell had she thought she could drive this ing? Why had she thought she could sell her work in a proper llery? Why had she thought she was okay with her and Theo just ing friends? She wasn't okay with any of it.

'It's all right, love.' The man from the barge was still talking to r. 'You're all right. Got a soft landing there on the bank. Are you ay to get yourself out?'

'No,' she said quietly. 'No, I'm not.'

'Well, give us a minute. We need to get you shifted fast. No other boats are getting past with you like that.'

Daisy's stomach plummeted as she saw just how much room she was taking up. She was practically perpendicular to the bank. With it being a sunny June day, there would be a tailback of half a dozen boats within minutes, all of whom would bear witness to her extreme and utter stupidity. Though, deep down, there was only one boat she didn't want to see. And it was exactly the one heading towards her.

'Daisy? Daisy, what happened?'

The *Narrow Escape* was still a foot away from the *September Rose* when Theo leapt across between the two. Without catching a breath, he walked over the top of her boat and dropped down next to her.

'What the hell were you doing?'

'I thought I could manage on my own.' She sounded like a child. A pathetic, wounded child.

Of all the things she didn't want Theo to do next, he did the on she feared the most: he wrapped his arms around her, pulled he head into his chest and held her. She could feel the tears leakin from her face into his shirt as she struggled to hold them in. Sh could feel his warmth flooding through her. And she didn't want t let go.

'Honey, I'll take the *Escape* back up the canal.' The voice cause Theo and Daisy to jerk apart. Now nearly level with ther Heather's head could be seen over the top of the boat. 'I'll t anyone back there just to give it ten minutes, so you have time clear this.'

'Thank you, baby. That would be amazing.'

Daisy watched on silently as Heather manoeuvred the *Narr Escape* perfectly out between the *September Rose* and the riverba before straightening up and disappearing.

'She knows how to drive one of these things,' she said, more to ıerself than Theo.

'She's been around them a lot,' he replied. 'You tend to pick hings up. Assuming you learn slowly, and don't stupidly assume ou can do everything by yourself. Honestly, if you wanted to go ut why didn't you ask me? Heather and I would have come with ou.'

Great, Daisy thought. *A boat trip with the beautiful Heather.* xactly what she didn't want.

'I've just had a bad day, that's all. I wanted to get away from it r a while.'

'You know I would've taken you.'

'I know, but to be honest, I'm a little tired of your crappy lvice.'

She hadn't meant to snap, and it wasn't fair that she had. But it dn't take long for Theo to figure out where the animosity had me from.

'The paintings?' he asked. 'What happened?'

'Oh, nothing,' she said, her voice laden with sarcasm. 'Unless u mean was I told my work was derivative and naïve and that I s clearly overreaching. And absolutely not special.'

'What?' Theo looked at her with disbelief. 'Who said that to ı?'

'A curator at a gallery. He said I was completely oblivious to the el of talent out there in the world and that I should stick to nting birthday cards for my granny. Not that I have one.'

'Daisy, I'm so sorry.' He lifted his hand towards her shoulder, she flinched away.

'Don't. Don't.' She took a long breath in. 'Can you just help me the boat moved? That's all I care about right now. The sooner I get the boat out of here, the sooner I can finish her off and be of her for good.'

The crash didn't appear to have damaged any of the recen work. She had simply run aground on the muddy bottom near th bank. Of course, to get that out meant to someone had to ge muddy. Very muddy.

'Leave the tiller exactly where it is,' Theo said, as he lowere himself off the boat. Daisy hadn't realised quite how shallow it wa by the edge of the canal, with the water only just reaching hi thighs. 'Did you hear what I said?'

'I'm not touching the tiller.'

'Okay, now push the throttle slowly forwards.'

If she thought the day couldn't have got any worse, The helping her out of this predicament was really the cherry on tl icing. At least, that was what she thought until she moored up.

52

Daisy had only just secured the *September Rose* when Heather came bounding down the riverbank. But rather than going to her boyfriend, as Daisy expected, it was Daisy who was constricted in a tight bear hug.

'Are you okay? Do you need any ice or anything? I can grab some out of the freezer if you're hurt.' She broke away, her face crinkled with concern. 'These bloody boats. They're harder to handle than you think, aren't they? I have to say, that was incredibly brave of you taking her out by yourself so quickly. I still get nervous with the *Escape* and she's twenty feet shorter. Now tell me, can I get you a coffee? No, a chamomile tea. That's better for nerves.'

Daisy didn't have time to reply before Heather was back on the towpath, this time pulling her by the hand to follow.

'Of course she's lovely,' she muttered to herself.

Inside the *Narrow Escape*, Heather continued to fuss as though she and Daisy were long lost best friends.

'Theo, go and get yourself cleaned up,' she said, automatically picking up the mop to wipe up the drops of mud he was spilling on the floor, before fetching Daisy her drink and sitting down next to her.

'I can't believe I'm only just meeting you. Honestly, I feel like I know so much about you already. Theo's told me all about what you've been doing with the boat. I think it's incredible. All that work. And he loves helping you.'

'I'm so grateful,' Daisy said. 'I'd be completely lost without him. To be honest, I feel guilty for how much help he's given me.'

Heather waved her hand dismissively. 'If I'm being honest, I don't know why he doesn't give up his job as linesman and just refit old boats full time. I'm sure he could make a killing.'

'That's what I said to him.'

'Well, great minds think alike.' Heather smiled. It was a stunning smile. Entirely warm and genuine, and one that Daisy received with mixed emotions. In other circumstances, she would have probably really liked her. Actually, she did really like her, but the fact that she was so at ease with Daisy spending hours of her time alone with her boyfriend only confirmed to her what the curator had said that morning. She was nothing special. Theo would never see her as anything special, just like Paul hadn't.

A couple of minutes later, Theo appeared in a pair of clean jeans.

'I made you an espresso, hun,' Heather said. 'It's by the kettle.'

'Thanks,' he replied. 'I just want to check the *Rose* over quickly. Make sure there's not any damage that I missed.'

'Why don't you have your coffee first? While it's hot. A couple of minutes won't make a difference.'

'Unless there's a leak. Then it could make a massive difference.'

'I'm sure she didn't hit the bank hard enough for a leak.'

'Well, I'll know that for sure once I've checked her.'

Daisy wasn't sure whether she was imagining it, but she w

sure she felt tension forming. She blew on her tea, attempting to cool it down so she could drink it as quickly as possible.

Heather stood up.

'Gosh,' she said, putting her mug down on the table next to her. 'I didn't realise that was the time already. I need to get my things together.'

'Already?' Theo asked. 'I thought you were staying for dinner?'

'No, don't you remember? I said I had to do those reports by this evening. And I'm going away on Tuesday.'

'But this is the first time I've seen you all week.'

Daisy shrank back into her seat. Heather being perfectly wonderful and kind was bad enough, but now she was caught between a burgeoning domestic and she couldn't help but feel that she was somehow the cause of it.

'I'm gonna get off now too,' she said, standing up forcefully.

'No, you stay.' Theo and Heather spoke in perfect unison.

Feeling like she had just been shouted at by a schoolteacher, Daisy dropped straight back onto the sofa.

'You should finish your drink,' Heather said, once again with that warm smile. 'You don't want to rush about after the shock of what you've been through. And I'm sure we'll catch up again. Maybe when I've got a little more time.'

'I'd love to know when that will be,' Theo muttered, just loud enough for Daisy to hear.

The tension was stifling, but Daisy hadn't appreciated how quiet it was until she blew the steam from her drink again. This time, the noise blared out between them, as if she had just clashed a cymbal.

'Well, do you want to walk me out?' Heather asked, looking at Theo.

As he nodded, Theo's gaze went to Daisy. 'I'll be back in a

minute,' he said. 'Then we can take a look at the boat. A proper look.'

Feeling like she couldn't move, even if she wanted to, Daisy continued to sip her drink and tried not to listen to the talk outside. But given how close the two were standing, it was hard not to.

'This has got to change.' It was Theo's voice. 'I never see you.'

'I told you this was how it would be,' Heather replied, far more curtly than Daisy had heard her speak before. 'I told you before I applied for the job. But you wanted to stay here on the boat.'

'Because it's my home. Which you had no problem with before you took that job and let it take every second of your time.'

'That's what it takes in my industry. If I don't give it everythin now, I'm never going to make it up the ladder.'

'Then how about you don't? How about you just start enjoyin life? Some days it's like I don't even know who you are any more.'

Daisy knew it was wrong to listen in, but she couldn't sto What she really wanted to do was turn around and look at ther After all, there was so much that you could tell about a couple fro their body language. Were they still holding hands? Perhaps h had his hand on her cheek? Or were they standing apart wit hands on hips or arms folded across the chest? But even if she ha found the courage to try to peek over her shoulder, it would ha been pointless, as Theo appeared back in the boat.

Without a word, he moved straight into the kitchen, where picked up his coffee and poured it straight down the sink.

'After the afternoon we've had, I think we both want somethi stronger than that.'

53

ɩven that Daisy now knew exactly how strong Theo's beer was, e had no intention of having more than one. Still, she took the ›ttle as he handed it to her straight from the fridge, not even thering to offer her a glass.

'Are you okay?' she asked quietly.

'You mean despite the fact you nearly wiped out all the hard ›rk we've done in one moment of stupidity?' he snapped back :ore dropping his hand and letting out a deep sigh. 'I'm sorry, t was uncalled for. That joy ride, it was about your art?'

'Amongst other things.'

'Do you want to share? I mean, I'm guessing you just heard at was said outside. My girlfriend of six years telling me that a she's had for eight months is more important than our relaɩship.'

'I'm sure she didn't mean it like that.' Daisy wondered if they kissed each other goodbye when Heather left. Immediately, tried to scrap the thought. Why did it even matter if they had? as their relationship and nothing to do with her.

'Trust me, that's exactly what she meant,' Theo said, taking another substantial gulp from his bottle. 'We've got so much history. But you can't base a relationship only on history, can you Surely, at some point, you need to start thinking about the futur too?'

Daisy couldn't tell whether Theo's questions were rhetorica or not.

'If you guys are meant to be, then I'm sure you'll work it ou she said, offering the most neutral answer she could.

With another swig, he dropped down on the sofa next to her. second passed before he spoke again.

'You know, that's what I thought. I thought we would work out because we were meant to be together. But to be honest, t longer this goes on, the harder I'm finding it to believe. Maybe we both be happier with other people.'

A swarm of butterflies took hold as she lifted her gaze from h drink to find that Theo was staring straight at her. His ey unblinking.

'I know what I should do. We both do. But we've always be each other's safe place, you know? It's hard to let go of t security.'

'I get it, I do,' Daisy replied. 'Not that I've ever had any r security other than the girls in a long time. I don't think I've e fitted in properly with anyone else.'

'You fit in with me.'

Static buzzed in the air around them and her heart pounding even more furiously than when she had crashed *September Rose*. Theo was looking straight at her still, but his g had changed. He wasn't thinking about Heather any more, D knew. He was thinking about her.

His head moved just a fraction at the same moment as hers

They were such minuscule movements, but they brought them that much closer together. She was close. She should smell the soap still on his skin after his shower. Just one inch more, and their lips would touch.

His relationship was practically over... Practically. But not completely.

She jumped up, springing from the seat and spilling her beer, but she didn't even stop to wipe it up.

'I should go,' she said, racing towards the door.

'Daisy, please, wait.' Theo was on his feet too, rushing towards her. But she held her hands out, as if that would be enough to stop him.

'I need to go. Thank you for all your help with the boat. But I should go. I should definitely go.'

* * *

Well, I hate to say I told you so, but I so told you so.'

Daisy had sent an SOS message the moment she stopped unning and reached the car. Then she drove straight from the lock ɔ Bex's place. Once there, it had taken her less than ten minutes to ll her in on everything that had happened, from the paintings to ɿe boat crash and then the moment in the *Narrow Escape*, which ad never felt more aptly named.

'I don't know that he was definitely going to kiss me,' Daisy ɩid, recalling the way her hands trembled.

'He was so going to kiss you. And even if he wasn't, you wanted kiss him. This is great news.'

'I have no idea how you can think that. Did you not just hear erything I said about his perfect girlfriend?'

'Who he was arguing with.'

'Who he loves dearly. If Theo was thinking of kissing me, it was because he saw me as some kind of rebound. That's not what I want.'

'I know, but this isn't good news about Theo. It's good news about you. This is the first time I've ever seen you hung up about a guy. Apart from you know who. I don't want to count our chickens before they hatch or anything, but it feels like you might actually have moved on from Paul.'

Daisy thought about what Bex had just said, sitting there nursing a cup of tea. All that time on the boat and she hadn't once thought about what Paul would think of this new her. This her that knew all these new things, like the use of bitumen on a boat and the importance of a bilge pump, and the fact that she would happily discuss either with anyone who asked.

'I was over Paul years ago,' she said finally.

'We both know that's not true,' Bex replied. 'But if you're no ready to talk about it, let's change the subject. How was driving th boat?'

Daisy not being ready to talk about a subject normally had n bearing at all on whether Bex pressed her on the matter. Still, sh didn't need asking twice to talk about the boat.

'Before the crash? Amazing. Seriously amazing. I mean, I kno I crashed and everything, but I really don't think it would take m that long to get the hang of it.'

'Great, because I've got an idea. I was thinking you real should do trips on it. Just until the summer season's through. The when it's winter, you can sell it. It seems like a complete waste get rid of it before then. By which I mean we really need a gi holiday on it, too.'

'I like the idea, but it's the mooring fees, remember?'

'Couldn't you ask your mum to cover you, just for a month? put it on a credit card?'

Daisy appreciated her friend's enthusiasm, but they were all ideas she'd already had herself. Realistically, the only sensible thing for her to do was to sell the boat.

'After I've done the roof, there'll only be the rest of the outside to do. Then she'll be ready to sell.'

'And you don't sound happy about that.'

Daisy thought about the time she had spent on the *September Rose*. Doing it up, painting it, learning about walking planks and how to steer. It was a period in her life she'd never forget. But for now, she was going to have to.

'I should get going,' she said, standing up, not wanting to face the question.

'You sure? You can stay here if you want?'

'It's fine. Thank you for today.'

'That's what I'm here for.'

After a long hug goodbye, Daisy headed home.

It didn't take long for the loneliness to creep in, loneliness filled with thoughts of that near kiss. She needed a way to refocus. To ut that moment to rest, or at least distract her for a while. And so ie picked up the phone. Her call was answered within two rings.

'Hey, Mum... No, nothing is wrong. I just thought it might be ce to have a chat. That's all.'

They spoke for a full hour. It wasn't like old times, and Daisy dn't bring up Theo or the paintings, but she did mention that her st attempt at driving the *September Rose* by herself had ended up th her landing it on a riverbank. At the end of the call, she actu-y felt a little better.

Daisy sat down and considered the day she had just had, ssecting the most disastrous part of it. While Theo occupied an healthy portion of her mind, nothing had actually happened tween them. There had been no actual disaster, and the only ng that was injured when she crashed the boat was her pride.

No, the most disastrous part of the day was definitely her paintings. With a spur of inspiration, she spread out the pictures on the table in front of her and studied them one by one, before grabbing her pad and pencil.

'I'll show you derivative,' she said.

54

aisy had definitely stayed up too late. So late that when her alarm ock rang, it felt as though she'd not slept at all. Last night, she d painted as if she was possessed. With her paints and paint-ushes littered across the table, she had thrown aside all the rules. e had cast aside her precision of shadows and light and played h dimension and perspective. She had treated the page not as if vas paper to be painted on, but as if it already had a story to tell. vas simply her job to find it.

By the time she finished, it was gone midnight and both her gertips and forehead were smudged with paint and charcoal. v on earth she was going to stay awake at work, she had no idea, she didn't care, not in the slightest. The curator was right: her painting had lacked soul. But this one? Her soul was practically ping off the page. Even when she crawled out of bed the next ning, her eyelids hanging from the lack of sleep, that single ting was enough to raise her spirits.

As she dressed, a lightness she hadn't felt in years filled her. ething had shifted. It was time to stop living in the past and creating the future she deserved.

During her journey to work, her mind whirred with ideas. Why did she even need a gallery to show her paintings? Wh even used physical galleries nowadays? People shopped on th internet. She could set up her own online store and sell th paintings directly. There'd be no losing commission that wa either.

She buzzed, lit from inside by the energy.

With the thought of money coming in, she allowed herself expand the dream further. As Bex had suggested, the *Septemb Rose* could definitely be used for boat trips and day rentals. Sh could put together a proper business plan and go to the bank for loan to pay off the mooring fees. It would take a year at most, wi the rental she should get. Then if she was bringing in an ext hundred or so a month from painting, she could keep going. S could make this work.

Her optimistic mood was enough to cause the tiredness abate, but when she reached the office, she stopped. Frowning, s checked her watch. It was the same time as she got here most da which was fifteen minutes before she was due. But today, the pl was rammed. She edged inside, joining a cluster of people t were gathered in the reception area.

'What's going on? Why is everyone here so early?' she aske woman she vaguely recognised from accounts.

'Did you not read your emails? They sent it yesterday morni

'Sent what?' Daisy had been told time and time again t didn't need to check their emails on the weekend and it was on the things she liked about working there. But that rule had ap ently changed.

'They've had an offer of a takeover. Which means they'll to downsize and get rid of a load of us.'

Daisy shook her head. 'But they wouldn't get rid of us, su It's not like that here.'

'It's like that everywhere. They're calling people in one at the time. Alphabetically. What's your surname?'

'May,' Daisy replied.

'You're luckier than me then. I'm Wilson. I've got to hang around all day to find out if I've got a job or not. I'm not sure if my nerves will take it.'

Redundancy wasn't something Daisy had faced before, though she knew the general rule: last in, first out. But did that apply at a small company? And surely they'd need someone to answer the phones and respond to emails, whoever took them over? The panic was causing her throat to tighten. Any bank would laugh her out the door if she applied for a loan when she was unemployed, and without it, she couldn't see how she could keep the *September Rose.*

'Who's giving the news?'

'The line managers,' the same woman from accounts replied. Those in the middle that are left. They got called in yesterday. I nean, at least we didn't have to deal with that, right? Who wants to et news like that on the weekend?'

Daisy didn't need to hear any more. She squeezed out of the roup and went to her desk, but like the rest of her colleagues, her nind couldn't rest. No doubt there was work she could do, After ll, she was still technically employed, but it took her less than five ninutes to realise she wasn't going to be able to focus. Instead, aisy took out her phone. Her plan was to look at online marketlaces to find somewhere she could sell her art, but a message from heo distracted her.

as a bit of a mess yesterday, sorry. Are you coming down to the boat er? I'd like to talk to you.

Daisy put her phone down on her desk. Even after everything at had happened, she still needed to work on the boat. Even more so if she was thinking about using her in the summer. But she wasn't ready to reply yet. Theo needed to get his head straight. That much was clear. They both had too much on to be messing around like this.

At just gone eleven, Amanda stepped out of her office and turned to Daisy.

'Daisy, if you're ready?'

'I don't know if you've heard,' Amanda said as Daisy took a seat opposite her. 'But several factors have been considered in making these decisions. It's not a case of just last in, first out.'

A slight wave of relief billowed in Daisy. The bank loan could still happen. Why else would Amanda say such a thing if not to put her mind at ease? She waited, still tense but with decidedly more hope.

'We had to consider how well we think all the members of staf will fit in to the new company structure. How they will fit in as a team. Not to mention factors like punctuality, professionalism.' Sh paused between each of these words, and Daisy couldn't help bu think of the way her mother had accosted her outside of work That was a long way from professional, but it had been weeks ag They wouldn't hold that against her, would they?

'I'm not going to drag this out any longer than necessary. W saw some good growth in you while you were here, these la couple of months especially. And it wasn't an easy decision make.'

'But you're going to let me go,' Daisy finished for her.

'We will write you a good reference, of course. But I have inform you that as you've been here less than two years, you wo be entitled to any redundancy pay. I realise this must come as blow.'

Daisy stood up, despite the fact that Amanda was still talking her. She couldn't hear what was being said, anyway. She was nun

She had no job. She was unemployed. Her chest clamped tight. She had been unemployed before, she reminded herself. She had quit jobs with nothing else to go to. But this was different. This meant it was over. Any dreams of keeping the *September Rose* were over.

55

When Daisy reached Wildflower Lock, she was met with a mixtur
of disappointment and relief as she realised Theo was nowhere i
sight. With all that had happened, she had completely forgotte
about his message, but there seemed little point in replying to
now. Either she would see him or she wouldn't.

With a heavy heart, she stepped aboard the *September Rose* ar
unlocked the door.

The smell of fresh paint had faded now, and the primer w
completely dry, ready for its next coat. But she wasn't ready for th
yet. Inside, she took a moment to observe what she had create
Currently, there was no furniture, and only an oven in the kitche
but in her mind, she could see it all. The comfy sofa with
arrangement of throw cushions. The pictures on the wall whi
picked out the colours in the wood. The simple curtains t
wouldn't distract from the views beyond. It was impossible not
smile at the image in her head. Even if it would never be real
Not for her, at least.

In the main cabin, she ran her hand along the mattress. Ag
the walls were still white, given that she hadn't decided on a col

scheme yet, but now there was no point. That was a decision best left to the new owners.

'I'm sorry, Dad,' she said as she sat on the corner of the bed, in he same place she had done all those months ago when she'd ound the box of cards. 'I'm sorry I never got to meet you properly. m sorry I don't remember the times we had together. I'm sorry I ouldn't keep your boat.'

Tears filled her eyes, and she made no attempt to wipe them vay, letting them drip down onto her cheeks. Even when dark rcles formed on the fabric of her trousers, she didn't stop. She obably could have stayed there forever, had she not heard the ll-tale footsteps on the bow. A moment later, there was a knock at e door.

'Daisy? Is that you? Are you in there?'

Sniffing back the rest of the tears, she stepped out into the open ing area and into view.

'You can come—' she started to say before changing her mind. e boat already felt claustrophobic. Having Theo so close would ly make it worse. 'I'm just coming,' she said instead, before ing one last look around her and heading outside.

The moment Theo saw her, his face clouded with worry.

'Is everything okay? You're not normally here at this time of .'

'No,' she said, expelling the word with a long breath. 'I got l.'

'Fired? What for?'

Well, made redundant, but it's basically the same thing, isn't it? jobless.' Her eyes started to well again, and she couldn't wipe ears away fast enough. 'Crap, I'm so sorry.'

There's nothing to be sorry for.'

They stood there silently. She had grown used to silences een the pair of them, particularly when they were working on the boat together. But this one felt different. As if there were thing going unsaid. Daisy scoured her mind for something to say whe Theo beat her to it.

'Well, I guess it's a day for change,' he said, looking straigh at her.

'Why's that?'

'Heather and me. We... we...' He left the sentence floating i the air. There was nothing more to add to it.

'I'm sorry—'

Theo waved her condolences away.

'It was a long time coming,' he said. 'I think we've been hangi on to the past for years now. I guess I just needed a reason to lo to the future to see that.'

He stared at Daisy, with that same hard fixed gaze from t night before. The one that caused tingles to spread down her spi And they were still there. The same tingles. The same static sp starting within her. But there was something greater that was ov whelming everything else. Grief.

'I've got to sell the boat, now,' she said. 'There's no way I make rent and pay the mooring fees. Not when I have no idea h long it's gonna take me to find another job.'

'You could give up your flat to start with,' Theo said. 'Live the boat. I know it's not 100 per cent there yet, but it's perfe liveable.'

'I don't think fridges are considered a luxury these days.'

'We can fix that easy enough. A fridge isn't hard to find.'

'If you've got the money to pay for it.'

'I'll find you one second-hand. There are loads of pe wanting to get rid of them. You can do this. *We* can do this. If really wanted to live here, you can make it happen.'

Daisy turned her attention back to the *September Rose*. It come a long way since the first time she saw it. The paint sanded down, the hull properly blackened. Any fool would be able to see what a beauty she was now. Her heart ached as she thought of the tin of duck-egg blue paint she had bought for the outside. It would look incredible. It just wouldn't be hers.

'Theo.' She rested her hand on his arm. 'I appreciate what you're doing so much. Please believe me. I know I wouldn't have got here without your help. And there is nothing I would love more than to spend my days on the river. Honestly, but it's just not practical. I have to have a job. I have to have some way of making money and right now, I can't think of one. I'd have to sell every painting I've ever done and I still don't think would be enough for the fees and to live on. It's no good dreaming. The sooner I can face reality, the less it will hurt.'

A new silence shrouded them. One that was full of pain. Daisy knew she and Theo would have needed time to figure out if they wanted to be more than friends. After all, he had a relationship to grieve. But even if it was what they both wanted, she knew she would never be able to see him while he lived so close to the *September Rose*. It would break her heart every day. She moved to tell him as much when a couple of dog walkers approached, chatting loudly.

'I mean, it's ridiculous,' one said. 'Don't you think? It makes no sense.'

'Oh, you don't need to tell me. I say it every time I come here.'

'Exactly, it's common sense. A place this busy needs a coffee shop. And how hard would it be to set up, really? There are enough boats. They could just sell drinks from one of these.'

The women carried on chatting as they walked, but Daisy wasn't listening any more. She had heard everything she needed to.

'Did you hear that?' Daisy said, as her eyes met Theo's; the small smile which curled up on his lips was an exact reflection of hers.

'I did.'

'And?' she pressed 'What do you think?' A swarm of butterflies took hold within her. 'Would it be possible? Could it work?'

It was no longer a small smile toying on Theo's lips, but a great grin, and Daisy could feel her cheeks desperately wanting to form the same expression.

'If it's what you want to do, I'm almost positive it will work. But you'll probably have to live here.'

'I know. And it will still be a risk.' The excitement had spread past butterflies now. Instead, her entire body was alight with anticipation.

'But a risk worth taking,' Theo added.

For a moment, neither of them spoke. The enormity of what she was about to say, about to do, felt too great to say aloud. But she needed to. She needed to hear herself say it.

'I guess that's settled, then,' she said, her pulse hammering in her chest. 'It's time to set up the coffee shop on the canal.'

ACKNOWLEDGMENTS

This book was so much fun to write and I want to say a big thank you to Emily Yau and entire team at Boldwood Books for seeing the potential in my crazy idea. To all the people whose brains I picked for boating knowledge: Kate, Magdalen, Kelly. Thank you! Thank you also to the volunteers at Papermill and Heybridge Locks who were always willing to share their time and knowledge with me. To Kath, who has helped me so much, to Jake and his unwavering support and lastly, to all my readers, who have been with me on this crazy, book-loving journey. I wouldn't be here without you.

MORE FROM HANNAH LYNN

We hope you enjoyed reading ***New Beginnings at Wildflower Lock.*** If you did, please leave a review.

If you'd like to gift a copy, this book is also available as an ebook, large print, hardback, digital audio download and audiobook CD.

gn up to Hannah Lynn's mailing list for news, competitions and updates on future books.

https://bit.ly/HannahLynnNews

Vant more feel-good romantic reads from Hannah Lynn? Why not explore The Holly Berry Sweet Shop Series...

Hannah Lynn
The Sweet Shop of Second Chances

Hannah Lynn
Love Blooms at the Second Chances Sweet Shop

Hannah Lynn
Family Ties at the Second Chances Sweet Shop

Hannah Lynn
High Hopes at the Second Chances Sweet Shop

Hannah Lynn
Sunny Days at the Second Chances Sweet Shop

ABOUT THE AUTHOR

Hannah Lynn is the author of over twenty books spanning several genres. As well as signing a new romantic fiction series, Boldwood will be republishing her bestselling Sweet Shop series inspired by her Cotswolds childhood.

Visit Hannah's website: www.hannahlynnauthor.com

Follow Hannah on social media:

facebook.com/hannahlynnauthor
instagram.com/hannahlynnwrites
tiktok.com/@hannah.lynn.romcoms
bookbub.com/authors/hannah-lynn

Printed in Great Britain
by Amazon